ALSO BY PAUL WATKINS

Night Over Day Over Night
Calm at Sunset, Calm at Dawn
In the Blue Light of African Dreams

THE PROMISE OF LIGHT

THE PROMISE OF LIGHT

PAUL WATKINS

RANDOM HOUSE
NEW YORK

Library of Congress Cataloging-in-Publication Data

Watkins, Paul
The promise of light / Paul Watkins.
p.   cm.
ISBN 0-679-41974-8
I. Title.
PS3573.A844P7   1993
813'.54—dc20   92-17865

Manufactured in the United States of America

24689753

FIRST U.S. EDITION

Book design by Carole Lowenstein

For PLW

Therefore take heed . . .
How you awake the sleeping sword of war—
We charge you, in the name of God, take heed.
—WILLIAM SHAKESPEARE, *Henry V*, I:ii

PART 1

CHAPTER 1

Ships were burning in the harbor. Their rigging became branches of fire, scattering sparks as the blazing masts toppled into the waves.

I stood with Monahan on the beach across the bay. The tide was coming in. It bubbled up white over our shoes, but we didn't bother to move.

Monahan ran the ferryboat between Jamestown Island and the mainland. The ferry hadn't been late once in the ten years he'd been running it and he knew it and the people over on Jamestown knew it, too. As far as Monahan was concerned, those people who stood now on the Jamestown dock hadn't come to see the fire. They came to see if the flames would stop him from making the crossing. Then all of us would remember the fire, not because it swallowed Dillon's fishhouse, or the Seaside Restaurant, or because it lit up boats like candles and then snuffed them out and sent them to the bottom of the bay. It would be remembered as the day Monahan's ferry didn't make the crossing. Not even the hurricane of 1911 had done that, and people had run to the water's edge to see him ride the greybeard waves in his flat-ended boat, which took on water and spat it back out through the scuppers. Monahan's ferry roared in so fast on the tide that it smashed the dock to pieces and ploughed onto the beach, but at least he had made the crossing. And what his ferry hadn't smashed, the hurricane took with its white-boiling water and wind that sounded like a train run off the tracks.

Monahan raised a pair of binoculars to his eyes. He kept his hair slicked back with Bay Rum, and it shone in a silver hood across his skull. "I could run aground on one of them sunk boats, couldn't I, Benjamin?"

"You could all right." I had been carrying my suitcase all this time. Now I set it down and kneaded the blood back into my knuckles.

"And I could catch a load of sparks on the wind and it could set my engine on fire. That would blast us right out of the sea."

I didn't answer him. By now he was talking to himself, weighing his boat against his reputation.

He dropped the binoculars onto his chest. They were German ones that his son sent back from the war. They had the name "Kruger" scratched onto the case. The binoculars reached Monahan in good condition, but his son had died and was buried in France, at a place called Château-Thierry.

I still remembered the shock when I heard about his death, as if a knitting needle had been run through one of my lungs. The news spread quickly on the island, from street to street and across the gardens like a huge black butterfly. I had been ready to spend the rest of my life catching sight of him around the island and stopping now and then to talk. In my mind, I had cleared the way for him to grow into a barrel-bellied replica of his father. Even years later, the space he left behind still hadn't closed up.

Monahan never took off the binoculars. People in town would touch their thumbs and index fingers together and raise their hands to their eyes, as if spying on something in the distance, and everyone would know who they were imitating. "I guess your father has about given up trying to put out the fire on the dock. I guess he's trying to make sure that the whole town doesn't go up."

"I'm sure he's doing all he can." My father was the fire chief. I knew he would be someplace close to the flames, sweat running so heavily off him that afterward he'd be able to pour it from his boots. It was the worst fire that had ever come to the island. I could see that from where I stood. My father's heart would be thundering out of control, and I knew he would be angry, vicious angry, if anything failed him now; man or woman or machine. He had an old scar on his forehead, from falling off a horse in his childhood back in Ireland. The scar would be red with his anger, as if it meant to split and bleed again.

"I have to go. You know that, don't you, Benjamin?"

"Yes, Mr. Monahan. People are waiting to see."

"Well, let's give them a show. I'm going to run this ferry clean into the flames and if there isn't a dock to stop me, I'll keep running until I've planted this boat on the steps of the Jamestown courthouse. I wish my son was here to see it, Benjamin. I swear to God I do."

I smiled and picked up my suitcase, thinking how cold the water would be if we had to jump over the side. The air was warm, but this water had spent its winter swirling around the crags of icebergs off Newfoundland and the brick-red Nova Scotia sand. The Labrador Current. It would be a while yet before the Gulf Stream returned, riding up from the south until it broke against the long beaches of Cape Cod. Then I could swim without the breath being punched from my body.

One car stood on the deck of the ferry, its axle chained to stop it from sliding around. The car was a new model Ford. It belonged to Mr. Dalrimple. He had been sitting in it, smoking a pipe, while Monahan made up his mind. But now he climbed out and came walking down the beach toward us. He had been to see his family in Saunderstown, as he did every week. His wife stayed behind, at the Sturgess Rest Home in Jamestown. Her mind was slipping away. "Are we going or not?" Fire winked on his glasses and for a moment his eyes looked like cinders.

"Of course we're going." Monahan stamped over to his ferry. "Benjamin and I were only planning the best route. Are you backing out, Dalrimple?" He climbed into the wheelhouse. "Because if you're backing out . . ." His engines broke into thunder.

Dalrimple turned to me. "This is the end of my car."

I touched my thumb to my lips and made as if to disagree. But he was probably right and it made no sense to argue.

"There's no backing out. Not now that Monahan's made up his mind." Dalrimple tapped the ashes from his pipe on the heel of his shoe. Then he stuffed the pipe in his pocket and took off his glasses. He polished them with the tail of his shirt. He looked tired. Having his wife go slowly mad, like a slow fog creeping down the corridors of her brain, had dug trenches of age across his face.

I stood at the bow with Dalrimple.

Waves charged out of the dark and smacked against the steel sides of the ferry. Veils of spray blew past us and left a taste of salt on our lips.

Something exploded in the dockyard. The roof of Dillon's fishhouse burst into a flutter of slates and wooden beams. In the shudder of light that spread across the yard, I thought I saw my father. A man stood by himself, too close to the fire for safety. His arms were raised at the rubble of the fishhouse. I thought I saw the gleam of my father's brass fire helmet, which I had polished each Sunday night for as long as I could remember until I went away to university.

I knew it wasn't Dillon, because he would be fall-down drunk by now. He did that at every excuse, and this was the best one he'd got. Besides, it was known that he'd bought insurance only six months before. There would be talk, whatever the truth, that Dillon had burned the place himself. I'd have been drunk if I was him.

We passed the first of the burned ships, wreckage drifting in clumps around the black stump of the mast. Timbers bumped the ferry's hull, and I heard Monahan swearing up in the wheelhouse.

People on the dock were pointing at us. They ran down to the water's edge.

I heard Monahan laughing, a great rumble from his belly that would send the binoculars bouncing against his chest. He didn't care if his ferry struck wreckage and sank. In the morning, perhaps, it would dawn on him that his business was ruined for life. But for now he knew he was famous on the island, the kind of fame that would reach to the grandchildren of people who stood on the dock. It might even have reached to his own grandchildren, if his son had not died in the war.

The ferry dock hadn't burned, except for some tar that coated the tops of the pilings. They lit the way for us, like torches. We pulled up alongside the dock, the ferry engines churning into reverse and sending a froth of white water onto the sand. The smoking tar left a bitter taste in my mouth.

Monahan ran to the bow and unhooked the car's chains.

Dalrimple started his engine. He grinned, with the pipe jammed between his teeth. A few sparks had landed on the roof of his Ford, but not enough to ruin it. Only enough to let him claim some fame from Monahan's finest hour since the hurricane of 1911.

The front end of the ferry slammed down onto the dock.

People were running toward us, trampling footsteps on the dusty ground of the dockyard.

"Climb on!" Dalrimple slapped the side of his door. "You'll get stampeded to death."

Monahan's belly-roaring laugh met the oncoming crowd.

I threw my suitcase into the car and climbed onto the running board. I gripped the window frame and Dalrimple gunned his Ford over the ramp and out into the dockyard.

Smoke was everywhere. It billowed over the dust, carrying the smell of burnt tar and rubber and wood. I had grown used to the smell of fires. Not the dry and sweet smell of pine logs in the fireplace, or the tobacco reek of white birch. I knew the stench of melting car tires and tar-paper roofs, with their strange squealing sound as the fire closed them like fists one after the other.

One shack next to Dillon's fishhouse stayed out of the blaze, while everything around it had burned. The shack was Dillon's icehouse, where he kept the ice for fish fresh off the boats. He also kept salt in the shack, for fish that would be sent up to the Boston market.

The fire truck stood off to one side. All the water in its tank had been used up, and now firemen manned pumps that sprayed seawater over the houses close to the dock. I saw carpets set out on the roofs. These would extinguish the embers before they had a chance to light.

Dillon was drunk like I'd thought. He kept running into his ice shack, dragging out football-sized lumps of ice and throwing them into the remains of his fishhouse. Salt spilled out into the yard. The ice in his hands was coated with it. As Dillon threw his ice into the blaze, the salt flickered blue for a second, before the ball crashed into the fire-belching guts of the building.

The crowd pulled back to let Dalrimple pass.

Voices were calling my name. Hands brushed past my shoulders. But the fire was in my eyes and I couldn't see who was calling.

———

I found my father standing in the ruins of the Seaside Restaurant. Pillars of smoke rose up around him. He took off the brass helmet, smoothed back his hair, then set the helmet once more on his head.

Two men stood with him. They wore long overcoats and carried their hats in their hands.

My father's head jerked from one side to the other as he spoke to each of them in turn. He kept jabbing at pieces of wood with his toe and I could tell he was angry with the men.

I set down my suitcase and stood in the dark, waiting for him to finish. I didn't want to muddle my good news with the bad news I figured that these men had brought. I had a job now. That was the good news. For weeks, I had been taking Monahan's ferry back and forth to the mainland and applying for posts at all the different banks. I bought special bonded paper and wrote out my résumé each night before I went to bed. My father didn't mind me living at the house, but he knew and I knew that it was time to be moving on. The house was plenty big enough, especially with my mother being gone. And he could have used the company, but he figured that after graduating from university up in Providence, it was time for me to pack up and leave.

It had got to the point where I no longer cared about what impression I made at the banks. I moved easily in my new suit and was not constantly fingering the knot of silk at my throat. It made a better impression not to care so much, and when I walked into the First Bank of Wickford, having polished my shoes on the trouser cloth that ran down behind my calves, I knew I would have a job by the time I left. I'd been getting superstitious. It seemed that the people who interviewed me had been trained not as bankers but as smellers-of-fear. At first I had plenty of fear, and they smelled it and didn't give me the job. By the time I made it to the First Bank of Wickford, I'd stopped being afraid because I had also stopped giving a damn.

But now that I had the job, it seemed to me as if the rest of my life stretched out like railroad tracks. It was the way I once saw the train tracks that ran up from Kingston toward Boston, and down towards New Haven. I discovered them one day through the woods of the Great Swamp, when Bosley and I were hunting for quail. For a while we had sat on the tracks, pulled sandwiches wrapped in wax paper from the back pockets of our canvas hunting coats and eaten them for lunch. We found pennies that children left on the rails to be squashed by the trains when they passed.

The picture of the tracks stayed clear in my head—smooth and without obstacles. Now this was my life. I had found the path that I would follow and once I'd seen the path, I knew it was the one meant for me. I would spend two years clerking, a year as submanager and in five years I'd be running the bank. I had a house picked out to rent in Wickford.

I was glad not to be straying too far from this bay and this island. I had never been restless to leave and stay away. Long before, back into the smudged memories of my childhood, I had claimed the place as my own. The red-leafed autumns and the waves frozen green on the winter beaches and summer and spring were all wound up in my blood. Sometimes I thought of myself as a guardian of the rocks and tides, as if the island itself had a heartbeat that only I could hear, and if I pressed my ear to the grey stones in the fields, I could hear its constant thunder.

My father slapped his hand down hard on the shoulder of one of the men. "I got nothing for you, Pratt. I don't even know what the hell you think you're doing showing your face around here. Suppose someone recognized you. What then, eh?"

"They wouldn't be looking for me, Arthur. I'm already gone

from their minds." The man kept his hands in his pockets. His shoulders were heavy and sloped.

"The hell you are!" My father turned away and said again, "The hell you are, Mister."

Now the other man held his hands palm up toward my father's face. "You can help us, Arthur. You know the ropes. You know the whole game. It's important to us, Arthur."

"But not to me!" My father jabbed his thumb against the chest of his black oilcloth fireman's coat. "I've done away with all that now. And I don't have any money for you. You ask Willoughby if you want money."

"We can't touch what he's got and you know it." Pratt nodded to the other man and both of them turned to leave. They stepped carefully in their good shoes over the puffed charcoal beams of the restaurant. "Well, maybe your son would have some interest in helping us."

My father swung around. He took hold of Pratt and pulled him back to where he had stood before. He took hold of Pratt as if the man was a doll and raised him in the air and shook him. "You say one word to my son and I'll put you in the place where everyone thinks you already are. I want your promise. I want it for old time's sake and for every damn favor you owe me, Johnnie Pratt. So what's it to be? Do I have your promise?"

"Yes, Arthur. I didn't mean to say it."

"I'm serious, now."

"I know, Arthur."

"It's because of my son that I can't help you. Because of him that I got out of all that. Does that not make sense to you?"

"It does. And could you put me down now, Arthur?"

My father dropped him in the ashes.

The other man had lit himself a cigarette. The tiny fire lit up his face and hollowed out his cheeks.

I had never seen him before. Never seen Johnnie Pratt, either.

My father slapped the dirt off his hands, as if grabbing hold of Pratt had somehow left more grime on his skin than any black dust painted on him by the fire. "Good luck to you," he called after the two men. There was a distant panic in his voice.

They didn't answer. They stepped into a car and drove away without turning on the lights. They reached the main road that headed up to the north end of the island, where the ferry owned by a man named Von Klug ran over to Newport. At the main road, they turned on their lights and the two white sabers cut along the road and they sped away into the dark.

My father watched them go. His mouth hung open slightly and I could tell that he was thinking hard.

I walked to where he could see me.

He squinted at first, because he couldn't tell who it was. Then he beamed a smile and spread his arms. "And how did the job market go today, Benjamin?" He hugged me and I felt his soot-grimy hands grip the cloth of my suit behind my shoulder blades.

"I got it. The man said I could start next week."

He stepped back, but kept his fingers pressed into my shoulders. "Yes? Next week. Good salary?"

"Good enough."

"Well!"

I knew he was impressed. He only said "well" when he was impressed. And riding across the bay into the burning Jamestown harbor, I'd had some time to think about it. I was beginning to be a little impressed myself.

"Who were those two men, Dad?"

"What men?" He walked me away from the restaurant and out toward the fire truck. The other firemen were coiling up the fire hose. The heavy bronze spigot dragged through the sand on its way back to the truck.

"The two who just drove off in that car toward the Newport ferry."

"Two old pals." He nodded, as if only just remembering. "They wanted to borrow some money and I told them no."

"You told them worse than that."

"I can't be expected to keep my temper all the time." He took off his brass hat and stuffed it on my head. "You've got the job. Well done, Benjamin. I knew it wouldn't take long."

"Why did you tell that man not to show his face around here? Would people get mad if they saw him?"

"Do we have to talk about it? No one wants to see him because he owes too much money. You know how people get when debts haven't been paid. Now look, you get home and change and have a bath or something. I'll be around in a bit. There should still be some supper on the table. This damn fire started when I'd just sat down to dinner."

"How did it start?"

"I'll tell you exactly. It's that insurance Dillon bought last year. Been driving him round the bend thinking he could get all kinds of money if his ratty busted-up fishhouse burnt down. So he sets the thing burning. But here's the jam. As soon as he's got a few drinks in him and sees the flames eating it all up, he remembers the stories of insurance companies not paying if there are suspicious circumstances. So he goes berserk trying to put it out by himself. Throwing slabs of ice into the fire and such."

"Did *he* tell you all that?"

"No, but I been in this job too long to make mistakes about a thing like that. Go home now, Benjamin. Go home and rest for a while."

The fires had stopped on the water. Night crept up close around the pilings of the dock and hid the bay behind it. There was no moon and I couldn't see the mainland. The only blaze still burning was the one in Dillon's fishhouse. I thought his tank of diesel fuel must have caught. It would be a while before that burned itself out. The crowds were thinning. People shuffled home, some in their nightclothes and wearing hunting boots. Monahan still stood at his ferry, alone now, but still hopeful that another stray person might appear to congratulate him on his finest hour.

The front door was open.

My father's dinner lay cold on a white china plate. It was pork chops and a potato, with some of Mrs. Gifford's apple jam for sauce. I left the door open and ate the food. It was too early in the year for mosquitoes to come in, and I liked the breeze blowing through.

After dinner, I pulled a bottle of my father's Irish whiskey from the mantelpiece. The bottle had a red label and said Dunhams Belfast. My father's friend Willoughby had brought it back from one of his trips to Ireland. I sat down in his chair with the horsehair stuffing. He had rubbed the leather seat dark and smooth with years of naps and pipe-smoking sit-downs and whiskey-drinking sit-downs with Willoughby and Monahan. From this chair, he would raise his glass whiskey mug into the last beam of sunlight coming through the room. He let the sun wink rainbows through its sides.

My father and Monahan used to go on and on about how you could taste the peat in Irish whiskey. I would be handed a glass of the honey-colored liquid and told to smell the peat and taste it and let it rest on my tongue. But I had no idea what peat looked like or smelled like or even tasted like on its own. As I washed the whiskey through my mouth, I would try to pull apart the different threads of its fire and let instinct tell me where the peat was hiding.

I pulled out the cork and took a drink. I swished it through my teeth before I swallowed, feeling it sting along the line of my gums. First there was only the heat, like embers scattered in my blood. But when I stood up to shut the door, the alcohol plowed through me so hard I had to sit back down.

An explosion echoed across the bay. Another slab of Dillon's roof must have shot into the sky.

"So you'd like to make a deposit?" I said to a reflection of my face in the window. "Will that be to your checking account or your savings account? Oh?" I slugged back another mouthful of the Dunhams and sat forward. The whiskey rocked in my skull. "You don't have a savings account? Well, allow me to explain our policy." I stopped talking and frowned at myself. It seemed as if the fun had already gone from telling people what to do with their money and I hadn't even started yet. For a moment, panic fluttered up inside me as I wondered if it might be a mistake to start at the bank. But I had been talking about a job as a banker for over a year now. I had no other plan.

I thought about my vision of the rails, how they were bolted to the land and raced like slivers of mercury into the future.

It was the Dunhams doing this to me. Making me think wobbly. I tapped at my chest to settle the fire. I saw myself walking into the bank in my new suit and sitting at a desk with my name on it. I heard the hum of business. The frown stayed on my face, but now it was the frown of responsibility and calm.

I'd be starting at the bank and that was that. I knocked back some more of the Dunhams.

Then a face appeared in the window.

I cried out and stood up. The whiskey went down the wrong way and its burning doubled me over. My eyes teared and I couldn't see the floor to put the bottle down.

The door opened and I heard from the swish of cloth that Willoughby had come to visit. He was the island's Catholic priest and I felt as if I'd spent most of my life trying to avoid him. My father sent for the man whenever it was time for a

long talk. Through every spotty-faced clumsy part of my growing up, Willoughby had been there. His arm was always creeping around my shoulder. I hated saying hello to him and I
hated saying good-bye. Shaking the man's hand was like grabbing hold of a glove filled with pudding. I used to squeeze
hard sometimes, to see if there were any bones inside at all. I
didn't know why my father sent for Willoughby. Most likely,
he didn't want to be the one who came trampling into my
memory whenever I thought back to the times when I put a
foot wrong and couldn't put one right.

"Hello," I was trying to say. The tears of coughing rolled
down my cheeks.

Willoughby drifted in front of me. "Ben, you must come
with me at once."

"I'm waiting for my father to come home." I jammed the
heel of my palm into my eyes to squash out the tears that
remained. Then I could focus on the old man.

"It's to do with your father. Now you must come at once."
He looked as if he combed his hair with a fork. It stuck up like
spikes on a hedgehog.

"What's the matter?"

Willoughby breathed in. The air rasped down his old throat.
"I don't really know, except that there has been an accident
and they need you at the hospital."

The comfortable rumbling of the Dunhams in my head suddenly stopped. It stopped so quickly that I thought I might
fall over. "What kind of accident?"

He didn't say. He took hold of my arm and led me out of
the house.

It wasn't really a hospital. Jamestown was too small to
have a hospital. Dr. Melville had retired here from Newport
three years before and then got bored with growing cucumbers

and digging for blue crabs in the mud. So he opened a clinic in the back room of his house. The back room was our hospital.

We had to run, because Willoughby didn't have a car. He said they hadn't been able to find one in time.

"There's been an accident," he kept saying as we ran.

I wanted to press him for details, but sudden fear had clogged my throat.

Bosley met me outside Dr. Melville's house. A crowd had gathered there, almost as big as the crowd that had come to watch Dillon's burn to the ground. The same people who had been shuffling home in their hunting boots and nightshirts now stood peering into Melville's living room.

I grew up with Bosley. Years ago, in the time when we met every morning at the Mackerel Cove bridge and shuffled to the one-room schoolhouse with leather satchels on our backs, he and I and Monahan's son had made a pact to be volunteer firemen and another pact to take turns driving the fire truck. Bosley was the only one who kept the pact, and he grudged me in small ways for not holding my part of the bargain. He even seemed to grudge Monahan's son for dying over in France.

Bosley still wore his black fireman's clothes, too-big boots flopping on the ground as he walked out to meet me. Soot cut through by lines of sweat looked like war paint on his face. He took hold of my elbow and pulled me to one side.

"What is it, Bos?" The last bee-hive hum of the whiskey left my head. "What's gone wrong?"

"Your father went into Dillon's to cap the diesel tank. He said if we capped it, we could save ourselves the trouble of waiting all night for the diesel to burn off. He walked in and a couple of seconds later, the whole thing went up. It blew him through the wall and landed him right at our feet. Melville says he should be all right. But he's lost a lot of blood, Benjamin. He's all banged up to hell." Now we were deep in the shadows.

The crowd had watched us go. I knew all of them. There was Mr. Quigley, who once dropped a brown-paper package in the street and it split open and postcards spilled out. On the postcards were pictures of naked women. Postcard Quigley. They damn near ran him out of town because of it. And there beside him was the lady who tried hardest to run him out—Miss Beecham, who taught us at the one-room school and once fell in love with one of her students, a boy named Henry Macintosh. He was only sixteen and he pretended to love her back. I saw them in the street once and it was the only time I ever saw Miss Beecham with her hair down. They made a scandal and then Henry left the island. Miss Beecham seemed to grow old so quickly, it was as if she'd strapped herself into a time machine. People said she played up the stuff with Mr. Quigley's postcards to give the island something else to talk about besides the sight of her and Henry Macintosh, arm in arm and Miss Beecham's face all filled with love. And in the dark I saw the face of Mrs. Gifford, who lived across the road from my father. She loved my father and brought him pies. People said they should have married after my mother passed away. At first the idea made me angry, but when my eyes had cleared enough to see how lonely they were by themselves, I saw that the people were right. I didn't know why they wouldn't marry. Nobody else did, either, but they all had theories.

Men and women on the island came to be known by their jobs, or by one or two things that they'd done right or wrong. They knew Monahan as the man who drove his ferry through the hurricane, and my father as the man who stood among the fires and swore at the top of his lungs as the smoke swirled all around him.

Soon enough, I figured, I'd be known as the banker. And I hoped only as the banker. The less I gave them to talk about, the better.

I knew all these men and women who had come to watch, but the way they gaped with their eyes as wide and unblinking as fish, made it seem as if they didn't know me. It made me angry to have them staring. They had crept out of their beds to gawk at the fire and now at my father's spilled blood. I thought about the blood and felt helpless. I wanted to gather it and get it back inside him, to seal his wounds without trace and for there never to have been any pain. Please, not my father, I thought. Please not him.

Bosley stopped walking. We both turned and looked back at Melville's. Willoughby stood on the doorstep, squinting around to see where I had gone. Some of the nightshirt gawkers pointed in my direction. "He's all banged up and talking funny. He's not making any sense, Benjamin. I just want you to be prepared for it is all."

I could barely see him in the dark. "Thanks, Bos."

"I hear you got a job." He wiped at the dirt on his face.

"They said they'd give it to me."

Bosley laughed; a quiet cough of breath. He didn't look me in the eye. "I'd been hoping you were coming to work alongside your dad and me."

"I thought about it, Bos." I started walking toward Melville's house. Already the crowd's pale faces were turning.

Bosley walked beside me. "I guess I just thought about it more than anyone else."

I couldn't make out any words in the constant mutter of the people who stepped back to let me pass.

Bosley didn't come inside. He shoved his way back into the night.

It was bright in Melville's clinic. The first thing I heard when I stepped through the doorway was my father's raging shouts. Not shouting in pain. He was howling in Irish, which I had not heard him speak for many years. The door that separated us was shut. For a moment, I stood in front of it, feeling the stares from behind. I turned and saw them, dozens of wide eyes peeking through the glass.

Then Willoughby opened the door and pulled me inside.

I tried to stay calm, but when I saw my father, the shock kicked at my ribs. I did not recognize his face. His forehead was blistered white through the layers of soot. The fire had taken his eyebrows and most of his hair, leaving only a brittle mess of orange crumbs, which fell across the floor as he shook his head from side to side. My father had been tied down onto the clinic table. Bandages were wrapped around his bare arms and legs.

He kept up the talking in Irish, his voice all spit and croaking, as if he had reached the last words of an argument before it came to blows.

Melville tried to wrap another bandage around my father's head, but my father moved so much that Melville gave up. The bandage slipped from his hands and unrolled across the floor. Melville's head snapped up to look at me. His eyes were gray like a sled dog's. "We need you to give us some blood."

I took off my shirt.

Melville went to his closet and pulled out a tube with a needle at each end. He also removed the biggest syringe I had ever seen. While he was uncoiling the tube, he shouted up at the ceiling for his daughter. It was going to be a direct transfusion, so I had to be in a higher place than my father. Melville cleared off his marble counter top. He moved quickly but with such care that each glass jar of tongue depressors and cotton balls made no sound as he set them down at the far end of the counter.

"I thought I was coming here to read him his last rites."

Willoughby's hands fluttered in front of him. "When they called me . . ."

"Last rites?" My father's voice boomed through the house. "You keep back from him with your last rites. You let the poor man die in peace. And you leave me out of this. When Hagan went away, I didn't hear any prayers for him, did I? And for his wife? We had to fight even to get her buried in the church-yard. You leave my son out of this!"

The marble counter was cloudy white with threads of gray woven into the stone. It seemed to grab at the bare skin of my back as I lay down.

"Keep away!" my father shouted. Then suddenly the belt that had pinned him gave way. The leather tore and flew off to the sides. He sat up and held his hands out in front of him. His palms were burned so badly that the skin had started to peel away.

It was seeing his hands that made me realize how badly he was hurt.

Slowly, my father lowered his outstretched arms. "Keep him out of this," he said. His voice was no more than a whisper.

Peg came running downstairs. She skidded into the room. She had arrived with such speed that I knew she must have been listening for his call, maybe with her ear pressed to the floorboards, hearing every muttered word.

I couldn't help staring at the blackness of her hair. Although it had been years, people still thought of her and her parents as strangers to the island. I did, as well. To me, Peg seemed to come from much farther away than Newport, although the island of Jamestown was separated from Newport by more than just the distance of the bay.

The chromium shine of the syringe blinked at me.

Melville tied a cord around my bicep. Soon the veins on my arm stood out, green-blue and crisscrossing. Then he poured ether onto a cotton pad and stepped behind my father.

My father's talking had died down. He was still sitting up, head bowed forward. His fingers twitched, as if he was trying to remember a tune on the piano.

Melville set his hand on my father's forehead and with his other hand, he held the pad against my father's face.

A shudder rocked down the length of my father's spine. The ether flooded through him like a tide.

Melville lowered him down onto the leather-covered pillow built into the table. Then he wheeled the table over to where I was lying.

I could smell the ether. It was sweet and peppery.

My father looked dead. I couldn't see him breathing.

Peg walked over to me and I tried to sit up, but she held out her hand and made me lie still. "Do you want me to cover your eyes, Benjamin?"

For a second, calm settled on me as I heard the softness in her voice. I didn't have time to answer. I wished we could be any place but this.

"Cover his eyes." Melville talked as he wiped alcohol on both needle ends of the tube. "He needs at least two pints of blood within the next twenty-four hours. One will do for now. Father Willoughby offered to donate, but we don't have time to do the tests to see if his blood type is right. If we give him the wrong kind of blood, we'd kill him in no time at all. So we'll be using yours for now, Benjamin. That way we'll be sure. Tomorrow, he'll be taken to the Naval hospital in Newport. They've already got a bed ready for him. He can't be moved now."

Peg's hands passed in front of my eyes and made me blind.

I felt the slap of Melville's fingers bouncing off my veins. Then came the pinch as the needle slid under my skin.

I could feel the blood being taken. It was as if Melville had hooked his finger under the vein and was tugging it out of my arm. "He'll be all right, won't he?" I said through Peg's fingers.

Through the cracks between them, all I could see was the brightness of the bulb on the ceiling.

"He is stable for now. Burns take a long time to heal and he's mangled his arm pretty badly. Parts of that diesel tank hit him like shrapnel." Melville's voice was toneless as he concentrated on drawing the blood.

It was quiet for a while. The others in the room had seen my blood and it extinguished their voices. The faint tugging at my veins continued. I knew that by now, they would have fitted the other end of the tube into one of my father's arteries and that my blood would be flowing into his. I thought of it mingling, reaching his heart and charging away into the caverns of his body. I wondered if somehow my thoughts might travel with it. Maybe I could talk to him through my blood. Perhaps, now, memories that belonged to me would flicker to life in his head. Perhaps even the Dunhams would reach him, speckled in the heavy red flood from my arm. What did my father say the whiskey did? Takes out the fire but leaves in the warmth.

The needle slid out of me and Melville folded my arm back. "Keep that there."

Peg's hand moved away. She helped me to my feet.

I kept my arm folded. Blood found its way out and dripped from my elbow.

The other end of the tube was still in my father's arm. The tube remained filled with blood and there was more blood on the floor. The syringe lay on the counter, by my feet. A fat drop of blood hung from the end of the needle. Melville had used it to start the flow into my father's arm.

Melville removed the tube from my father, and then lifted the two needle ends, so that the blood in the tube didn't pour out on the floor. "You should go home now, Ben."

"I ought to stay here, don't you think?" Dizziness swirled at the back of my head. "Jesus, is he going to be all right?"

"There's nothing for you to do but rest." Willoughby's hands settled on my shoulders. "You save your strength for the morning."

"Goodnight, Benjamin." Peg was leaving the room.

I wanted to tell her to stay. As Willoughby guided me out of the room, I saw my father lying on the table, legs still strapped down. The bandage had covered his eyes and wound once under his chin. It looked as if Melville had been trying to embalm him.

I wished I could take some of the pain for him. It would get worse before it got better. He had told me himself about burns. The healing took months and all of it was pain. He could fend off the shrieking of his raw nerves with anger and shouting, but he didn't have the strength to hold it back for long. Nobody did.

The crowd had gone. All that remained of them were footprints in Melville's flower bed, his early summer flowers stamped into the mud.

CHAPTER 2

The sweat of a nightmare was still on my face.

I opened my bedroom window and stared out at the darkness. Flowers showed like chips of bone among the honeysuckle bushes.

I had been expecting nightmares, but not this soon. A few days lag-time before the images caught up with me, of seeing my father's flesh peel off his bones. I knew it wouldn't be long until grotesque mirror images of him and myself came stumping like cripples into my dreams, badly acting out what hurt me most.

But the nightmare that came charging down the alleys of my sleep was not from the present. This dream had followed me through childhood and I'd thought it had long ago been put away for good.

For more than two decades, the pictures had rested harmless and forgotten in some wrinkle of my brain. I could not believe how clearly it had burst from cover and spread like wings behind my eyes.

My mother once told me about a famous knight in Ireland. This knight had spent his life saving the kingdom from invaders. When he saw that his work was done, he took fifty of his best men, all of them strapped into armor plated with gold, and he led them to a mountain cave that overlooked the kingdom.

He made them all lie down, and one by one he sprinkled sleeping dust into their eyes. They fell into the deepest, calmest dreams.

Then the knight hung a bell from the roof of the cave. He sealed off the cave's entrance with a boulder and lay down like the others. If the kingdom was ever in danger again, the bell would ring and wake them. Until then, they would sleep, safe in the promise that one day they would return into the light.

Nobody knew where the cave was. No one would ever find it.

One night after she had told me the story, I surfaced from the black of my sleep into the strange light of my dreams and found myself inside the cave. An oil lamp was burning on a shelf dug into the rock, as if I'd been expected. I saw the knights stretched out on the dusty ground. The lamp bounced light off their gold armor. Their faces were calm. I heard the creak of the armor's leather bindings as the knights breathed deeply.

I could find no way out of the cave. A boulder blocked the entrance and a bell hung from the ceiling.

I was only there for a moment. Then I sank back down into the river of my sleep and woke with the dream still clear in my head.

This was not the nightmare. That came a few days later, when I returned to the cave.

This time, no light was burning. I stood in the India-ink darkness and heard only the breathing of the knights. I was afraid to move, in case I stumbled into the bell and woke the knights. I knew they would kill me before I had a chance to explain. I could feel their breath around me. The shine of their gold had been extinguished in the black. I waited for the dream to end, to fall away, and for me to wake up in my bed. But the dream wouldn't end and panic was closing around me.

When I did wake up, I found myself smothered in blankets and unable to move. For a while, I couldn't breathe or even open my eyes.

In this same nightmare that returned and returned, I visited the place where the knights lay sleeping. I had time to think about what would happen if the bell suddenly rang. The boulder would roll aside. The knights would wake and the dust would fall from their shields. They would all charge out into the blaze of green that my mother had told me was Ireland.

I had a sense that if I went with them, I could never return to my family and friends. But if the bell rang, I would go. I knew it like an instinct.

My father had laughed when he heard about the dream. "Wasn't that King Arthur? He wasn't Irish? Well, was he?"

Willoughby was there. He leaned forward through cobras of smoke that rose from his pipe. "Of course he was Irish. In his heart, he was. And they say the same legend goes for Finn MacCool. Don't you listen to your father, Ben. You'd better believe that it's true."

Then my father leaned back and his chair's horsehair stuffing rustled. "Well, I say that bell's been ringing nonstop for five hundred years, and those knights have got so old they're deaf as posts."

"They don't grow old," I told them.

Then Willoughby nodded, "And the bell hasn't rung yet, for sure."

In time, the dream faded. The fear it brought grew stale. But the nightmare stayed like a pool of deep water in my memory, that I sidestepped whenever it came close.

Thoughts of my mother and her stories kept me from falling

back asleep, so I climbed up to the attic, stepping along the cross beams. I knew what I was looking for.

My father kept a box of things that used to belong to my mother, whose name was Mae. He couldn't bear to throw them away.

It had been a long time since I'd dreamed the dream of the knights in the cave and a long time since I'd thought of my mother. I wanted to find the box and go through it, to see what memories of her it jolted to the surface of my mind.

I knew what the box contained. I could tell the story of every item. There was a scarf that still smelled of her. It was this scarf that killed her. She had just bought it and got it wet in the rain as she walked home from the shops. Halfway home, she bundled the scarf in a ball and held it between her chest and her raincoat. The damp scarf chilled her, and two days later she came down with pneumonia. She didn't last long after that. I wondered why my father kept it. There was a pair of shoes, worn so you could see how she had walked on the inside of her heel. I had once seen my father take these shoes off my mother's feet. He set them softly on the floor and then gently squeezed her feet with his big hands. He kneaded them and made her close her eyes, as the pain-shut nerves hummed back to life. There was an umbrella with black lace at the edges and clothespins she had painted red so as not to lose them in the grass. The clothespins made me think of years before, and of playing hide-and-seek with her among the sheets hung out to dry.

For my father, these were the keys that broke open pictures of my mother and made him love her again as if she were alive. Of all the things I'd helped him carry out to the dump after she died, each one a key of its own, I wondered why he kept the glossy red clothespins, and the scarf with her perfume distant and wound into the threads.

I found the box and took out the clothespins and clipped them one by one onto each of my fingers, the way I had done years before.

It didn't help much to see these old things. I could no longer remember much about my mother. I had lost the pitch of her voice and the tone of her skin and I knew her eyes had been brown but not which of the dozens of shadings of that color. Everything I had taken for granted, I lost.

So I shoved the box back into the dark and began to rummage through trunks and stacks of books.

I dug through the pockets of my father's old oilskin fireman's coat, but found only sand and the crumbs of stale tobacco. Then I put on the coat. It was worn through at the elbows and the brown corduroy collar.

I found his bamboo fly-fishing rod that he only used once, one late September near a town called Roscoe in the Catskill mountains, but he talked about the time as if he'd been going there for years. It began to rain. Drops trampled the tiles close to my head.

I opened a book and a scrap of paper fell out. It was a flyer for a meeting of the Boston Chapter of the Ancient Order of Hibernians in October of 1917.

Suddenly I remembered standing in front of my father and holding out the leaflet. It had arrived in the mail that day.

I was in his bad books then. My friend Bosley had borrowed his father's service revolver and the two of us went into the woods to shoot it. We carried a stack of old pie tins, set them up and shot them from twenty-five paces away. The pans made a smacking sound as they were hit, and spun away into the trees. Bosley got himself a whipping for taking the gun without permission, and I was in trouble now, too. It was the first time we'd been caught, but not the first time we'd used the gun. Over the dozen times when we had taken the gun into the woods, we had taught ourselves to shoot and we were good at it now. The pie tins were so full of holes they looked like cheese-graters.

My father had just come back from putting out a fire. A dairy farm had burned on the north end of the island. When the fire truck ran out of water, they threw buckets of milk on the flames. He sat in his chair, still wearing his fireman's clothes, boots splashed white from the milk and starting to smell sour.

I tried to make conversation, to break through his sulking and silence that I'd been out shooting pie tins. He had yelled at me that there was no place here for guns. He yelled until he was hoarse and then he shut up for a few days.

He took the leaflet that I held out to him, read it and then wedged it into his book as a marker.

"Are you going?" I asked him. Talk to me, old man, I was thinking. Enough of this grizzly quiet.

"No. I got nothing to say to them up in Boston." He pulled the suede tobacco bag from around his neck and undid the mother-of-pearl button that held the bag shut. From a pocket, he took his pipe, and with one finger scraped shreds of mahogany tobacco into the bowl. "The Boston boys talk too much and when it comes time to do more than talk, they do nothing."

I set the flyer back inside the book. The rain was coming down hard now. In the gloomy corners of the attic, I heard droplets plipping on the old trunks and boxes, having found their way under the slate.

As I walked downstairs, seeing the wind-blown rain run silver on the windows, I tried to think about what possessions would one day fill a box of someone's memories of me.

I sat in the leather-backed chair and watched the sun come up bloody through the trees.

Once I fell asleep and for a few seconds when I woke, startled by the wailing of a seagull overhead, I felt only the happiness of finding a new job. There were the shining rails again, and I was on them now, on the path I would follow through life.

Suddenly I remembered my father. A heaviness settled back onto my shoulders. It was knowing the pain he was in, and being helpless to prevent it.

I walked into the kitchen and cranked the handle at the side of the telephone. I held the dull black earphone to my ear. There was a space rubbed dirty on the wall from leaning there as my father or I spoke into the phone. Not many people on the island had telephones, but we did because of my father being the fire chief.

Hettie snapped onto the line. She had just started as operator for the Jamestown circuits. I heard she had already electrocuted herself twice. "Ho?" Her mouth was full of something. "Hu oh? Yes?"

"Hello, Hettie. This is Benjamin Sheridan. I wonder if you could put me in touch with . . ."

"The hospital. Of course."

"I guess everybody knows, then."

"Well, I should say so." She crunched at what sounded like a piece of toast.

"How are you, Hett?"

"Fine."

I waited for more, but she had nothing else to say. Hett and I used to be friends. There was a time when she thought we were more than friends. But I wasn't thinking that way, and we began the slow drifting apart that I'd already begun from Bosley and the others after I went away to university. Now when I returned to Jamestown they treated me like a tourist. The beaches and the cliffs that had belonged to all of us, only belonged to them. The truth was that they weren't leaving the island, not now and not ever, so they grudged me my escape and would no longer share what they had.

I heard the burble of the phone ringing at Melville's.

"Go ahead." Hettie's voice was brittle.

"Hello? Dr. Melville's. Hello?" This voice wasn't brittle. It was Peg's voice and it flooded my head. She always answered the phone. I thought that if it was possible to fall in love with someone only by hearing them speak, it would be a voice like hers.

"Hello, Peg." I watched my breath condense on the telephone's mouthpiece. "This is Benjamin Sheridan and I'm calling to see how my father is doing."

She told me to hold on.

I wondered if Hettie was listening, hiding someplace in the rush of static on the lines. "Hettie," I whispered into the breaking waves of telephone silence. "Hettie, are you there?"

"Mr. Sheridan, this is Dr. Melville."

Then I knew something was wrong. He didn't call me Benjamin.

"Hello, Dr. Melville. I was calling to speak with my dad. How's he doing today?" I narrowed my eyes, waiting for the word. I felt the worry at the base of my throat, clumped behind my Adam's apple. It sparked along the notches of my spine.

"Are you adopted, Benjamin?"

"Of course not. You know that." I leaned against the worn patch on the wall.

"I have no idea what happened." He sighed and the sigh roared in my ear. "That's not exactly true. I do know what happened, but I don't understand . . . Again, that's not quite true . . ."

Someone took the phone away from him. Then Willoughby's gravelly voice popped onto the line. "Benjamin, your father passed away last night, about three hours after the blood transfusion. He went into some kind of arrest, as Melville here has been calling it. Are you there, Benjamin? Can you hear me? Blast everything, has this line gone dead again?"

Suddenly I felt as if I was breathing the smoke of Dillon's fishhouse as it tumbled into ashes and shoved back the crowd with its heat.

"The line's gone dead." Willoughby clicked his tongue.

"No." The air was thin and didn't feed my blood. Smoke seemed to barrel out at me from the telephone's mouthpiece, jamming my windpipe with soot.

"Benjamin, I'm coming right over. There's something that needs to be explained."

"What needs explaining? Stand where you are and explain it." I thought of my father tumbling far into the past, still in his fireman's clothes, cartwheeling away into the dark. Already time had raced ahead and was covering him up.

"Dr. Melville is saying that . . . now let me get this right . . ."

Again the phone was snatched away and I found myself listening to Melville again. "He went into arrest after the blood transfusion. It was the wrong kind of blood. You put the wrong blood into someone and you might as well be feeding them poison. What I'm trying to say is that your blood should not have had any bad effects on him. That is to say, I know your father's bloodtype, and I even have your mother's type on file. And those two types together could not have produced your type. Based on all that we know in the medical world. . . ."

"Oh, get on with it, Melville!" Willoughby shouted in the background. "Just tell him what you told me."

"I don't think he was your natural father, Benjamin. I know this must sound absurd."

"Revive him!" I shouted.

"I can't, Ben."

"Revive him!" I didn't even know for sure if it was me shouting.

"He's dead, Ben. You must understand."

"Revive!" The word burst from my mouth like a command to my father himself.

"If there was any possible way, Ben. But there isn't. Do you see?"

Finally, a flicker of understanding passed like a shadow through my mind. But for now, it was only a flicker.

Melville's words beaded up along the miles of telephone wire and fell like sand into my ears. I found myself thinking about Peg, how her hair was so black it sometimes shone blue in the sunlight. The normal running of my thoughts had not been interrupted. I wondered when I'd get the call from the First Bank of Wickford and I wondered if Hettie was still listening. "I'll be there in a minute," I said. My tongue stuck to the roof of my mouth. "I'm giving you more blood and I want you to test it again. I want to see the test. I want you to be wrong." All the moisture had drained out of my body. I felt it in my dried-out eyes and in each crossed thread of my skin. I knew that if I clenched my fist, the knuckles would crack open and bleed.

"Your father lived a long and healthy life, Benjamin."

"No, he didn't, you damn liar. Excuse me Melville, but you're a damn liar about that." I would apologize later. But for now he was a liar and we both knew it and Peg knew it and Hettie hiding out there in the raining static knew. The fire had cheated my father out of decades and there was no denying it.

His hand was like a river stone. Its cold bled into my palms and my fingers, not just a chill but deep, glacier-water cold.

They had pulled a white sheet over his head. It covered his whole body. But his arm had swung loose just as I walked in the door. Willoughby lifted the arm and put it resting on my father's chest.

I walked straight over to his hand and held it between my

palms. It wasn't just cold on the surface, but cold all the way through. It gave out cold and chilled the blood in my palms. His scars were still raw pink and bubbled white. The pain was still in them, still raking at his nerves.

I didn't need to see his face. On my way past the smoke of Dillon's and the tiny flood of Dillon's melted ice, running in trickles from his ice shed, I had told myself that I had to see his face. From his face, I would know for myself if he was dead. It didn't matter what they told me on the phone. I didn't trust anyone then. I was ready to call them all liars until I saw his face. But now that I had touched his hand, I didn't need to see the face. Didn't want to. If the pain had marked itself on his eyes and his mouth the way it had done on his hands, I would never be able to get it out of my head. It would be fuel for nightmares for the next thirty years. So I let the blanket rest where they had put it, and I didn't call them liars, but still I couldn't look them in the eye.

"There's no need to draw any blood." Melville had his test tubes ready. There were three tubes, each half-filled with blood. "This is your blood, this is your father's and this is mine."

"Take some out of me now." I rolled up my sleeve and held out my arm, fist clenched and the veins already bulging to the surface. I didn't care about his test. I wanted them to take my blood and channel it into my father's veins. It would warm him, I thought, and bring him back to life. I wanted to pound on my father's chest and start his heart beating again. I'd beat on him until his ribs began to crack.

Melville took my blood. He did his test and said it was proof.

I felt my father's hand again. River stone.

People were talking at me, but I could not hear what they said.

Willoughby had on his purple sash. He was saying prayers over my father.

"Beat on his chest." I sat in a chair in the corner, hands clamped onto my knees, as if I meant to prise off my kneecaps.

"Eh?" Melville was filling out a form on the marble counter top. The nib of his pen scraped on the paper.

"Hit him in the chest and start his heart again."

"It's too late for that, Benjamin."

"Well, did you do it when it wasn't too late? Did you try at least?"

Willoughby's muttering prayer was like an insect buzzing in the room. He kept his eyes closed as he prayed.

Melville put the cap carefully back on his pen. He walked across to me. "I can assure you that correct procedure was followed at all times. If I had known you weren't related to your father, I would never have made a direct transfusion. You have to believe that. But I checked your records and your father's and your mother's, and in all of them it is indicated that you are their natural son."

I stood up to go. "Are you saying that my mother slept with another man?"

Melville sighed and pinched the bridge of his nose. "No, I'm not. But I can't rule that out. It looks to me as if you were adopted. Somebody has lied to you, Benjamin, and maybe they had a good reason. Whatever it was, we might never know, but the lie cost your father his life."

I walked through the house with nothing to see by but moonlight. I didn't know where the day went. It seemed to me I had slept through most of it. The times I woke, I couldn't stand the daylight in my room. I pulled curtains across the windows and lay with my arm crooked across my eyes.

It was the sense of movement that I couldn't stand. Time grinding forward. News of the death crackling through the streets like some electrical current. The more time ground forward, the more I lost sight of him. In my sleep, I watched him falling away, the same as I'd seen him before. He grew fainter and fainter and the last fool hopes of feeding him my blood and punching his heart back to life began to disappear. I could feel the cold that had settled in his body, as if the blood I'd given him could send back messages of the stillness in his veins.

Not my father and mother. Suddenly they were like strangers. Her death had come too soon for me to know her. And now, with him gone, I felt his life distilling down to a staggering of half-completed motions and words. It seemed to me then that soon he would have shrunk in my mind to a single picture—perhaps the raising of his whiskey glass toward the sun and all the honey-tinted rainbows that would spread around the room.

I knew what Melville had told me, but I couldn't make sense of it, as if he'd spoken in a different language. I tried to shove the news far away into a distant corner of my head, but it dragged itself back into the light.

For a while, I forced myself not to cry. It kept him somehow closer to life to clamp my jaw shut and stare at the ceiling until my eyes were painfully dry. I held it back with anger at his vanishing, the same way he had raged against his pain. But as pictures of him grouped in my skull, massing in ranks and charging, I could not hold back the sadness. His face that shimmered in front of me was kind but helpless, and it was this feeling of not being able to help him that snapped the last threads of my strength and blinded me with warm and salty tears. Grief prised open my mouth and leaned into my chest, so that the sounds of my crying leaked out. I had cried more easily for things far less important, but in my lock-jawed silence I had hoped to keep him anchored to the world.

When my eyes finally cleared, and the barbell weight had

lifted from my ribs, I knew he was gone. I could feel only the calm emptiness that he had left behind, not shrieking in pain and ugly with wounds.

He was leaving me now. He was saying good-bye. His brave and smiling face rippled and scattered like a reflection stirred up in a flat-calm pond. When the calmness returned he was gone.

I heard people knocking on the door downstairs. Once I even heard someone come in quietly and leave and, a while later, a smell of apple pie drifted up the stairs.

Not my parents. Each path of my thinking broke down suddenly into the echo of Melville's toneless voice. If this kept up, I knew it would drive me mad. Even as dreams slumped down on top of me, the voice still marched on my brain.

When I woke, the sun had grown paler and fallen through the trees. I was hungry, so I went downstairs to find the pie. It was good and Hettie had made it. I knew it was hers because of the shape of the crust, which was latticed in strips like the pulled-apart threads of a blanket. She was the only one I knew who made lattice crusts. Mrs. Gifford from across the road made thick crusts on her pies like roofs on sturdy houses.

I sat at the kitchen table and ate with my fingers, drinking cold milk from the bottle. Pie tastes better in the dark.

Not my father. Each time my eyes came to rest on a corner of a room or a piece of furniture, a picture of him would spark into view like struck flint. Already this house was haunted.

I heard footsteps outside.

I knew from the walk, that it was Willoughby. I sat down in the horsehair-stuffed chair, put my hands on the sweat-polished arms, and waited.

Willoughby walked in without knocking. He stood for a moment on the doorstep, then saw me in the chair and gasped. "Oh, Benjamin. You gave me a shock."

"I'm just sitting here." I felt like a troll, crouched in the shadows and waiting.

He stepped into the room and closed the door. "I'm sure he really was your father."

There it was again. The babble of a foreign language.

"Melville's just made a mistake. And that's the way we should leave it. There's no good in dredging up the past."

"Do you think I'm just going to shove this aside? We're not talking about some rumor. I gave my father a transfusion of blood and it *killed* him." I kept my hands locked tight on the arms of the chair, as if the room would fall out from beneath me and leave me drifting in space. "Was he my father or wasn't he? And how about my mother? Who the hell was she?"

Willoughby's hand shrank away. "I don't know. That's God's truth. I don't. I came over from Cork and that's a long way south of where Arthur lived. I didn't know him until I came to America."

"He's my father until someone proves to me that he's not." I said it, but the words were hollow in my mouth. I would still call the man my father, but it was because I had no other name to give. An earthquake had come to my vision of the smooth, shining rails and their clear path into the future. The land beneath them had been cracked and blown away. I no longer saw myself moving steadily forward. Instead, I began hurtling into the past, chasing the last fading trace of the dead man. I ransacked the warehouse of my memory, looking for a sign that would have told me of this sooner. But there was nothing.

"Right you are, Benjamin. I'm not believing any chemistry of Melville's." Willoughby pulled a scrap of paper from his pocket. "Does this mean anything to you?"

THE GREY DOG IS FOLLOWING ME. It was Willoughby's writing. I handed back the paper. "Should it mean anything?"

Willoughby sat down in a rocking chair by the fireplace.

"He said that to me before he died. I thought it might hold something for you."

"I don't know any grey dogs." The room had dissolved around me. I felt myself shunted back and forth in my chair by vicious poltergeists.

Willoughby smoothed his brown-spotted hands across his face. "He said a number of things before he passed away. He asked to be cremated."

"If that's what he wanted." Every damn place my eyes settled in the room, there stood the dead man, locked in some action from the past.

"You don't quite understand. The Catholic church does not cremate people. Your father must have known that. He was raving."

"But that is what he asked for?"

"Well, yes." Willoughby took off his collar. It was held to his shirt by two gold studs. He set it down and it lay like a white sickle blade on his knee. "This is a very difficult request, Benjamin. It would never be allowed if we went through the proper channels."

I pictured his ashes as the fine grey dust of burnt pine. I held my breath even against the imagining of the smell. "He should have what he wanted."

Willoughby stood up suddenly. "You idiot! Do you see the spot you've put me in?"

I blinked at him. My mouth fell open a little. He had never shouted at me before. But then I realized he wasn't yelling at me. He was yelling at my father, whose face still seemed to drift in front of Willoughby's old eyes.

"I can't allow it!" He raked his nails across the bare wood of the table. "And still I must allow it. This will have to be kept very quiet. Isn't that right, Ben?"

I nodded, wondering where my father was now. I felt him to be close. It seemed to me I could even hear the faintest rustle of breathing, a sound that did not come from Willoughby or me. I did not understand why he had asked to be burned, after all his life of dousing other fires.

"He also asked that you carry his ashes back to Ireland and scatter them near the town where he used to live. He was quite specific about the place. He wants his ashes scattered on the beach at the town of Lahinch."

I let the words sink in. Then I raised my voice. "But that doesn't make any sense! He hardly ever spoke of the place." There seemed to be some hidden reason in his asking to be cremated that maybe someday would come clear to me. But Ireland? I thought he had long ago shrugged off the place and everything that went with it.

"He didn't speak of it to you, perhaps. But you see, Benjamin, it was where he grew up. It was a kind of holy ground. He didn't need to speak of it, and least of all to you. Of all the things he said and did that make no sense to me, that much I do understand."

I had thought this island was his holy ground, the same as it was for me. I believed it was a thing that joined us across the crevasse of years and misunderstanding. The further I had gone away from Jamestown, the more I found myself returning to it in my mind. My heart beat smoothly here. I felt the rising and falling of the tides in the roar of blood through my body. I had some strange communion with the ghosts of Conanicut Indians, who had lived here and slid without sound across the bay in their white birchbark canoes. And no matter how much Bosley and Hettie treated me like a tourist for going away, I knew and they knew that I was not one. A part of me was anchored here and they could not dislodge it.

Now I realized that I had not spoken of this to him, or to anyone at all. This knowledge of a holy ground could not easily be gathered into words, and even to try was somehow to devalue it.

Even in his pain, he had not been raving. I understood what he wanted. Now I would bring him to the place where his heart had once beat smoothly, because I knew that if anyone could tell me the truth about who he was and who I was, it would be there in that place. I could not go forward until I knew one way or the other. There would be no peace. It could not be swallowed and forgotten. If the people I had called father and mother all my life were not my blood, I had to know why it stayed buried like my nightmares until now.

I walked to the window and looked out into the garden.

My father stood in the moonlight, arms spread wide and his mouth open ready to scream.

I cried out and stepped back.

"What is it?" Willoughby rushed to the window. "What?"

I looked again. It was a scarecrow in the vegetable patch, with a wretched sackcloth face. Floppy-gloved hands stretched palm up, as if waiting for rain. It was my father's coat. My father's hat wedged onto its straw head. I had forgotten about the scarecrow. It had only just been dragged from its winter place, propped up against the lawnmower in the garage.

I stared at the scarecrow. "The only way I'm going to settle this is by going to Ireland. I was born there, you know. A month before my parents left the country."

"I know that." Willoughby's hand settled like a bird on my shoulder. "But what would you do when you got to Ireland? Who would you talk to?"

"There must be town records. There'd be people who remembered my parents."

"There's a war on over there." Willoughby scratched at the back of his neck. "It costs more than you have to get passage on a ship."

"I'm selling the house."

"Oh, for crying out loud!" Willoughby stamped away back to his chair.

"I don't want to live under this roof anymore." I knew that if I came back some day to live on the island, I'd choose the other side or maybe live out toward the cliffs. But I wouldn't come back here. This was his house and it would never be mine. From now on, the murmurs of voices and pictures and smells would keep me from feeling at ease. It wouldn't help to clear out the furniture and repaint the walls, the way some people did when they inherited a place. Then the furniture itself would turn to ghosts.

"You'll be murdered if you go to Ireland." Willoughby began to rock in his chair. He stared straight in front of him. "I'm saying to you there's a war on."

"What are you not telling me?" I paced slowly toward him. "What do you know?"

"Nothing that could help you." He started to put on his collar. Years of wearing it had left a permanent crease in his neck, as if he'd been hanged but survived.

"Let me decide that."

"I believe,"—he cut the air with the knife-edge of his palm—"I believe he was active in trying to get the British out. I don't know how active. I only heard some stories and I'm sure they can't be true."

"What are they?"

"If he didn't tell you, then he didn't want you to know."

"Tell me!" My shout punched off the walls and left behind a shuddering silence.

"I heard he spent some time in prison." Willoughby got up from his rocker and walked into the kitchen. His fingers scraped in the pie tin as he gathered together some crumbs. "You should leave well enough alone."

"What did he mean about the grey dog?"

The scraping stopped in the kitchen. "There's something in my memory that speaks of a grey dog. Some awful godless thing."

"It doesn't matter, then." I could hear the old man's raspy breathing.

"Perhaps not, but the thought of being followed by a grey dog at the hour of my death does something to me in my bones."

The scarecrow's gloved fingers twitched in the wind. It was as if the last spark of my father's life still rested somewhere in the widespread arms, ready to strike out at crows when they dropped squawking from the trees.

CHAPTER 3

A man with pale-blue eyes stood on the doorstep. He was wearing a Panama hat.

"Hello, Thurkettle. What can I do for you?" After Willoughby left, I had fallen asleep with my head on the table. Now the wood grain was printed on my cheek.

Thurkettle tried to smile, but only bared his teeth. He worked for the Maxwell family. Harley Maxwell, the family's only son, was my friend at university. Thurkettle wasn't their butler or chauffeur or gardener, but at one time or another I had seen him being all these things. The Maxwells spent their summers in Newport, just across the bay.

Thurkettle tried to smile again, jaw muscles straining from the effort. "Mr. Maxwell is inviting you over for lunch."

"Why couldn't he come here and invite me himself?" I looked over Thurkettle's shoulder at the Ford in the driveway.

"Mr. Maxwell is practicing his fly-fishing cast on the lawn, sir. He did not wish to be disturbed."

"I swear to God, Thurkettle. I don't know how you put up with it."

Thurkettle's smile flickered on and off, as if he was hooked up to some faulty electric current. "Well, sir." He sounded as if he might have more to say. But that was all of it.

I walked out and stood with him on the doorstep. I looked down at the top of his head. He was going a little bald on top, and combed his hair forward to hide it, while the rest of his hair had all been combed toward the back. "For once, you're not going to call me 'sir.' You're going to come in and have a drink of Dunhams. Powerful stuff. Come in for a drink." I set my hand on his shoulder and guided him inside. I wanted someone to talk with. It didn't matter who, but I felt as if someone was playing tricks on me. Of all the people to send here to my door. If I'd had a thousand people to choose from, stone deaf, blind, and dumb, Thurkettle would have been last on the list.

His neck hunched down as he stepped into the house. He held his hat against his chest. "I was sorry to hear about your father, sir."

"How did you hear about that?" Suddenly I didn't want a drink. The taste of old whiskey had come back into my mouth, its fire long since out. The bitterness it left behind was even a little like soot.

"It was in the paper, sir." Thurkettle fanned his eyes across the living room, at the bare mission-oak furniture that my father had preferred.

"I haven't seen a paper in a while, Thurkettle." I didn't want to go to Belmar. That was the name of the Maxwell's summer house. It was a place so big, it had a name that people mentioned as if of course you had to know what they were talking about. And so big, that BELMAR was blocked in iron letters on the gate that cut off their driveway from the rest of the world.

"Mr. Maxwell has expressed some urgency, sir. He asked me to drive you both ways." Thurkettle looked suddenly hopeful, as if giving me a ride would make the difference.

"It might do me some good to get out of the house." I wished he would sit down and talk with me. I wished to hell he would not keep calling me "sir" all the damn time.

"Oh, indeed, sir." He gripped his hat so tightly that the blood had drained out of his fingers.

"When does he want to see me?"

"Now."

"Important?"

"Always." Thurkettle fitted his hat on his head. He knew I'd given in.

Monahan wrapped chains around the axle of the Ford to keep it steady on deck. When the ferry pulled out into the bay, waves broke against its flat end bow and sprayed across the car's windshield.

I sat next to Thurkettle, gripping my lower lip as I always did when I was thinking hard. "Was there anything in the paper about a blood test?"

"No, sir. It was an obituary."

"I asked you not to keep calling me 'sir.' "

"No, sir. Excuse me. No."

The first time I ever saw the Maxwell's house was on my tenth birthday, long before I'd ever met them. As a birthday present, my parents took me on a bus tour of the Newport mansions. A man with a bullhorn stood next to the driver, calling out the names of the mansions as we passed them. The bus was a double-decker and had no roof. That was why I had wanted to go on the tour. I didn't care where we went as long as I got to sit up top with the wind in my face.

Their house stood on a hill, overlooking the sea. Its driveway ran in a semicircle, through the black iron gate that looked as if it had been forged from old javelins.

Two white marble pillars held up the roof on either side of the doorway. The doors were open. Now, as Thurkettle and I drove up, I could see straight through the house and out across the water. The hall seemed to be lined with mirrors, but it was only the afternoon sunlight, reflected off the rows of family portraits.

The people in the paintings all had the same surprised look, as if they'd been slapped in the face. The frames were crusted with gold-leaf grapes and cherubs holding out fat baby fingers.

I hoped Clarissa wouldn't be there. She was Harley's sister. I could not have stood getting the air kissed in front of my face again. Least of all from Clarissa. I fell in love with her the year before. I fell so hard and fast that last August, I dropped down on my knees and asked her to marry me. I hadn't even introduced her to my father. He barely knew she existed.

My life had been going perfectly until then.

I remembered it all very clearly. I was not the sort of person to get down on my knees. But there I was. And there she was, standing with the sun behind her back. I couldn't really see her in the glare. All I could make out was her silhouette, and the molten gold which seemed to pour from her hands and her face and down the smooth line of her shoulders.

"Marry me," I said. "Marry me." I had only meant to say it once. But a nervousness appeared that I did not expect. It scrabbled up my ribs and showered goosebumps down my back. So I said it again. "Marry me."

Something came unhinged inside. The energy I'd stored away so carefully, stacked like vials of gelignite, came tumbling and breaking down the white path of my bones.

I could no longer help myself. "Please marry me," I said. "I want to marry you. Oh God, I want to marry you."

Then she sighed and the molten gold shuddered around her. My voice trailed away into mumbling.

I don't remember exactly what she told me. The words came with tears and hands jerked open to explain and maybe one of these words was friendship, but with the vials of gelignite still bursting one after the other, I couldn't be sure. I know they were words meant for comfort, but they bounced off my head like marbles off a corrugated iron roof.

Mrs. Maxwell called for me the next day. She started off kindly enough, telling me about the differences between our two families. Catholic and Protestant. Then her patience slipped between the cracks of neatly folded hands. "What did you think you were doing, Benjamin? Was it a joke?" She didn't wait for a reply. She knew what she was going to say, made sure of every word before she came to find me. It had been gathering inside her like clouds. "How, for example, did you think you would support her? I mean, in the manner that she is used to. How did you imagine that we would take the news?"

I knew I didn't have enough money. Their garage was bigger than my house. But I hadn't been thinking that way. I lived next to Harley for five years at school and the differences had not mattered between us. But between Clarissa and me, they were everything.

The hard part about going to the Maxwell's now was that I would always be the person who had proposed to Clarissa. And if Clarissa and I had been friends before, we would be less than that now. People would see to it that we were never alone together again. It would ring along the vines of gossip and never grow dull in the telling.

In the beginning, even after my talk with Mrs. Maxwell, I was still in love with Clarissa. It made no difference that she did not love me. I knew I would make any kind of fool out of myself just to see her again. There was no silence in my head. My skull had become like an orchestra pit, with instruments all playing out of tune. Over and over, I saw myself drop to my knees and heard myself beg her to marry me. Each time, I felt a groan rise out of me, trying to stop the memory. I had to prevent myself from climbing on the next train to New Canaan, reaching her house and not caring what trouble it caused because at least I would be near her.

It was as if she stopped being real. She splintered in my memory. When I thought back on the time, I only recalled shimmers of laughter, glimpses at her eyes and hands and feet.

Now that same angry restlessness had broken open inside me again. I felt the vertigo dizziness of my sanity slipping away. But this time it was worse, and it had nothing to do with Clarissa. Last year, even at the worst acid tide of worry in my guts, I could say to myself and believe it, that I would someday get over this.

Not now. It seemed to me that if I did not find out the truth, Melville's voice would dog me for all time. I thought I'd caught a glimpse of the way my life would unfold, and I took comfort in the smooth unbroken path. It had all dissolved overnight. Chaos gibbered at me from the dark corners of my mind. The longer I waited, the louder it became.

It was a waste of time going to see Harley. What I should have been doing was selling the house and buying a ticket to Ireland. War or no war, someone would be there to tell me the truth.

We stopped on the blinding white stones of the driveway at Belmar.

Thurkettle stayed with the car. He took off his linen jacket and set it carefully on the front seat. Then he opened the car's hood and looked inside. Red-and-white striped braces stretched tight across his shoulders.

I could see he was resting. He knew that no one would bother him while he inspected the car. He stood very still, eyes closed, face bowed slightly forward.

Mrs. Maxwell called me into the study. She stood by the window, looking out at Harley and several others who sat at tables on the terrace. Her breath condensed on the glass. She was barefoot and blue veins coiled around her calves.

She turned when I walked into the room. "Benjamin!"

She spoke with such surprise in her voice that I thought there had been some mistake. They hadn't invited me after all. I pointed out toward the Ford. "Mr. Thurkettle"—I cleared my throat—"drove me all the way here." I let my hand drop. "Nice to see you."

"Nice to see you, too." She looked too young to be Harley's mother. She traveled to Italy every year, to a place called Monte-catini-Terme, and lay in baths filled with black mud to stop her skin from wrinkling. "Did Thurkettle regale you with jokes and stories?"

I narrowed my eyes. "Thurkettle?"

She laughed and her teeth flashed white for a second. "I didn't think so. I once offered him fifty dollars to tell me a good joke. He looked as if he was going to have a heart attack. He went all red." She touched the tips of her fingers to her cheeks and puffed them up. Then quickly her right hand slipped back into the pocket of her dress.

Her right hand was mangled. She had once gone with her husband to the factory where Mr. Maxwell made guns called Krags for troops in the Spanish-American War. Journalists came, too. Mr. Maxwell picked a gun off the assembly line and handed it to his wife. They walked outside to test fire it. Maxwell thought the journalists would be impressed. The gun was loaded and Mrs. Maxwell aimed it at a bank of sand where the test-fired guns were aimed. The gun exploded in her face. It took the thumb and part of her index finger off her right hand.

Harley told me this. He said that the journalists were all paid not to write about what had happened. They were paid and then they were threatened.

The flash burns healed on Mrs. Maxwell's face. But there was nothing to be done about her hand. Now all of her dresses had pockets. Harley said they were lined with rabbit fur. Sometimes her shattered hand found its way out of the pocket, when she wasn't thinking. It waved or pointed or tried to pick something up. Then shock would appear on her face, maybe the same shock as when the gun's jammed breech had burst, and the hand slipped quickly away.

"I wanted to talk with you, Benjamin." She walked onto a Persian carpet in the middle of the room. "Come here and take off your shoes."

"My shoes?" I thought about the black mud on her skin. I kept seeing Clarissa in her eyes and her mouth and her forehead.

"Come and walk on the carpet in your bare feet. This is how Mr. Maxwell bought his carpets. Not from the way they looked, but from the way they felt under his feet."

I kicked off my shoes, rolled my socks into a ball, and walked out next to her. The carpet seemed to shift, bristly against my toes. A waste of time, I wanted to say. Let me be on my way now, so I can sleep without needing Dunhams to cremate my insides and so I can get the hell back on the rails.

Laughter reached through the closed windows. Harley got out of his chair, picked it up and threw it across the lawn. The chair rolled out of sight. The others applauded, three women and two men. They all stood and threw their chairs away. Harley stuffed a cigarette in his mouth. A woman held out a match. Harley bowed forward to the flame, cheeks tensed as he pulled in the smoke.

Mrs. Maxwell bounced slightly on the balls of her heels. "I wanted to say how sorry I was to hear about your father."

"Thank you."

"Clarissa sends her best wishes. She has gone out for the day." I nodded. Clarissa. I couldn't say the name anymore. It was like gnawing on steel wool.

"I wanted to talk to you about Harley. He has always thought of you as a good friend and his closest confidant." Mrs. Maxwell was all out of focus. She was Clarissa for a second, until the age returned to her face.

I had been watching the pattern of the carpet, eyes following lines the way a squirrel runs from branch to branch in a tree. I tried to imagine Harley's father tiptoeing barefoot across the design.

"Harley, as you know, is heir to a rather large sum of money." She raised her eyebrows and the slapped expression of surprise appeared on her face, as if it was news to her, too. "What I am looking for, I should say we are looking for, is someone to handle Harley's accounts. Now I understand that you are soon to be employed at a bank."

"And how do you know that?"

"It was in the obituary." Mrs. Maxwell walked to a red velvet couch and sat down. She sank so far into it that her knees almost banged against her chin. "We would like you to come and work for us. I believe we could do a little better for you than the bank."

I imagined myself in a little room next to Thurkettle's, writing out checks on all of Harley's accounts. I thought of following him into New York City nightclubs, my pockets heavy with change for tipping waiters and busboys and hat-check men. I thought about having to be kind to Harley all the time, even when he was drunk and being an idiot. I glanced at Mrs. Maxwell, and it seemed to me she looked a little desperate, as if a battalion of people had already passed through here this morning, all of them receiving the same job offer and all of them refusing.

Harley and the others had moved to a different table. Now they were playing cards. Only the women were sitting. The men stood behind them, heads tucked in close to their necks, whispering advice and throwing bright red and blue chips out onto a pile.

"I do hope you will consider it, Benjamin. You see, as much as anything, we are anxious to find someone who might help Harley control his expenditures." She smiled and Clarissa flickered again across her features. It was a witch's smile. It could make you do anything, even spend your life helping Harley spend his money.

Something clacked against the window. It was Harley, tapping the glass with a poker chip and trying to see into the dark room. "Benjamin? Is that you? Is my mother holding you prisoner?" He pretended to blow a bugle and ran out of sight.

"I am so sorry about your father," she whispered to me across the bristly red tundra of carpet.

Then the two huge doors swung open and Harley marched into the room. "I am liberating you, Benjamin. From the bonds," he looked around. A poker chip slipped from one hand to the other, a hardened drop of blood between his palms. "Jesus, Mother, do you ever turn the lights on in here?"

Mrs. Maxwell didn't answer. Her toes curled and uncurled on the carpet.

I walked with Harley down the lawn. We each dragged a chair.

The poker players fell silent when I walked past. The smiles froze on their faces.

"Was she giving you a lecture?" Harley set down his chair and slumped into it.

"No." I watched a sailboat coming in to moor at the Max-

well's dock. A man in a blue captain's cap was pulling down
the sails. He misjudged his approach to the dock and his bow
thumped into the pilings.

"Yes she was, you liar." Harley grinned and rummaged in
his pockets for a cigarette. "She was trying to get you to work
for her and stop me spending all the family's money. It's my
fault. I made the mistake of calling you frugal at dinner a few
nights ago."

"I didn't know I was frugal." I sat down in my chair. Two
women and the sailboat captain climbed out onto the dock.

The unlit cigarette wagged in Harley's mouth. "Well, I suppose anyone looks frugal next to me." He began patting his
pockets for a match. "I hear your dad passed on. That's very
bad news. My dad died almost twenty years ago. He was an
old man."

The sailor was walking up the lawn. He wore white trousers
with a blue blazer and had a gold anchor stitched to his cap.
The two women had been swimming and wore towels wrapped
around them.

They stopped when they reached where Harley and I were
sitting.

The captain kept his hands balled in the pockets of his blue
sports coat. "We were thinking of sailing over to Narragansett.
I hear they're racing horses on the beach." Then he looked at
me and nodded.

Harley swung his arm across my shoulder. "This is Benjamin
Sheridan. He and I were at school together. He's eligible!"

I looked down at my feet. "Oh, Jesus."

One of the women laughed as if she had gone mad. Then
she turned red and shut up. She bent down to me and kissed
the air in front of my face. "I've heard Clarissa talk about you.
Isn't Sheridan a local name? Is your father the fire chief over
on Jamestown?" Her face was starry with freckles.

"No. I think that must be someone else."

When they had gone up to the house, Harley went back to patting his pockets. "Matches?"

I shook my head. "Is there anyone who doesn't know I proposed to your sister last year?"

"Hell, I doubt it. She told just about everyone. My kingdom for a light." Then he took out the cigarette and threw it away. "Why did you say your dad isn't the fire chief when he is?"

"Because he's not anymore. And besides, I know what it means to these people to have a father who's a fire chief. It means nothing at all, and they'd just laugh about it. I'm tired of giving these people things to laugh about. And there's another thing, Harley . . ."

"You can't just abandon your family!" Harley's forehead crumpled. You can't deny who they are. I mean, look at me. I know I was a walking goddamn farce at university. I couldn't have just shrugged off being the son of Albert Maxwell. People would have said I was a fraud. So I went the other way." He stood up and spread his arms at the house. "I fucking went and wallowed in it!"

For a second, I saw him again in the smoke-foggy air of a university club called Rudolph's. It was his birthday. He stood at the head of a table, drinking champagne from a trophy cup while the rest of us pounded on the table with our fists. The tables were deep carved with names, and when the wood became so hacked that the tables could no longer be used, they hung them from the walls instead. Harley kept drinking. Champagne dripped from his chin. Fists kept up the drumbeat until his cup was empty.

Harley's arms were still spread. People on the terrace thought he was waving to them and waved back. "You can all go to hell," he told them in a voice they couldn't hear. "That's right. Straight to hell."

"The obituary didn't say how my father died, did it?"

"It said he died in a fire."

"He died when the doctor gave him a transfusion of my blood. It poisoned him. This means it's almost impossible that he was actually my father."

Harley scratched at his chin. "So your mother was a naughty girl."

"The doctor said he couldn't be sure. He said it was his guess because of the blood types that I was adopted. It means that my real father is probably still over in Ireland. Maybe my mother, too." I put my hands in my pockets and looked up at the cloudless blue. "The priest on Jamestown said I should just forget about it, but I've alrady made up my mind to go to Ireland and find out."

"You'll get no peace until you do know. I can tell you that much just on instinct. You can't leave your blood. It's one thing to be adopted, and maybe you were. But not to know. Who could stand that? Your blood is running through somebody's veins over in Ireland. If you try hiding that, either to others or to yourself, you'll drive yourself mad before long. Even if the truth is bad, at least it's there. I'd rather know that my father made his money selling useless guns that blew up in the soldiers' faces and in my mother's face than know nothing at all."

"I've always thought that must be hard to live with."

"It is. But it's given me a purpose in life. It's not even the guns that bother me so much. It's that when my father was called up for duty in the Civil War, he did what was legal at the time and paid a man three hundred dollars to take his place. I remember him saying that at the end of the war the man came back to my father and asked for another three hundred dollars. My father told him that wasn't in the contract and to leave before he called the police. I remember he said 'Why should I pay you twice what we agreed?' The man said 'Because I was at Antietam.' 'So?' my father yelled. And the man kept talking. 'Because on that day the entire regiment that you were supposed to be in were running in a fixed-bayonet charge through a cornfield at the Confederate lines. None of us could see anything but cornstalks. Then suddenly we were out of the corn and in front of us were hundreds and hundreds of Rebel men in their butternut-colored clothes. They all had their guns raised and ready to fire. There were cannons too,' the man said, 'and then those men in butternut were gone all of a sudden behind smoke and the noise made me deaf and the regiment, *your* regiment, Mr. Maxwell, didn't exist anymore.' My father said to him, 'I'm not paying you a damn thing.'

"So spending this family's money the way I do is like a way of paying him myself. I'll keep paying until it's all gone."

He was quiet after that, and I stood up to go. "I have to leave now, Harley."

"Yes." He wasn't really listening. His mind was far away, running with the soldier through the cornfields of Antietam.

Thurkettle and I were just leaving the driveway, when I saw Clarissa walking toward us. She wore an off-white linen dress and was barefoot.

I had been saying something to Thurkettle, but when I caught sight of Clarissa, I fell silent. I waited too long, letting my vision blur around the paleness of her dress against the dark, waxy green of rhododendron bushes that lined the avenue. Strange how even now she seemed to live more clearly in my mind than when I saw her with my eyes.

I turned to ask Thurkettle just to please keep going, but Clarissa had already flagged down the car. She'd been across the road, at one of the other mansions. In her hand she carried a floppy Panama hat, with flowers woven into the brim. She laughed, and smiled as if there had never been any awkwardness between us. She leaned into the car and kissed my cheek and asked me how I was doing.

I didn't remember what I said. Maybe nothing at all.

And I didn't remember what she said, except that her last words to me were to take care of myself. It was as if she knew already that I was going far away. She smiled as if we were friends and would always be friends and maybe she believed it was true. I didn't recall any mention of the death and was glad of that.

The way the light settled on her face reminded me of when I had given her swimming lessons the summer before. I held her body in waist-deep water, while she paddled at waves that crumbled all around us into foam.

Every time I saw her now, I thought of something in the past, even when she was standing there in front of me.

Then Thurkettle and I were driving on toward the ferry. I twisted in my seat to watch her disappear onto the chalky dazzle of the driveway at Belmar. I saw her body outlined through the linen of her dress as she walked past the iron gates. Then I faced forward again and saw how Thurkettle kept his gaze straight ahead at the road. I wanted to ask him what I'd said, but I kept quiet and his face gave nothing away.

We drove along the avenue of mansions. Sun flickered down through the trees.

It was not a mistake to fall in love with Clarissa. I didn't blame myself for doing that. My mistake was trying to leave behind everything I had grown up with and burying it and expecting it all to stay buried. The reason I never introduced her to my father, although I always invented excuses to her and myself, was that I felt ashamed. I was proud of my father and his reputation on the island, but I knew it meant nothing to her and would never mean anything to her. And she never saw our house because in front of her I was ashamed of that, too. I never brought her out to meet my old friends from the island and I never talked about her to them. Even as I asked

PAUL WATKINS 60

Clarissa to marry me, I had somehow convinced myself that none of these things mattered. The shame I felt then didn't come close to the shame I felt now.

My other mistake was not falling out of love, even though I knew I did not belong with Clarissa among these mansions. Having money would not change that, and Mrs. Maxwell asking me to take care of Harley's wealth only rubbed it in deeper.

I couldn't have said just then where I did belong. I used to think I knew, but this death had jolted me off course. Now the island seemed dark and unfamiliar, to me who had called myself its guardian and listened to its heartbeat in the rock.

I hoped that going to Ireland would show me something of where I belonged, even if it pointed me straight back to the island of Jamestown and the house that I wanted to leave. Perhaps it is that way for everyone, I thought. You start out with the whole world to range across and claim, and you end up returning to the place where you started, choosing a few square feet of land, the way that my father had done.

I told Thurkettle not to bother taking the ferry across with me. I said I could walk home from the Jamestown landing.

When he had gone, I listened to bandstand music coming from the town. Soon the café people would move from their metal chairs on the sidewalk to the indoor rooms as the evening chill drifted in off the sea.

Jamestown clumped quiet and shadowy across the water. The music from Newport could be heard all up and down the bay, but you never heard any coming from Jamestown. Instead, you would hear waves breaking on the cliffs at Beavertail, and wind through the rigging of boats in Jamestown harbor. Those sounds were drowned out in Newport. All you heard there was the music.

I stood at the bow of the ferry, tasting salt that sprayed up in my face. Sunset turned the bay into a field of boiling copper.

The ferry was almost empty. The Newport people never came to Jamestown, unless it was to pass through on their way to the mainland. Then some of them took the Kingston train back up to Boston or down to New York and Philadelphia.

They almost never walked through Jamestown village, because there was nothing to buy except hardware from Briggs's general store or groceries from Allington's. So they moved quickly past the squat houses with their sun-bleached paint and lobster pots set out to dry in the backyards.

To the island people, downtown Newport was a bubble of laughter and songs, which they could touch now and then but which was not theirs. When winter came, the bubble disappeared. Half the shops closed down. The metal café chairs that used to jam the sidewalks lay stacked inside the closed cafés. Sailors in their dark wool coats shuffled down Thames Street with their collars turned up against the wind. Fishermen waited out storms in their drafty dockside huts.

I used to wonder what the Newport people did all through the winter. I imagined them hidden away in rooms with dark-paneled walls and green felt-covered card tables, impatient for the snow to melt and for the Gulf Stream to return.

A nurse stood on deck with me. She wore a blue cloak with a red trim over her white clothes. She was pushing an old man in a wheelchair. The old man's head was tilted to one side. A tartan blanket covered his legs.

They had come from the Sturgess Rest Home, which had a little wooden sign out front that said—DROP IN FOR A SMILE. So when we were younger, we used to walk past and give our version of a Sturgess Home Smile, which was a mindless slobbering grin.

Often the old people would be wheeled out to the dock to watch the ships come in. The old people seemed mostly to be interested in themselves. I'd seen men and women slumped in wheelchairs, pushed into patches of sunlight, and the only part of them that seemed to be alive was their eyes. Sometimes they studied their hands, fingers wafting gently like weeds in the current of a stream. With nothing else to do, the nursing-home residents became students of their own disintegration.

Sometimes my father had spat out how miserable he thought they looked, but I wondered if he would have said it, if he knew how much time he had left.

Two men were standing in my driveway. The engine of their car was still running.

I recognized them as the same two men my father had been yelling at, the night Dillon's fishhouse burnt down. They wore the same long raincoats and kept their hands stuffed in their pockets.

They watched me coming closer. Then one man said "It's him," and walked across to meet me. His hand slipped from his pocket and reached out to me like the blade of a knife. "We come to say we're sorry about your da." He was Irish, with a faint American twisting of the words. "I'm Pratt and this is Duffy. Come here out of the dark, Duff."

Duffy shuffled over. The tight curls of his hair were mashed down on his head with brilliantine. "Your father was a great man."

Pratt nodded. "An inspiration to us all."

Pratt slapped Duffy on the arm. "Anyway, that's all we came to say."

"You were talking with my father the night of the fire."

Now Pratt turned. "Yes, we were. Did he mention that?"

"He said you owed him money. He said you were crazy for showing your face around here."

"Money was it?" Pratt chewed his lip and then laughed. "Well, I'm sure I might owe him a bit."

I moved to the front door at the house and swung it open. "Would you like to come inside? I'd like to talk with you."

"No." Duffy took a step toward the car. "No, we got to be going."

I stood in the doorway. It was dark behind me and I felt as if I was standing at the entrance of a tunnel. "How much do you know about what my father did in Ireland?"

They were quiet for a while. I heard waves breaking on the beach. I stood very still, barely breathing, frightened that they knew everything but wouldn't tell me.

Pratt's hands found their way back inside his pockets. "It really is time we were going."

I wanted to force them to stay. "What did he do? I heard he was in prison."

"If he'd meant for you to know these things, then surely he'd have told you himself." Duffy opened the car door and sat behind the wheel.

"Don't go. Please. Who are you two? How did you know my father?"

"We're old friends is all." Pratt had reached the car. He rested his hand on the door. "And if you heard us talking the other night, you'd have heard us promise to keep you out of it."

"But what harm is there in telling now?"

Pratt slipped into the car and before the door was shut, Duffy had already started the engine.

First I only walked after them. Then I ran. I chased them

down to the edge of the road and saw Pratt turn to look at me. "Why won't you tell me?" I shouted after them. "For Christ's sake, why?"

I wouldn't be able to catch them. And even if I did, they wouldn't tell. I had seen a window, when they paused and thought it over. They had come close to talking. The words were already forming in their minds. But the window shut quickly and they knew they had to leave before they broke their promise to my father.

They could have told me everything. I knew it. I could see it on their faces. And I knew I would never see them again.

I knew nothing about Ireland, except that my parents came from the west coast. They never spoke of it, and they were not the only ones to start again as they passed through the gates of Ellis Island. I had friends at university whose German or French or Italian parents seemed to have forgotten where they came from. It had not troubled me until now, but suddenly it was all I cared about.

I started packing. I threw a suitcase on the bed and crammed in socks and trousers and shoes. There was no time to waste. I didn't know how long it would take to sell the house. I'd have sold it for one ticket, if the boat was sailing that day.

Perhaps in Ireland there was also a window, and if I didn't get there soon, it too would close. The country seemed an impossible distance away, anchored out of reach somewhere in the past.

CHAPTER 4

The masts of sunken sailboats jutted from the harbor like dead trees in a flooded field. Dillon's fishhouse had almost disappeared. Its roof lay slopped into the guts of the building. Paint had blistered on its walls. The breeze lifted ashes from the rubble and blew them across the dockyard.

I stood at the ferry landing. The ferry was halfway across the bay, its bow snubbing the waves. I could just make out the figure of Monahan, in his red-and-black check coat, standing outside the wheelhouse with his hands tucked behind his back.

I had written out an ad for selling the house and now I was going to Wickford, where I'd place it in the paper. It was strange to think of leaving the island. But in my mind I had already sold the house and left. At the bank, I would tell them that I needed some time before starting. If they turned me down, I figured, I could always work for Harley.

The area around Dillon's had been roped off, but children ducked under the rope, grabbed pieces of wood and steel and ran away with them as trophies. There was nothing worth taking, but the fire had made the junk special. I knew it was also because my father had been blown through the side of the building by the exploding diesel tank. Its closeness to his death had turned the melted iron and charcoaled wood into talismans.

As the ferry dodged past sunken boats and made toward the landing, I caught sight of Willoughby. He wore a coat over his black robe. The collar was a flash of bony white across his throat. He carried a small suitcase hugged to his chest.

Seeing Willoughby reminded me of unfinished business. I knew about the rush of documents and bills and funerals to be organized from when my mother died. Dying was expensive. It cost my father two weeks' pay to have a decent tombstone set above her grave.

It could all wait. I had no patience for it now.

Willoughby lifted one hand and showed me the paleness of his palm. Then he walked off the boat straight toward me. "I was just coming to see you, Ben. See how you've been getting on."

"Not too bad." Cars started their engines and climbed off the ramp. They kicked up dust on their way into town.

He held up the suitcase. "This is for you."

"I was just heading into Wickford to put in an ad for the house." I watched him closely, waiting for creases to slice across his forehead and for the blood to drain from his lips as he pressed them tight together. I had stopped caring or even wanting to know why it made him so angry for me to be selling the place. I wished I could have made him stand in the living room and see the pictures of my father and the odd and distant image of my mother, sparking off the walls and chairs like a squadron of fireflies. That would have made him change his mind.

"I think that can wait for a while." The creases split his forehead into strips. He handed me the suitcase.

It was heavy. Somehow I had thought that it was only filled with clothes. "The paper only comes out twice a week. If I don't place the ad in now, I'll have to wait a long time before they can fit it in."

"You don't need to sell the house. Not to get your ticket." His hand found its way to the familiar perch of my shoulder. "I've got you a place on a boat leaving from Boston. It's heading to Galway with a load of farm equipment."

"When?" Suddenly I saw myself walking down a gangplank into Ireland. The picture was so clear and sudden that for a moment Jamestown seemed to disappear out from underneath me.

"Three days. The captain is an old parishioner of mine. It won't be comfortable. It's only a cargo ship."

"That doesn't matter. Thank you."

"I daresay you're already packed."

It seemed to me sometimes as if my skull was like rice paper to Willoughby, with thoughts lit up like candle flames behind it. "What's in the suitcase?"

"The ashes."

I slammed the case down on the ground. The flesh cringed on my arms.

Willoughby bent slowly down and picked up the case again. "I took care of the cremation."

We reached the road and started heading toward my house. I kept looking straight ahead, not wanting to catch sight of the case in Willoughby's hand. I could not see a man reduced to this.

"Have you had many people stopping by?" His overcoat rustled as he walked. Sea spray still clung in beads to the cloth.

"Two men came by last night. They were talking to my dad the night of the fire. I'd never seen them before that. They were Irish. Their names were Duffy and Pratt."

"That doesn't sound familiar."

"My father was angry with them about something. They wanted money but he wouldn't give them any. He said they were mad showing their faces around here. And he said if they wanted money, they should come to you, but they didn't want to do that. I guess they drew the line at taking money from a priest."

Willoughby walked on a few paces and then suddenly stopped.

A car drove past us, clunking through its gears. Leaves flickered in the breeze. All around us, the grass was thick and heavy in the first green blaze of summer.

"Did you say this man was named Pratt? With a nose like a bird? About as tall as me?"

"That's him."

Willoughby seemed to be watching me, but then I saw that he was staring out across the bay. I even turned to see what had caught his eye, but there was only the white-capped water and Monahan's ferry, heading back to the mainland.

Then Willoughby changed direction. He began walking back toward town. "Come with me," he called over his shoulder.

He turned down a side road before we reached town. We walked down a dirt lane crowded at the edges with purple-flowered chicory and black-eyed Susans with petals so bright yellow-orange that they seemed to fizz in my eyes.

Willoughby led me to the cemetery, stepping fast beside the thunder-colored tongues of old graves, past my mother's, where I thought he was going to stop. He kept going until he reached the far wall, where poison ivy had already begun to creep its oily leaves across the stones.

The suitcase thumped down in the grass and he swept back the tall weeds that had grown around a stone.

The stone said: JOHN THOMAS PRATT. BORN ARAN IRELAND 1878. DIED JAMESTOWN JANUARY 7th 1904.

Then he cleared away another stone. MICHAEL DUFFY. BORN CONNEMARA IRELAND 1881. DIED JAMESTOWN JANUARY 7th 1904.

Willoughby pulled up the weeds and threw them over the wall. "They must think that no one would remember after all this time. They didn't even bother to give you false names." He swung around and faced me. "You see, these aren't their graves. These are only memorial stones. Which your father and I paid for, I should add."

"So why did they need memorials? How could you think they were dead?"

"Do you remember when the bay froze over in the winter of 1904?"

"Yes." I remembered walking on the beach with my mother. Waves were frozen into green humps on the sand. I couldn't touch the brass buttons of my coat because my mother said my fingers might freeze to them. Steam rose off the ice, climbing so thickly that I couldn't see the mainland.

"Duffy and Pratt had just come here from Ireland. God knows, they were in some kind of trouble because even the Ancient Order of Hibernians up in Boston wouldn't help them and they helped almost any Irishman who'd been in trouble back in the old country. I don't know what these boys had done. They shacked up with your dad for a few days. He must have known them in Ireland, but he wouldn't say and warned me not to ask questions. Well, when the bay froze, your father and these two men decided to run across for a lark. I was there when they started their crossing. It was fine for a bit. The ice was as solid as paving stones. Then I started hearing cracks when they put down their feet. The ice was splitting. The sound was almost like gunfire. I lost sight of them in the mist, but I was calling at them to turn back. Then after a bit, I saw a shape running toward me and it was your father. He said that Pratt and Duffy had gone ahead and were still trying to cross. And that was it. Nobody ever heard from them again. Nobody saw them reach the mainland. We waited for their bodies to wash ashore in the spring, but they never did. We all assumed that they'd been carried out to sea when the ice melted. So there was nothing to bury. And nothing to assume except that they had died. That's why we put up the stones."

Moss had filled in their names. Willoughby bent down and carved it out with his thumb. "Your father must have known. He never said a word about it to me." Then he stood, knees cracking. The blood had run into his face. He tried to smile, as if to show it didn't matter any more.

"I wonder why they needed to disappear." I started walking back toward the road. Bees belly-flopped into the chicory flowers, and rolled around in the pollen.

"They needed to make a new start, same as your father."

"Well, then why did they come back?"

"They need another favor. And who do men who are supposed to be dead go to when they need some help? To the only person who knows they're still alive. There's a lot going on now in Ireland. I'm sure that many favors are being asked." He raised a finger and held it out to me in warning. "It's a war, Benjamin."

"I read the papers."

"Yes, but do you understand? There's Catholic gunmen fighting in the streets with English soldiers and some of the Protestant Irish who want the English to stay. I think of that, and I ask myself why I'm helping you go to this country."

"You want to know as badly as I do what he was hiding. That's why."

Willoughby stayed quiet for a while. Then he breathed in deep and said, "Perhaps." The heels of his heavy black shoes dug into the road.

The suitcase contained a cylinder. Its nickel sides had a soft yellow-silver shine, smudged by fingerprints. The ashes were inside.

I set it on the table. The cylinder wasn't large, but its weight was like lead.

A man reduced to this, I thought again. I couldn't see it. No strength in me could cram the memory of my barrel-chested father into a space so small.

Maybe in time, I thought. But for now the smooth gleam of the cylinder was so far from the dullness of ashes and even farther from the solidity of my father's body, that I could only think of it as a strange piece of furniture.

"Mr. Sheridan? Hellooo! This is Arnold from the bank."

I had forgotten about the bank. Instead I had become lost in the muddle of packing. I was only bringing one suitcase, but couldn't figure out what things to take. I'd spent the last hour sitting on the end of the bed, my hands tucked into different pairs of shoes, inspecting each one as if I'd never seen it before and wondering which would be best for the trip.

I could hear Arnold thumbing through some papers as he talked to me over the phone. "I'm just calling to say you should be here a clear half hour before the bank opens tomorrow. It's your big day."

Arnold had a gut. It was so much like a pregnant woman's belly that in the middle of the interview, I had thought about reaching across and patting it. He had a salesman's voice. New customers at the bank were always sent to Arnold. I heard that he was important to the bank because he could drink anyone under the table and still make sense. He spent most of his days taking important clients out to lunch and drinking them under the table, but not before he made them buy more bonds.

The trouble with Arnold's salesman's voice was that it never stopped being a salesman's voice. I knew that already, and I had only met him twice. I wondered how his wife could stand it. Living with Arnold, I imagined, was like living in a nonstop auction house.

"Hello, Arnold."

"Hellooo!"

"I can't come to work for the bank for another month. Maybe longer." I spent a few minutes telling him why. I leaned against the rubbed patch on the wall and left out as many details as I could.

He clicked his tongue whenever I paused for breath.

It wasn't going well. I told him I knew it meant he might have to reconsider giving me the job. I said I understood. But it couldn't be helped, I told him.

Arnold clicked at me like a slow-running clock and then said he'd have to call me back.

I'd lost the job. No doubt about that. It surprised me how little I cared.

The house seemed strangely quiet after I'd hung up the telephone. I had been hoping he might become angry. Tell me I was fired even before I had started. Then I went back upstairs and kept packing.

I was not afraid of the war in Ireland. I didn't really believe that it was a war, not like the headlines of 1916—Verdun, Jutland, Ypres—burying the Irish rising of that year under barrage after barrage. It barely seemed important, when the whole of Europe was being plowed underground, with twenty thousand casualties in one July day on the Somme. The only thing I could clearly recall about the Irish rebellion was my father reading an article at breakfast, then rolling up the paper and slamming it down on the table. "They're shooting the poor bastards!" he yelled.

Instead of fearing the war, I was afraid that I would travel all the way across the Atlantic and find that no one could tell me what I wanted to know. I had no plan for what to do if that happened. I didn't even have a plan for what to do if they did tell me. All I had now was the impatience to be gone. It blanketed all other thoughts.

———

Hettie stood on the doorstep. She had a ledge of breast. In her outstretched arms she held a pie with steam still rising from the crust.

"Good morning, Hett." I remembered when she used to be skinny. The bones of her ribs stuck out. Then she had started to grow, skin piling on skin, and it seemed for a while that she would never stop growing. At first, she was ashamed of her breasts. Then, for a while, she was proud of them. But when they grew too big, she went back to being ashamed, and wore baggy dresses to hide them.

Years before, she and I used to hunt for steamer clams in the low-tide mud of Mackerel Cove. We threw stones onto the wave-smoothed rocks and wherever a jet of water shot up, a clam had closed shut against the shock. We dug in the black sand to find them. Grit scraped our fingernails white. Sometimes we dug up the heavier quahog clams, which the Indians used to make wampum. We broke them on the rocks and ate them raw, skimming the purple-rimmed shells back out into the water.

Hettie smiled and the pie was heavy in her outstretched arms. "I baked you another." Then the smile peeled away. "Oh, Benjamin. Are you all right? Are you coping here all by yourself?"

There was only the sound of forks clicking through pie-crust and touching the china plates.

The pie had been made with blackberries picked out on Dutch Island the year before. They were picked in late summer when the jellyfish came to the bay, waves of them, first clear ones and then pink ones, washing up on the sand.

I'd helped her pick the berries. She and Bosley and I had all sailed out to the island in Bosley's homemade boat and gathered them in buckets made of tin. Then Hettie bottled the berries and stored them in a closet under the staircase. The closet was filled with bottles, holding the dark sweetness of strawberries and raspberries and peaches.

Hettie's face had gone red with the warmth of the pie. "You can taste the summer in these berries, can't you?"

"I was just going to say it myself."

She stared at me now.

I knew what she was thinking. "He died in his sleep, Hett. There wasn't any pain. I'm coping very well."

"It must be so difficult."

"It's not difficult all at once. I think it's more a thing that's difficult in small ways for a long time." I set a berry on my tongue and crushed it against the roof of my mouth. It was true you could taste the summer in them. I thought back to the sea-rose bushes and their shabby pink blossoms that came in late August and the northeaster storms that blew all the petals away. For as long as the berry lasted in my mouth, I let the old summer spark back to life in my head.

"I always missed you when you went away." Hettie cut herself another piece of pie. She set the slice carefully on her plate. The dark juice seeped slowly out from under the crust. "Do you know, Benjamin, I used to be in love with you."

I grinned awkwardly and did not know where to look.

Hettie spoke with a mouthful of pie and her teeth were a little bit blue. "It's true. I can say it now because it was such a long time ago. Well, maybe it was and maybe it wasn't. I used to think that someday we'd be married." She raised her head and scanned the ceiling. "I used to think we'd live here in this house."

"Did you, Hett?" I followed her eyes to the ceiling, as if something might be there to change the subject. "Well, I'm sure I used to think about it, too. Back in the days when we went clamming. Do you remember?"

"That far back?" Her fork clacked down on the plate. "I'm not talking about that far back! I'm talking about last summer!"

"Were you, Hett?" I smoothed sweat off my face with the palm of my hand. "I didn't know."

"I should have told you then. Right when we were picking berries on Dutch Island. Before you went and asked that Newport woman to marry you."

I sighed and swallowed the mouthful. Now the summer had gone from the berries. I didn't know how she had found out. Probably she'd heard it on a telephone line. There was a time when her knowing about it would have sent a corkscrew feeling through my guts, but all it drew from me now was a pinch at the back of my neck, like I felt sometimes when the weather was thundery.

"Do you still love her, Benjamin? Do you love her like I loved you last summer?"

"Oh, Hett. Please." I tapped my fork on the plate.

"Oh, Hett nothing! You give me an answer." She looked as if she might lunge for me. Her legs seemed braced to spring.

"I don't know. I thought I loved her but that was a long time ago."

"If you loved her, then you should never have let her go. You should have done whatever it took to keep her." Hettie owned the silence that followed. She let it drift for a while.

I thought back to the times when I had to lock myself in my room so as not to get on the next train to New Canaan and be near Clarissa. A vial of acid fell shattering through my body. Maybe I should have gone. For the first time in ages, doubt scrambled my nerves.

"I should have done the same to keep you, shouldn't I?"

I shrugged. I wished things could have been simple again between us. Back to the time of clam digging in the mud.

"But I lost you, didn't I?" Her hands were spread flat on the table. "And now you're probably moving away from here, and I will have lost you for good. It's true, isn't it, Benjamin?"

I met her eyes and it was painful to keep up the stare. But I could not look away. I thought I owed her more than that. "It is true, Hett."

"Yes." Now she looked down at the mashed remains of the pie. She began to cry without sound.

She did lose me, but long before she thought she had. I lost her, too, and I wondered if I would regret it someday.

When she had gone, I felt a vast, black quiet settle on the place. It was this quiet that she had come to chase away— Hettie who had brought pies before to this house and to others and who knew the silence of houses of the dead.

Bosley delivered the mail. He would make his deliveries until the fire bell rang. Then he'd sling the udder of his mailbag onto his back and run with flat feet to the volunteer fireman's house. He wore his oilcloth fireman's coat over the sky-blue mailman's uniform, as if to remind me that I had betrayed him and he was not yet ready to forgive.

Bosley had always been the clumsy kid. He was the one who would tangle his kite in the trees or crash his bicycle in the first week that he got it. Bosley's elbows and knees were always bloody from his clumsiness.

To prove that he wasn't clumsy anymore, Bosley had built himself a boat. It was a dinghy with a mast and sail. On the stern, he painted *Mary-Sue*. The letters started out big but grew thinner and smaller as he ran out of space.

On the summer weekends, he took his boat out on the bay. *Mary-Sue* wobbled through the harbor, square sail thrashing on its lines. One time he sailed to Saunderstown. Then he had to take the ferry back, dragging his dinghy up the car ramp, because he didn't know about tacking against the wind to cross the bay again.

"How's your boat, Bos? Did it survive the fire?"

"I don't know." He raked his fingernails back and forth across the mailbag. It left cloudy trails in the leather. "When the fire started, I rowed out to the mooring, but it was already gone. I don't know if it sank or if it got loose. I like to think it got loose. I think about it drifting out to sea. Maybe it will wash ashore on a desert island and save some castaway."

"Who was *Mary-Sue*, anyway?"

"My boat. Just my boat." He pulled a roll of paper from his tunic and handed it to me. "This is because I feel bad about your father."

It was a scrolled certificate, painted with angels and crosses and the first letter of every paragraph bloated with gold. The certificate said that the name Arthur Sheridan would be mentioned every day in prayers at the church of St. Anthony in Boston.

"They do it for a penny a day. I paid them a year in advance. I figure you could hang it over the fireplace if you wanted to."

"Could do." The angels all had clown-smiles, with grins reaching up to their ears.

"You know what I found in the attic yesterday?" He pulled a revolver from his mailbag. It was the one he and I had used to shoot pie tins in the woods. "Do you think we still remember how to use it?"

I took Hettie's pie tin and wedged it upright in a crack of the wall that ran behind the house. I counted back the twenty-five paces. Then I handed the gun, butt-first, to Bosley.

"You go ahead, Benjamin. Let's see if you remember."

I shot it off the wall and shot it again in the air. The smacking sound of bullets punching through tin brought me back for a moment to the time in the woods and the sulking of my father when he learned what I had done. I handed the gun back to Bosley and we didn't shoot it again. I knew I could shoot for the rest of the week and not hit the pie tin in the air the way I had just done.

Bosley knew it, too, and he didn't want to try. He stuffed the gun back in his bag. "So you'll be leaving town now, I reckon."

"Yes, Bos." The gunshots made a distant rumble in my head.

"Seems to me you're always leaving some place, Benjamin."

"You're right, Bos."

Bos nodded. "I know it."

I looked back at the island as I headed for the mainland. I thought of the stillness of the house, all doors locked and windows shut. The dust was already settling.

Willoughby said he'd keep me company across the bay. He stood next to me, his back unnaturally straight, the way he did when he was giving sermons. He stuffed a heavy envelop into my hand. "The *Madrigal* will drop you off in Galway. You'll find a man there to meet you. I sent a wire last night. The man's name is Justin Fuller. He's an old friend of mine and your father's. There's several letters in that envelope, that I've written over time. I've included a note that will explain everything to him. He'll take you south to the town of Lahinch. That was where your father and mother used to live. I want you to promise me something."

Justin Fuller, I was thinking. I tore through my mind, hunting for a memory of the name, and there was nothing.

"Promise me, Benjamin, that you'll scatter the ashes and head back to Galway and come home when the *Madrigal* leaves port. That should give you about three days. She'll pick up a cargo of crystal and wool in Cork and then she'll head straight back to Boston."

"But what about the questions? What about talking to people and finding out who my father is? Do I have any family in this place Lahinch?"

"Not as far as I know." Willoughby smoothed his fingers through his silver hair. He was trying to remember, but if there had been names in his memory, they had slipped away long ago. "When you board the ship now, you'd perhaps do best not to mention that you're carrying the ashes. They're a superstitious lot out on the water and they're liable to see it as bad luck. You'd just do best to keep it to yourself."

"So what should I tell them when they ask why I'm going?"

"Well, there's a hundred reasons why someone should wish to cross the Atlantic. Tell them you're going to visit family. Now, you've got your papers?"

I patted the chest pocket of my coat.

"And you've got money?"

I patted my other chest pocket. It was all my savings.

"And the ashes?"

I had packed the urn into my suitcase, safe among the trousers and the shirts.

"You stay if you have to, Benjamin. You do as you see best. Sometimes I forget that you're grown up now. I still remember you in your short trousers, down at the Narrow River, raking up clams for dinner. It's true, I do. The time"—he held out his hand, palm up and shaking from old age—"it pours through your fingers like little grains of barley."

I looked at him and thought, You're falling away, too, just like my father did. How does it feel to fall away?

All across the bay, wind carved out waves, the crystal of melting icebergs drifting down from the north. I tried to imagine my father running across the ice of the frozen bay, how he would have laughed to make himself brave, listening for the groan of the cracking surface. I wished I had been there to run with him. Closing my eyes, I pictured the dark below the ice, where blue crabs waited blind in the stillness, tapping their way from rock to weed to rock, hearing the strange thump of footsteps overhead.

Railroad tracks reflected sun, like lightning bolts captured and straightened and laid out side by side.

I sat on a bench at Kingston station. The stationhouse was small, with a blurred window at the ticket booth and benches like pews in a church but arched to fit against the small of a person's back.

The bone-snap sound of a car's parking brake made me turn. I saw Thurkettle stepping from the Ford. Thurkettle walked around to the other door and opened it to let Harley climb out.

"I have arrived!" Harley spread his arms wide.

"Hello, Harley! Hello, Thurkettle!" I was glad to have company.

Thurkettle started to wave hello. He flapped at the air with one hand, then stopped and fidgeted and flapped with the other.

"You mustn't do that to him. You catch the poor man off guard." Harley pulled a handful of coins from his pocket, selected three pennies and put them on the nearest rail. Then he stood back on the platform and pointed to the bright spots of copper. "The train squashes them flat as postage stamps."

"Thanks for coming to see me off."

"You didn't think I would, did you?"

"No." A chevron of Canada geese flew past, squabbling in the pale sky.

"Shows how much you know. As a matter of fact, Benjamin,

I came here hoping I could talk you out of going. I know I've left it to the last minute, but the last minute is often the only time a person can see something clearly." Harley stepped out onto the tracks. He ran his shoe along the polished rail. "You've got a nice, calm life here. But if you get on this train, your life is going to change. You may find calm again, but it's not going to be the same as you have now. Your parents didn't just forget to tell you about their life before they came to America. They did it for a reason. And they loved you, so the reason must have been a good one. I know I said a lot of things earlier about how you can't run away from the truth. But maybe I was wrong. Maybe the truth is that you were never supposed to know. You can't dig up the past and go back to living the way you were before."

"I don't want to go back to the way I was before."

"But how far are you prepared to go? Have you thought about what it might cost? People might not want the past to be uncovered. Their own nice calm lives might be at stake. And they'll fight you for that calm. They'll fight you with everything they've got."

I watched the coins on the tracks. "Yes, I imagine they would."

"So it hasn't worked. I haven't talked you out of it?"

"No."

"I don't think I've ever tried to talk anyone out of something before. Mostly it's been people trying to talk me out of things. I needed more practice. Then it would have worked."

"Maybe so."

The stationmaster walked outside. He wore a red cap with a black brim and carried a brass whistle on a cord around his neck. He pointed south down the tracks, rolling and unrolling a yellow flag attached to a baton. "See it?" A column of steam frothed above the trees. Then the train came into view.

I set my hand on Harley's shoulder. "Thank you, Harley."

The tracks began to ping. The pennies shuddered on the mercury-shining steel.

Harley squinted at the approaching train, which swallowed the lightning-bolt tracks and hid us in curtains of steam. He said something, but I couldn't hear what it was. Then he turned and walked fast toward his car, hands in pockets, shoulders hunched. He didn't look back.

Thurkettle opened the door.

I picked up my suitcase and climbed on board. I looked through the window, hand raised to wave good-bye, but Harley had already gone.

PART 2

CHAPTER 5

Thunder.

I climbed from my bunk and swung open the porthole. The night air was thick with fog. Waves barged out of the dark and broke against the *Madrigal*'s hull.

Thunder. There it was again. I pulled on my clothes. They hung like a fireman's from a wooden peg, shirtsleeves inside coatsleeves, trousers dangling from suspenders.

I stopped on the gridded iron stairs that led up to the deck. From here, I could see down into the engine room. The constant trample of the engines had long since made me deaf. The reek of diesel fuel was in my spit and clothes and sweat.

I tried to remember how long I'd been at sea. One by one my fingers uncurled as I tried to mark each day, but time meshed together and I couldn't keep count.

Thunder. I walked up to the deck. The fog seemed to rush at my face. Three crewmen stood near the bow, looking out into the fog.

"Is there a storm?" I asked them.

Only one crewman turned. His name was Baldwin. "The cliffs!" he yelled. "Waves against the Cliffs of Moher!"

"I thought it was thunder." I felt my weight shift from foot to foot as the *Madrigal* rolled in the waves. "How are you ever going to find the port in this fog? Is there a lighthouse?"

Now Baldwin walked closer. "I tell you what. You go back to your room and get dressed in your shiny shoes and your

Big Town Yankee suit and prepare for going ashore." He took his hands from the pockets of his heavy black coat, slowly and with a strain on his face, as if it was a favor that he didn't want to do. He reached his hands up to my shoulders. "We'll ask for your help if we need it."

I thought about strangling Baldwin, imagined closing my hands on the tough elephant leather of his neck and digging my fingers in deep.

I wasn't welcome on the boat. Most of the crew just ignored me, but Baldwin seemed to enjoy his constant volley of half-insults, never quite enough to start a fight, taunting me as if I was an old bear tied to a tree with no way to defend myself.

I had a small bunkroom. Six paces to the window and three from side to side. The walls were paneled with dark wood. I had the place to myself, which pleased me at first, but then began to drive me mad.

Each time I walked into the galley, following a path of mumbling voices and pots clattering on the stove, all talk stopped and eyes shifted down. The only sound then was the scrape of spoons in bowls, and chairs scudding back across the floor as men got up to leave. I counted nine men on the crew, including the captain, who had shaken my hand when he boarded the ship and then completely disappeared. All of them were Irish.

For the first three days, while I could still keep track of time, seasickness hollowed me out. I had bruises on my collarbone from rushing at the porthole to throw up.

Now and then, Baldwin would knock on the door and ask if I wanted to eat, listing off combinations of food that he thought would make me feel worse.

After four days, the sickness went away. I slept through one night, and when I woke I lunged out of my bunk, making for the porthole. I swung back the latch and stuck my head out. It was only then that I realized I didn't need to be sick.

That evening, Baldwin carried in a tray of food. There was soup and buttered bread and an apple and tea.

While I ate, he sat cross-legged on the floor. His face was round and he had blond hair cut so short it stuck up in pine-wood-colored spikes.

I lifted the bowl of soup to my mouth and drank it all. The bread went next, then the apple and the tea. It went down fast and half-chewed and barely tasted. "What have I done to get you so angry at me?"

Baldwin patted a rhythm on his knees, as if he had a song in his head that wouldn't go away. "Captain says we're not supposed to bother you. He said no questions. Told us to mind our own bloody business. These days it seems as if every trip we make to Ireland and every trip back to Boston, there's someone coming along with us who we're not allowed to talk to. It's a risky business carrying people like you and it makes a bad job worse."

I remembered what Willoughby had said about not mentioning the ashes, so I told him I was going to see my family.

"Are you?" His expression didn't change.

"Yes, as a matter of fact."

"Well." He climbed off the floor, and slapped the dust from his backside. "There we are, then."

"You don't believe me, do you?"

"No." He walked away into the guts of the ship. "As a matter of fact."

Boredom took the place of sickness.

I began to think of how it might have been to travel on a liner. Drinks before dinner. Chefs with butcher knives who cut slices from roasts set out on buffet tables. In my daydreams, I pointed to the parsleyed potatoes, holding out an imaginary plate. I heard the clink of glasses and silver knives and forks.

When the daydreams were over, I wandered the corridors to the crew's mess and sat at a metal table eating what the crew had left behind. I watched ladles and copper mixing bowls swinging constantly and evenly on their hooks with the motion of the waves.

Signs appeared on doors. CREW ONLY. They were handwritten signs, stuck up with white tape that looked as if it had been borrowed from a first-aid kit.

Maybe a liner wouldn't have been as expensive as all that, I thought. Not if I traveled second class. At least they might have a library. I thought of green felt-covered tables in the reading room and brass buzzers you could press which would bring a waiter up from below. Then I'd ask for coffee and the waiter would bring it on a tray with silver tongs for lifting crumbly sugar cubes into my coffee, holding them there until the cubes vanished. And maybe once I'd slide a silver teaspoon up my sleeve and carry it to my room and study the liner's crest engraved on the handle.

I imagined myself walking the liner's deck, hands behind my back, nodding hello to people sitting in chairs.

The *Madrigal*'s deck was not a place where I could walk with my hands behind my back. The times I climbed up from below, I moved from one clump of tarpaulin-covered crates to another, feeling the hammer of waves more sharply here than in my cabin. Iron-gray sky seethed above the ship. A small tractor was tied down on the bow, blanketed with wornout tarps, which were held around the crates with lengths of ginger-colored hempen rope.

My lungs filled with the emptiness of ocean air. Before this, the farthest I had ever been out to sea was half a mile beyond Narragansett Bay. There, I could still smell traces of land and the horizon was bubbly with trees. But here it was only the sea.

The cylinder lay nestled in my suitcase. Sometimes I caught

sight of it as I unpacked a clean shirt or unfolded a new pair of socks. Once I took it out and held it. The weight of it strained at my wrists.

I tried to imagine how Ireland would be. I painted pictures of it in my head, but the pictures were blurry and vague, like watercolors. All I came to know was how little I'd been told about the place.

A plan formed in my head of how I would go about uncovering my parents' past. I phrased the questions I would ask, and even designed a poster to be nailed up on the local noticeboards. I would be persistent but polite. I would circle and keep circling until I had uncovered every layer of what I didn't know. There was enough money to stay for a while. I'd even pay bribes if I had to, as soon as I could get to a bank and change my dollars into local currency.

It was my great adventure. I started to enjoy myself, and I found a resolve that I had never felt before.

In the long, midocean nights, I convinced myself that I would have no difficulty. The hard part, I thought to myself, was getting to Ireland, and I had as good as done that already. The people of Lahinch would be as interested to know about the lives of my parents after they had reached America as I would be interested in knowing how they were before they left. I imagined a breathless exchange of stories, which I promised myself I would write down and save and pass on to my own children some day. And if it turned out that they were not my true parents, then I wouldn't waste any time in finding my real mother and father. I knew it might make for some awkwardness. I felt I was ready for that. But I wouldn't let anything get in the way. If one person did not want to answer my questions, then I would ask someone else and keep asking until the truth was finally spat out. I tried to picture a different set of parents, but I couldn't. I only saw the same two faces that had softened so gently with age as I grew up beside them.

———

Lifeboats had been lowered on deck. Crewmen unbattened tarpaulins and stacked wooden crates in the boats. They lifted the crates by their rope handles, showing the weight with grimaces dug into their cheeks.

I had put on my suit, the same one I wore when I'd landed my job at the bank.

I realized now that we would be mooring offshore and rowing the supplies in. Perhaps the port was too small for their ship, or too crowded and they didn't have time to wait for the docks to clear. I snuffed out the idea of myself walking down a gangplank and onto the quay.

The captain stood outside the wheelhouse, hands in pockets. He nodded down at me.

Mist hedged us in. Each movement of legs and arms and lips sent a smooth stream of particles twisting away to regroup.

The only sound the crewmen made were grunts when they lifted boxes and more grunts as the boxes swung into the lifeboats.

I walked over to them. "Need some help?" I took off my hat as I spoke. Water had made drops on its felt brim and ran across my fingers.

"Help? You can help if you want, Yank." Baldwin tweaked the buttons on my coat. "Got into your city clothes, have you?"

"So we'll be rowing to shore?" I tried to make conversation.

"We'll be rowing in. That's right."

"How are you going to deliver that tractor?" Engines drummed up through the deck plates.

"We're making two stops. We deliver the tractor to Galway city. This stuff in the boats, this is the first stop. Lahinch. Your stop."

"But I'm getting off in Galway."

"You get off where the captain tells you to get off. Either that, or swim ashore from here."

It was three-thirty in the morning. Land bunched in a dark wave just beyond the mist. The heavy smell of plowed fields drifted in.

I sat on my suitcase and smoked a cigarette. The captain would show up sooner or later and then I would have words with him.

The lifeboats had been loaded. They hung in their cradles, ready for lowering into the water. More crates still lay on deck.

"Evening, Mr. Sheridan." It was the captain. He stepped out of the shadows in his heavy rubber boots.

I pulled the cigarette from my mouth. "I'm getting off in Galway, aren't I?"

"No, sir. We received a radio message to let off our passenger here instead. You'll be met."

"Why the change?"

The captain shook his head. His close-cropped beard looked as if it had been chipped off a slab of flint.

"Did Willoughby tell you why I'm coming to Ireland?" It seemed stupid to keep the thing secret any longer. I wished I hadn't taken Willoughby's advice.

The captain squatted down. He balanced on the balls of his feet. "Mr. Sheridan, I didn't want to bring you here. When he first asked me, I told him I wouldn't. But Father Willoughby insisted. I owe him a favor or two. I didn't ask questions. You kind of get a feeling for when questions aren't meant to be asked."

"It's really quite simple . . ." I rapped my knuckles on the suitcase, ready to explain.

"Well, if it's all that simple, you should have gone on one

of those big ocean boats that have brass bands and shuffle-board."

"I didn't have the money." The cigarette had started to burn my fingers. I flicked the stub over the side.

The captain watched the arc of the falling cigarette, as if he didn't like to see even those few shreds of tobacco wasted. He aimed a finger at a lifeboat that had been lowered to the water. "Time to go ashore, Mr. Sheridan."

"But where's the port? I don't see any lights."

"We've gone as far as you're going."

Worry fluttered in my chest. Then suddenly it was every-where, racing through my veins. "This isn't right."

"Either you go in that lifeboat or I'll have Baldwin throw you overboard. I had to stop him from doing that once already."

I stared at where the captain's eyes had been before the shadows took them away. "What the hell's going on?"

The captain ran a finger along the bridge of his nose. "Mr. Sheridan. I'm not going to ask you again. I've done you too many favors already."

I climbed down a rope ladder, using one hand to grip the bristly hemp and the other to hold my suitcase. The lifeboat rose up with each wave and clumped against the hull. Baldwin sat in the boat, ready to set out the oars. As soon as I stepped into the boat, Baldwin shoved the boat away and started row-ing toward shore.

The sky was purple and gray. A beach showed pale between the water and the clouds.

A wave struck the boat sideways. It fell on us in heavy rain. I tried to brush the water off my clothes before it soaked in.

"What's the matter with you?" Baldwin's fists tightened around the oars.

"What the hell are we doing, Baldwin? Where's the port?" I hoped that the anger in my voice would jolt the truth out of him. And I hoped he could not hear the panic that had taken over my heartbeat and my breathing.

"Well, if you don't know by now, then you're better off not knowing at all."

"All I know," I leaned forward and shouted, "is that you guys aren't delivering any fucking farm supplies!"

Baldwin laughed in my face. "Well, you're right about that. You must be academic."

"So what is it then?" I grabbed a crate and tugged at the lid. The nails groaned in the soft wood as they started to come loose.

"You leave those alone, you stupid bugger! You'll get us both killed." Baldwin jammed his oar blades deep into the coal-black water.

I gripped the crate and tugged again. The lid tore off. A smell of oil wafted up in my face.

"Now look what you've done, you bloody idiot!" Baldwin stopped rowing. He pulled in the oars. Silver threads of water trickled from the oar blades.

I squinted at the crate. I ran my hand across the cold metal and wood inside. Rifles. "You sons of bitches." The spit dried up in my throat.

"Well, what did you think was in there? Did nobody tell you back in Boston?"

I lifted one of the rifles from the crate. They were new Springfield '03s, the same gun that Bosley used to go deer hunting each year in the Great Swamp.

"And there's plenty more than that." Baldwin jabbed me with his boot. "We got fifteen crates at twelve guns to a crate and that makes . . . makes a lot."

"We're all going to jail." My eyes had dried out, too.

"No, we're not. If they catch us, they'll kill us."

"Damn you, Baldwin." I heaved the rifle into the water. It slipped into the waves and disappeared.

"Here!" Baldwin lunged forward. "You can't do that!"

I swatted him aside. I took another gun and threw it over. "They're all going in! You're not stopping me."

Baldwin knotted his hand into a fist and swung and missed. Then he swung again and struck me on the temple. "You fucking useless cowboy. You don't know what you're doing!"

My ear felt as if it was on fire. I grabbed another gun and threw it over. Baldwin's fist smacked into my other ear. Now my head buzzed as if it was filled with wasps. I grabbed another gun.

A strong light appeared suddenly from a hillside across the bay. It swung like a branch of ivory across the water.

Baldwin's face was suddenly bleached in the glare. "Oh, Jesus."

My eyes wouldn't focus. The boat seemed to be dissolving in the harshness of the light.

"That's the British army." Baldwin grabbed the oars and sank them into the water. He began rowing toward shore, leaning back to make the boat go faster. "They'll shoot us before we get anywhere near a jail."

I gaped at the beam. It swung back and forth through the fog. Searching.

Another wave exploded on the lifeboat. Light turned the spray into splinters of glass.

Baldwin heaved at the oars. "As soon as we hit the beach, you've got to get the crates out. There should be people there to meet us. You got to work fast."

I breathed in, ready to spit out my anger at Baldwin. But the anger had gone and only fear remained.

Now there was movement on the beach. Men waded into

the surf as the lifeboat came into shallow water. Their arms swung above the waves as they came close.

"There's people coming toward us." My throat had tightened so much that it hurt to speak.

"Now you got a choice, Yank." Baldwin pulled in the oars. "You can help us get these guns out of here. Or you can stand here and do nothing. And I swear to God you'll never get a word out of your mouth before the English shoot you and leave the seagulls to peck your bloody eyes out!" Then he stood up, ready to jump over and haul the boat through the surf.

I pulled him back. "Tell me who they are!"

"It's the Irish Republican Army. At least it would be if you'd leave them something to fight with." Baldwin struggled free of my grip and vanished into the water. He grabbed hold of a rope that looped along the length of the lifeboat and started hauling the boat. Now men from the beach joined him. Their faces barged out of the dark. All of them were breathing hard. Their soaked clothes slopped in the water.

For a moment, I stayed sitting in the boat. Baldwin was telling the truth. The worry on the faces of these men was proof enough.

The searchlight blazed on the curved planks of the lifeboat. I could feel it. It sapped all the blood from my skin. I swung myself overboard.

The water was freezing. It came up to my waist. Breaking waves shoved the lifeboat forward so that I found myself pulled toward the beach. My cramped hands gripped the ropes.

We heaved the boat forward through the surf, coughing when the waves slapped our mouths.

"You said there wouldn't be any soldiers!" Baldwin yelled at the others.

The man closest to me called across. "They got a tip. We did everything we could." Salt water coursed off his chin.

The beam swung out to sea. It found the *Madrigal* and burned along the hull. Men stood on the deck, their skin gone bony in the light.

Then the lifeboat's hull struck sand. Spray showered the crates and my suitcase.

More men appeared from the dark. Some wore trenchcoats with thick brown belts. Others carried bandoliers with loops for shotgun shells.

A wave burst against the back of my head. Water squelched in my ears. Another wave shoved me and I tripped. I went down into the surf and my fingers dug into the sand. Then hands closed on my arms and I felt myself lifted from the water.

A man with a broad, flat forehead stood in front of me. He wore a sweater that drooped with the weight of seawater. "All right, are you?" he bellowed.

I nodded and coughed up salt. Black waves crumbled into white and thundered up the beach.

The engines of the *Madrigal* hammered up. It started heading out to sea. The searchlight followed, draining the darkness around it.

"They're leaving me," Baldwin called from somewhere in the dark. "The bastards are leaving me!"

I waded onto the land. Foam boiled around my shoes as the tide pulled back.

The lifeboat lay stuck in the sand, filling with water as each wave barged over its stern. Men unloaded the crates, carrying them by their rope handles toward the dunes.

Now Baldwin was running toward me. "There he is! Get hold of him."

"What for?" It was the man with the waterlogged sweater. He heaved a gun crate over the side and tried to drag it up the beach.

"He's been throwing the bloody guns into the water!" Baldwin's drenched trouser legs trailed along the beach, picking up sand. "I'll fix your trolley now, Yank!" He grabbed hold of my arm. "I'll fix you!"

Before I knew what I was doing, I had punched him in the face and my knuckles cut on his teeth. Then I realized I'd been waiting to do that for a long time.

Baldwin tipped back into the water. A wave curled over him.

"Help me here!" The man in the sweater couldn't move the crate by himself.

I grabbed a hemp rope handle and began running with the man toward the dunes. The beach was wide and flat. My shoes filled up with grit and the drenched coat twisted around my legs. Salt burned at the back of my throat.

New thunder roared out of the night-black hills. I looked up into the sky, but saw only clouds hanging down.

The man in the sweater dove away into the dark. His end of the crate smacked me in the knee.

Pain slashed at my leg.

Then there was a shriek. A trunk of water sprayed up near the *Madrigal*.

Men ran past, carrying rifles and crates. Their footsteps dug into the sand.

Another distant thud reached my ears. I could feel it—a shove against my chest as the earth shook underneath me. This time I knew what it was. I saw the flash of an artillery piece set up in a field above the far end of the beach.

Then came a sound like a hammer banging inside an oil drum. The *Madrigal* lit up in fire. A flicker of darkness followed and then more fire. Flames blasted out of its hull.

The man in the sweater rose up to his knees. He looked toward the hills.

I reached for my end of the crate. The sweater man grabbed the other end and we ran again toward the cover of the dunes. We scrabbled up the slope, which gave way underneath us. Our clawed hands gripped the razor grass.

Another explosion sent me down on my face. I let go of the crate and covered my head with my arms. I felt the detonation. It clapped at the air but was not close. When I raised my head, the sweater man was looking at me.

The man held out his hand. "I'm Tarbox." He wore a glove of sand.

"Sheridan." Grit crunched between my back teeth.

Tarbox beat at the crust of sand on his chest. "I should never have got out of bed this morning."

"What's going to happen to me?"

"Happen to you?"

"Yes," The weight of my clothes dragged me down.

"Same things as will happen to us, unless you decide to lie there all morning. In that case you'll be dead by sunrise."

I watched his thick boots disappear through the razor grass. I tried to be calm and think straight. Tried to imagine my home, at least long enough to settle down my heart. But no pictures came. It was as if home had never existed, as if the island and Willoughby and Monahan and Harley had all bled into my mind through a dream. And now I was awake and they were gone and had never been there at all.

Another cannon blast. Then a thump and a hiss of water raining down. I turned my head, eyelashes flicking away grains of sand. They were aiming for the lifeboat now. I saw a ragged hole where the shell had come down on the beach. Men were running for the dunes.

Then I remembered my suitcase. I climbed to my feet and swayed under the weight of clothes. I started running.

"Where you going?" Tarbox pulled a rifle from a crate.

I jumped the last ripple of dune and headed out across the mud flats. The beach was huge and empty. The first smudge of dawn showed in the sky.

The cannon fired again and its flash jabbed at my eyes. I let myself fall, hands splashing down into a tide pool. The blast howled overhead.

Then I was running again.

Sand still rained back to earth as I reached the lifeboat. I found my suitcase under the forward seat and pulled it out.

As I turned to run again, I caught sight of the *Madrigal*. It burned under a patch of smoke, pressing against the clouds. Slithers of flaming gasoline threaded in and out of the waves. No voices came from the ship. No one cried for help. For a second everything seemed calm as I wheeled about, suitcase flying through the air.

Then I was sprinting. The damned suitcase was filled with water. My voice became a rhythm of obscenities.

Another cannon blast nudged at my ribs. I heard the shriek and a clap and knew from the sound that the shell had found the lifeboat. I craned my neck around and saw the lifeboat cartwheeling into the air. Smashed planks and oars skipped across the sand. Then the bow struck ground and a wave rushed in to claim it.

I slumped in the dunes and lay gasping with my face on the suitcase. Its leather was soggy and disintegrating. There was sand between my toes, in my crotch, against my chest and jammed into every crossed thread of my coat. Slowly my breathing grew steady. My eyes drifted back into focus.

Inland the sky showed lighter blue. Silhouetted against it was a man with a pair of binoculars. Others in trenchcoats crouched near him. They all carried rifles.

The crates were stacked nearby. Tarbox still rummaged through the rifles, as if to find the best one. Water dripped from his hair onto the polished stocks.

The *Madrigal* had started to sink. Detonations echoed inside it, more hammer strikes inside an iron drum. Still no sign of the crew. Pale rollers scudded up the beach.

A truck engine grumbled someplace in the shallow hills. It changed gears and appeared suddenly from behind a fold in the earth.

"Why haven't they hit the Crossley yet?" The man in the binoculars stood on top of a dune. "They're taking their damn time about it."

Shivers trampled on my back.

Gunfire rattled in the hills. The fast clumping of a machine gun.

The truck's brakes squealed. Its windscreen exploded in a shower of glass. The truck swerved into the ditch. Paint chips flew off the hood, leaving punctured bare metal beneath. Its engine raced and then quit. Bullets tore its canvas roof to shreds. Shouting. Three men jumped out of the back and as soon as they hit the ground, it seemed to fly up in their faces. Their bodies twisted and they fell.

The machine gun quit. Its firing echoed across the sand.

The truck's burst radiator hissed steam.

The men around me slung rifles on their shoulders. They started moving out toward the road.

"Are you hit?" Tarbox looked down at me.

I stared up, still hugging the suitcase. "No. Not hit."

"Grab a gun and come along." He handed over a rifle, holding it out at arm's length. "You're probably just concussed is all. That's the thing about being concussed. You don't think you are, but you are." He latched onto my lapel and pulled me to my feet. As Tarbox's hands dug into the soaked wool, its black dye squeezed out and bled across his fingers.

The gun stock was slippery with oil. As I followed Tarbox through the dunes, I used the Springfield like a walking stick. In my other hand I held the suitcase. Water trickled from its seams.

A pistol shot came from the road. Then another and another.

Scattered beside the truck were the three soldiers. They wore khaki uniforms with black belts and hobnailed boots. Another body lay behind the steering wheel. All dead.

I stared at the bodies, forgetting the cold and the sand. It would have been easy to blind myself with panic. Easier than understanding where I was and what I had just done, lugging guns up a beach in the middle of the night. But I did understand and Baldwin was right. There would be no time for explanation, not to men who were sending down an artillery barrage to welcome me into the land.

Tarbox talked in whispers to the man with binoculars. The man looked at me, eyes narrowed. Then he walked over. He stopped a few paces away and turned his head a little to the side, as if listening for something. The buttons had popped off his trenchcoat. "Who the hell are you?" He stepped over a body.

"My name is Benjamin Sheridan."

"Who?" The man barked in my face.

I said my name again.

The man pursed his lips and looked down for a moment. Thinking. Then his head snapped up. "You're the one who was supposed to meet Fuller, aren't you? We got a cable from Willoughby. You're Arthur's son, aren't you?"

We both turned as Tarbox dragged a body across the road. The dead man's head lolled back. Iron heelplates left white lines on the road.

"No looting the bodies now, Tarbox. Remember what I told you."

Tarbox ignored him. He dropped the man and rummaged through his pockets, taking cigarettes and a brass-cased pocket watch.

I dug in my coat pocket, where I'd put Willoughby's letter before I left my cabin. "Are you Mr. Fuller? I have a letter for Mr. Fuller."

My gaze kept drifting back toward the dead man. I still

couldn't believe what I saw. But I was too afraid for my own life to feel the weight of sadness and shock that I knew I should have felt at seeing this.

Another explosion came from the ship. Deep and far-away rumblings that blew fire from its smokestacks. I closed my eyes against jets of color that flickered across the water and smudged orange on the wet sand.

"I'm Harry Crow," the man said. "Your father said he'd come back, but I see that he sent you instead." He took hold of my shoulders and spun me around to face the other men. "This is Arthur Sheridan's son!" he shouted to them.

Their talking died away. The men stood staring now. A smell of spilled gasoline seeped from the truck. Pebbles of rain slowly darkened the road.

I looked from face to face, struggling to focus through the salt that burned my eyes.

CHAPTER 6

What do you mean you didn't know about the guns?" Crow's face stayed hidden under a short-brimmed wool cap. His lips were chapped and bloody.

I held my collar to my throat. My inner thighs were chafed raw from the damp trousers. "All I know is that I was supposed to get off the boat in Galway and meet a man named Justin Fuller. That's all Father Willoughby told me."

I had to concentrate to understand Crow when he spoke. I'd heard accents clipped with Irish before, but nothing like the singsong of the way Crow twisted words. It was a lulling voice, a voice for lulling children to sleep at night.

Cold rested like wet towels around my bones. Often I turned to look back down the road, expecting to see khaki-coated soldiers, bristling with knives and guns. I waited for the gravel road to shudder underneath me as artillery fired in the distance. But the fields spread out empty and thick with grass. In the hollows, reeds stretched from soil so dark brown and damp it looked as if it had been soaked in tea. I wondered what happened to Baldwin. Maybe he didn't get up after I knocked him into the water. I might have killed him. I had never hit anyone before, and it made me a little sick to think of how much I'd enjoyed paying Baldwin back for his days and days of bearbaiting.

We had been walking for an hour already. The sun was up, but mostly it stayed muffled in the clouds. Harry Crow had walked beside me all the way. His heavy, shapeless boots made him look as if he had just wrapped pieces of dead cow around his feet. Men left the group in twos and threes, heading out across the fields. Crow said that these were the ones who had to show up for work on time, so no one would know where they'd been. Soon the fifteen men were down to eight.

I didn't try to make talk. It took all my strength just carrying my suitcase and the two rifles I'd been given. Again and again, I tried to think of what to do next. It was like striking sparks from a flint to start a fire, but no fire came and no comfort and no plan.

Hedges thick with brambles lined the road. Where the road ran next to a field, thick walls blocked them off. The wall stones were almost flat, patched with lichen and moss. It looked as if thousands of books had been stacked across the countryside and painted dark grey. In places, the walls had collapsed. Sheep with gnarly wool and black faces gathered at the openings to watch us pass. Their tiny round droppings speckled the road.

On the ocean side, the land was bordered by cliffs. Headlands jutted out into the water. Waves smashed into the rock and spray unraveled in the air.

Crow fingered the brim of his cap. His nails were lined black with dirt. "Perhaps Willoughby didn't know about the guns, either. It doesn't matter now, though, does it?"

I thought about turning myself in to the police. I imagined a place noisy with typewriters and people who would listen. But the picture of the dead soldiers swept that aside. I had come into the country illegally and that meant the only way out would also have to be illegal. I couldn't do it without help. Couldn't do anything in this place without help. My money was no good. My clothes were no good. With my accent, I might as well have been wearing a flag. I was afraid to tell Crow about the blood test. From the way Crow treated me, I knew it carried weight to be Arthur Sheridan's son. If I told him the truth, I worried he might throw me aside.

My life had become so fragile. It seemed as if the slightest pressure would shatter my bones.

"I was sorry to hear about your mother passing on. Willoughby wrote us a letter about it." Wind skimmed over the hedge tops, flattening grass in the fields. Sheep huddled for warmth. "And how's your old dad?"

"He's dead. That's why I'm here. To scatter his ashes, Mr. Crow." The cold had a grip on my jaw.

Crow's fingers spread and rustled through his beard. "I was afraid of it when I saw you. I wondered what news you were bringing. And how did he die?"

"Blood poisoning."

"I suppose that's as good a way as any." It looked as if Crow had spent his life outside. Wind had cut grooves in his face and his eyes stayed narrowed, almost shut, as if walking into a storm wind that only he could feel.

"Are you taking me to see Mr. Fuller?"

"Fuller was taken to prison. I'm here in his place."

"Then this is for you. I don't know what it says." I took Willoughby's letter out of my chest pocket. The ink had smudged from black to blue to pink at the edges. On the *Madrigal*, I tried to read the letter by holding it up to a light, but the envelope was too thick.

Crow stuffed the letter in his pocket. "I was sure your father would come back. But I never thought he would be dead when he arrived. He never wrote, but Willoughby kept us in touch, about you going away to university and how you were looking for a job as a banker. I even knew what you looked like. Willoughby described you very well. And sure your dad would have spoken of me. Of Guthrie and Hagan and the others."

"No, sir."

"I can't believe it."

"Neither can I, Mr. Crow." I felt pebbles on the road through my sponge-soft, ruined shoes. "How am I going to get home?"

"That's not an easy thing." Crow bumped his knuckles over his chin. "I'd say the only way you're going to leave this country is when the English do. And that might never happen. It's a war now, you see."

"I didn't come to fight. Surely you can see that for yourself."

"Well, I'm telling you now that you'll have to fight. Because they'll come for you before they come for us."

A cigarette found its way down the line. As I took the stub from the man in front, I looked for a second at the man's face. He was smiling. Crow had puffed on the stub with his bloody lip. Its paper was pin-pricked with red. I inhaled, feeling the tobacco smooth out ragged edges inside me. Then I returned the butt to Crow, who pinched it between his thumb and index finger and breathed in until the ashes burned his skin.

I held down the smoke, then let it leak from my mouth. "Is it possible we're not talking about the same Arthur Sheridan?"

"A scar like this?" Crow raked his thumb across his forehead.

"Right. That's him. He got that scar when he fell off a horse."

"Not that scar, he didn't. An Englishman did that to him in Belfast prison. With a blade. One of these." Crow pulled a straight-edge razor from somewhere in the folds of his trench coat. He opened it with one hand. Its blade caught light from the egg-yolk sun. "I wouldn't be the one to call your father a liar, but I saw his blood run out across the blade and I remember the policeman shook it and the drops splashed on the floor. I saw your father's eyes closed with the pain."

Another slab of my childhood fell away, like a pane out of

a window. It seemed to me I knew more lies than truth. "Where did these guns come from?"

"From people in America who know we need them."

Crow folded the razor and hid it somewhere in the lining of his trenchcoat. It seemed he didn't want to say any more about it.

We came to a slate-roofed house. It had a bright-blue door. The windows were shuttered, but smoke leaked from the chimney. Wind batted it down, making it pour like grey liquid from the roof onto the road. The smell of it was heavy in my lungs.

Against the side of the house was a mound of black bricks. The bricks were made of earth; crumbly and faded to deerskin brown at the edges where the moisture had run out of them. I knew these were peat bricks, used instead of wood or coal to keep the fires burning. Willoughby and my father had talked about them, as they tried to make me taste it in their whiskey. Their fingers had fluttered up to their faces, as if following the wisps of burning peat. And now with the smoke's tobacco-sweetness clear in my senses, it seemed to me I could recall its taste, slipped into the amber of the Dunhams.

The line stopped. Now there were only six of us left, I set down my suitcase and looked at the blisters on my palm, bulging like white grapes from the skin. I worked my hands into my pockets. They were filled with sand.

Crow pounded on the door with a rifle butt.

A moment later, a man in overalls walked out carrying a teapot. Two mugs dangled from his fingers. He looked down the line and then back to Crow. "Well, for God's sake, Harry! I thought it was just you." He held up his arm, crooked fingers curled around the mug handles. "I don't have enough cups!"

I pinched the blisters and popped them one after the other, then pressed my palms together to stop the stinging pain.

"There's been some trouble in Lahinch," Crow said to the old man.

"The buggers in Lahinch are always trouble." Shreds of steam reached from the teapot's spout. "I'd rather cross all the way to Ennistymon than . . ."

"We don't have time for talking, Will." Crow raised his hand to silence the man.

Will's face grew suddenly pale, as if Crow's heavy-boned fingers had drained all the warmth from his body. "Well, why bother me at all, Harry Crow? You and your County Clare gunmen."

"Sooner or later, the Tans will be coming up this road and asking after us. And you didn't see anything."

"I didn't?" Will raised his eyebrows.

"No, you didn't."

The man's ears turned red in the breeze. They looked like wedges of tomato. "All right, then. So what am I supposed to say when they point to all these bootmarks in the mud?"

"I want you please to run your cows down the road for a mile and then run them back. That'll take care of the tracks."

"I'll do it soon as the wife and I have had our breakfast."

"Now, please, Will. We need it done now."

Tarbox walked up to the man. He gripped Will behind the neck and shook him. "You'll do it now or you won't have any cows left to run. Are you understanding me, you old fart?"

Will hunched down like a turtle into its shell. "Oh, it's you, Tarbox."

Crow tried a reassuring smile, but instead he grinned like a skull. "There's a good man, Will. We're all very grateful, I'm sure."

Tarbox unhooked a mug from Will's hand, poured himself tea and sipped at it as the rest of us filed past up the road.

We walked for another hour, footsteps finding rhythm in the hammer of waves on the cliffs. The air was thick with sea spray.

Then we shuffled to a stop outside a low-roofed house. Its walls were bone white and thatch carpeted the roof, patched with pea-green mold.

Tarbox walked down the line, two rifles on his back. His sweater was still clotted with sand. He stopped in front of Crow, but kept his eyes on me. "Mrs. Fuller says we should all go inside and warm ourselves. Is it really Arthur Sheridan's son?" Tarbox spoke slowly and carefully, as if we wouldn't understand him otherwise.

"Ask him yourself, Tarbox."

He turned to me now. Behind the bumpy leather of his skin, his eyes were bright blue and staring. "I met your dad once."

"You never did, Tarbox."

Tarbox slapped off Crow's cap. "I did so, you old bugger."

For the first time, I saw that Crow was completely bald. There was not even the blueness of his hair having been recently cut off. He had been bald for some time, and the sun had tanned his scalp the same as it had tanned his face.

"You pick up my hat, Tarbox." The baldness made Crow's eyebrows stand out thick and black.

Tarbox had been smiling. Now it flaked off his face like old paint. "Oh, stop pretending that you're in charge. It's only temporary for you. I'm sure they'd have put me in charge if I'd wanted the job."

Crow bent down and picked up his cap. "Nobody in their right mind would put you in charge of anything, Tarbox. We've only got to ask your wife about that." He fitted the cap on his head. Its lining was polished with sweat. "You'll be wondering why it is that I'm bald, Ben."

"Like a bloody hard-boiled egg!" Tarbox made as if to slap off Crow's hat again, but Crow gave him a stare that made him change his mind.

"I had a bad case of the lice in the war, and so I shaved my head to make them go away. I kept it shaved for so long that I must admit I prefer it this way now."

"I did see your dad, you know." Tarbox nodded, as if I needed more convincing. "It was in a pub. I shook his hand. And I read Willoughby's letters about you. I heard you was going to be a fireman, but then you decided on the banks instead. Myself, I would have stuck to putting out the fires." Then without waiting for me to say anything to him, he turned and ran up the road. The rifles crisscrossed his back.

Through Willoughby's eyes, they had all kept watch on me, as if through some trick mirror in my house. I had earned their friendship and their trust, without ever knowing who they were.

"Did he really meet my father?"

"I doubt he can remember. Tarbox keeps crab pots out in the bay off Lahinch. You'll hear people calling him Crabman. He throws the crabs in baskets and puts them on a cart and then he sells them in town. Over the years, they've pinched his fingers so all that's left of them is scars. He doesn't seem to mind. He talks to himself when he's out on the bay. Sometimes his voice carries across the water and you can hear him in the town." Crow folded his arms. "It's a shameful thing."

"What is?"

"You here in this country, breathing the dust of your ancestors and not even knowing their names."

Heat coiled in bands around my body as I stepped into the house. The roof was low and heavy-beamed. Its walls were plastered stone.

A woman barely contained by her dress stepped in front of me. Before I could put down my suitcase, she swung her arms around me and pressed her face against my chest.

I could smell her hair. I saw the tight-curled threads of grey and rusty brown. Her hands pressed at my ribs. Then she let go and stepped back and sighed. "They told me you were here." She handed me a mug of tea and showed me into the front room, where the other men had gathered. They rested their rifles against the fireplace and eased themselves down on the floor. A man crouched on his hands and knees in front of the fire, blowing on embers.

"Are you Mrs. Fuller?"

"Yes." She filled up the doorway. Her feet were tiny, wedged into cloggy brown shoes. The flower pattern on her dress had almost washed away.

"I was supposed to meet your husband." The white powder of dried salt clutched at my face.

"He's in prison, Mr. Sheridan. But they're letting him go soon and he'll be pleased to see you then. Now drink your tea before it goes cold."

First I tried to sit down on the suitcase. But I could feel it giving way, the neatly balled socks and folded spare trousers and white shirts buttoned and starched, all of it pasted with sand now and wrapped around the cylinder. So I sat cross-legged on the floor and sipped at the tea. I spread my hands around the mug. Heat buzzed my nerves back to life.

We brought with us the smell of the outside, the mustiness of damp wool and rain. Dreary sky flooded steel-grey through the windows. Another three men left for home. Now it was only Crow and Tarbox and me.

Tiredness rushed through my head. I tried to shove it away, enough to clear a space where I could think. But I didn't have the strength. It was like trying to push back water. Voices seemed to echo through a length of cardboard pipe. My eyes closed.

As I dove off the precipice of sleep, I searched for my father, peering through the veil between the living and the dead.

"Ben?"

My blurred eyes looked up at Crow. I seemed to be looking through a layer of oil.

"There's a man outside who has some news for you." The shredded lining of Crow's coat hung down over his knees.

I looked at my watch. It had stopped. Water condensed into tiny silver bubbles on the inside of the glass. From the shadows on the ground, I knew it couldn't have been much past noon. Then I followed Crow outside.

A man stood in the road, leaning on a bicycle. He wore a green uniform with silver buttons. "One of the Tans from that truck you people shot up on the road back at Lahinch wasn't dead. He just lay in the ditch and as soon as you lot marched off, he came running into town. He said he heard the name Sheridan, but he was lying on his face so he couldn't see anything. Now he's telling everybody that your father's back in town."

Crow held his hand out toward the man. "This is Sergeant Stanley."

Stanley nodded again. The wool of his jacket looked coarse, as if it had once been part of an old blanket. He carried a gun on a brown belt around his waist, the same kind of gun as Crow's.

I didn't understand why a man in uniform was talking to Crow. Then I heard someone breathing behind me.

Tarbox leaned against the wall of the house. "We should do what you bastards do, Stan. We should shoot the wounded."

Stanley took off his cap, which had a tiny metal harp pinned to the front. His hair was red and curly, but cut so short that the curls were only frazzles on his head. "I know what you do to your prisoners."

"Peeler!" Tarbox spat out the word.

Crow aimed a finger at Tarbox. "You say one more word and I'll have you on report."

"And what kind of report would that be?" Tarbox was so angry that his jaw had locked and he could barely speak. "I can't see you putting anybody on report."

Stanley gripped the levers on his bicycle, squeaking the brakes. "They're burning Lahinch."

"What?" Tarbox took a step forward. "Burning the whole town?"

"I don't know about that. The Tans were getting ready to start some fires when I left. That's all I know."

Tarbox's boots dragged on the flagstones. "We've got to go back. They might burn the dairy. My cousin lives in Lahinch."

Crow scratched the back of his neck. "The dairy's already gone. That's the first place they'd head for. Isn't it, Stan?"

"Probably." Stanley wheeled his bike around. He was ready to leave. "And I know they cut the lines to all your crab pots, too, Tarbox. In case you were hiding stuff down there in the seaweed."

"You fucking Peelers!" Tarbox swung his fist in Stanley's direction.

"You're on report, Tarbox." Crow didn't raise his voice.

"There's no such bloody thing as report out here, Harry Crow." Tarbox's mouth twitched, gathering saliva as if he meant to spit in Crow's face. "Now stop trying to rule the whole fucking world."

My stomach cramped into a ball. At home, when people cursed at each other this way, it was always the beginning of a fight. And here there was none of the slow-speaking politeness between people who carried guns.

Stanley climbed onto his bicycle. "You make me laugh sometimes, Harry. You act as if you were still in the service, putting people on report and saluting and all the other crap. You're nothing but a bunch of crooks, and whatever you pulled out of that boat in the harbor today isn't going to change anything."

"Careful what you say, Stan."

"No, you be careful." Stan set his bike rolling. Then he looked at me. "And you be careful, too."

Tarbox made choking noises. "But we got to go back. We can't just let them burn the town. I got . . ."

"Cousins, Tarbox. Cousins in Lahinch. Yes, I know. And your wife." Crow took the rifle off Tarbox's shoulder. "But if we go in there now, the Tans will be waiting for us."

"My crab pots . . . What am I going to do without my pots?"

Crow pushed him gently back into the house and shut the door. "I wouldn't have wished this on you, Ben."

My teeth were still clenched, waiting for the shock of gunfire. I couldn't believe that the anger in their voices would only end in this. "Who was that man?"

"He's a sergeant in the RIC. Royal Irish Constabulary. Irish policemen working for the English."

"Well, what's he doing here? I thought you were fighting against them."

"We are. Supposed to be, anyway. Stan was with me in the Great War. We were in the Irish Guards. When Stan and me came home two years ago, he joined the RIC. He was just looking for a job. But now that the troubles have started here, he's afraid he picked the wrong side. So every chance he gets, he lets me know what's going on with the RIC and the Tans. And besides that, I pay him. He's an old bastard, really. He'll probably get killed by someone like Tarbox, if the RIC don't catch him first."

I walked back toward the house. I didn't feel safe in the open.

"When we started giving the RIC a hard time over here, the British army enlisted thousands of ex-soldiers and sent them to Ireland. They were mostly left over from the Great War and couldn't get jobs when the fighting was finished. They make good money. One pound a day, for some of the officers. Poor old Stan in the RIC earns less than half of that."

"How could you and he be friends after something like that? You didn't join the RIC."

"Sometimes I look at the job I have now, washing dishes at the Dunraven Hotel, and I wonder how I stayed away from them. If you can't understand why Stan joined the RIC, it's because you didn't sit around after the war for months and bloody months with no job and no hope of a job. It wasn't any different for the Tans, for some of them, anyway. No job. Trying to pretend that we were back to being civilians. At least in the trenches you didn't have to go around making believe that your life was worth something. I had meant to settle down when I came home from the war. I had plans for a business of my own, building houses and thatching roofs. But there was never a chance for it. The war just kept going. I got dragged back into it again."

"How about Tarbox?"

"He's the only man I've ever met who enjoys all this and isn't ashamed to admit it. He's never had a break from it, not since the day he was born. He told me once he wouldn't know what to do with himself if the fighting ever stopped." Crow unbuckled the heavy brown belt from around his middle, and held it out to me. On the belt was his gun in its holster. It was a long-barreled revolver with a swivel ring at the end of the handle. "It's a Webley. I meant to give it to you sooner."

"I can't take that."

"And why not? Don't you know how to use it?"

I thought of the pie tins flipping through the air, and the smack of the bullet striking them. "I don't want to carry a gun."

The gun was heavy in Crow's outstretched arm. His hand was beginning to shake. "I'm not asking you to do it for some high moral cause. I'm asking so you can keep yourself alive. Keep yourself alive," he said again.

I took hold of the gun. Its leather holster was warm from resting against Crow's body. "Is there no one I could talk to? No one who'd listen to me?"

"You should have seen us when we tried to talk with them. Reason it out. Negotiate. We went all the way to Dublin as the representatives of County Clare. We wore our Sunday suits. It was me and old Guthrie and Tom Hagan and Fuller was there as well. Guthrie made us all polish our shoes until we could see our faces in the shine. Fuller's wife stuck flowers in our buttonholes. Hagan was supposed to do the talking. If anybody could have made them see our way, it was him. He had his points all written out on a piece of paper. You see, we believed they would listen. But they made bloody fools of us. Bloody fools." Crow's tongue slipped across his cracked lips so he could talk. "You don't forgive a thing like that."

CHAPTER 7

I stood naked in the middle of a room. My hands stayed double-fisted against my chest, shielding my heart from the chill. One foot stepped on the other. Toes curled over toes.

Mrs. Fuller lifted a basin of soapy water from the stand where I had washed. She pushed open the window with her forehead and poured out the water.

Sunlight spread in yellow sails across the walls.

Needles of cold drew goosebumps from my arms.

She threw me a towel. Then she began pulling clothes from a cupboard and setting them out on her bed. "Now these." She held out a pair of heavy wool trousers. They were grey-and-black herringbone. "These should last you."

I pulled them on. Then I took a flannel shirt without a collar, a waistcoat made of the same heavy wool as the trousers, and a tan wool jacket with leather buttons. It all carried the smell of another man's sweat and tobacco. These were clothes for living outside and walking through the fields, baggier clothes than the ones we wore at home. You'd have noticed if a man walked down the street in Jamestown wearing a waistcoat like this. But I needed them. My own clothes were ruined and the jumbled colors of this tweed were my first step into hiding.

Mrs. Fuller smiled. "My husband is a little smaller in the chest than you. All you Americans are fed on steak, I hear."

I tried to put my hands in the pockets but found they wouldn't go. The pockets were stitched shut.

She emptied the cupboard and the drawers, holding jackets up against my chest and then throwing them on the bed. "Last year, the police were so worried about men walking around with hidden guns that they said they'd shoot anyone with their hands in their pockets. And Justin was always walking around that way. So I stitched them shut, you see."

"Do you think he would mind me wearing his clothes?" I felt I had to ask. But even as the words were coming out of my mouth, I was staring at the heap of my suit. It lay in the corner, crumpled like a raisin. I'd rather have walked around naked than try to put that on again.

"Oh, do hush, Mr. Sheridan."

I stood at the bottom of the stairs, hugged by flannel and wool.

"You look like an Irishman now." Crow sat by the fire. Spread out at his feet were stacks of money. It was American money.

Tarbox sat next to him, holding slices of bread over the flames. The bread was spiked on the end of a log iron. "It doesn't look like real money. It looks like lottery tickets."

"Where did it come from?"

"It was in that note from Willoughby." Crow's face was lit up in the sharp-gold sun. "He wrote a note to say you didn't know about it."

"He told me that envelope was filled with letters." I pictured Willoughby again on Monahan's ferry, stuffing it into my hands. I saw his clear eyes looking straight into mine as he breathed the lie into my face. I had thought of him as old and tottering, the gears of his mind all ground down and slipping. But I saw now that his creased skin was only a cloak, and his

black priest's robe, that made him seem to drift across the
ground, was one more layer of camouflage. He lived two lives,
blessing and preaching and burying and christening, and then
sending off money for guns. I wondered which life his heart
was in as I didn't think it could be in both.

"One letter. That's all it was. The rest was these bills. It was
for your own good that he didn't tell you about the money.
He sends us some from time to time. There's people in Boston
who all pitch in, then give him the bills to send."

Tarbox pulled the bread out of the fire and looked at it. He
nibbled on a smoke-greyed crust. "What are we going to do
with all of this? I say we should divide it up between the three
of us. No one would be any the wiser."

"We're going to buy Clayton Guthrie out of prison, before
they take the poor bastard over to England and we never see
him again." Crow handed me a piece of toast. "Clayton is
commander of the local IRA brigade. He was taken prisoner
of war by the British last week. According to Stanley, they've
still got him at the Lahinch police barracks. They haven't had
the chance to ship him out yet. Stanley said he'd take the
bribe."

Tarbox held a bill up to the light. "And how much is that
going to cost?"

"All of it, Crabman."

"But there's damn near three hundred dollars here!" Tarbox
spoke so slowly, even in his anger. "What's he going to do
with all that money?"

I wanted to finish his sentences for him.

"I think he's going to buy his way across to America. He
wants to own some land in Oklahoma, although I don't think
he knows where it is exactly. That's what he told the brigade
commander, anyway."

Tarbox slapped the bill on the floor. "Stop with calling
Clayton a brigade commander! Give this poor bastard Yank a

chance to see how things really are before the Tans take him in and kick the living shit out of him. You have to understand, Ben. When Crow here starts talking about prisoners of war, you'll get in your head the idea that we're all gentlemen on either side. As if all you've got to do is stick your bloody hands in the air and call it quits and they let you go home at the end of the day. I say it's no use pulling Clayton out of prison. That money's better spent on guns."

Mrs. Fuller walked into the room. Her lips shuddered, as if she was getting ready to say something.

"We need him!" Crow spat out.

Tarbox crunched at the bread. Crumbs bounced from his mouth as he talked. "You need him, Harry. We all of us know that the only reason you're in charge is because he's in prison, and you've just got out of prison yourself. Clayton's a good man. He's my friend, too. But he's gone."

"Oh, you mustn't say it." Mrs. Fuller shook her head.

It seemed to me that the ranks didn't matter, anyway. Crow was too worried about hurting anyone's feelings to give orders. And Tarbox would do whatever he felt like, no matter who was in charge.

I looked at Tarbox and saw he was a dangerous and ugly man. It was as if he had been born in someone's nightmare, then kicked his way out of their head.

"The—Lahinch—barracks—is—a—bloody—fortress!" Tarbox measured the space that his words filled in the air. "Show Sheridan the barracks! Let him decide! We can buy guns with that money. Or dynamite or uniforms for boosting the morale. There's factories in Dublin building bombs out of jam tins, Mr. Sheridan, and we're lucky if we get any of those. With three hundred Yank dollars we could buy real hand grenades. Right now, we got all the plan-makers and able men we need. But we don't got the guns. If the *Madrigal* hadn't gone down, we might have enough, but we don't." He ran out of breath.

"My Justin!" Mrs. Fuller shouted. She was red in the face. "Couldn't you buy my husband out?" She took hold of my arm. "He wouldn't cost much. You could buy him out with your American money, Mr. Sheridan."

"It's not his money, Mabs." Crow gathered the bills and stuffed them in his pocket. "They've got your husband out of our reach."

"Oh, but he wouldn't cost much." Mrs. Fuller bent over into Crow's arms. Tears squeezed through her shut-tight eyelids. "He wouldn't cost much."

Crow led her upstairs.

I sat down next to Tarbox. "I came ashore with a crewman named Baldwin. You saw him on the beach. Do you know what happened to him?"

Tarbox swallowed and the bread slipped down his throat like a piece of broken glass. "I don't know. Perhaps he ran off on his own."

When Crow came back down, he shut the door behind him.

Tarbox picked at his nails. "When are you ever going to tell her, Harry?"

"Tell her what?" I walked to the window.

Crow spoke quietly. "They hanged Fuller in the courtyard of Ennistymon prison. I was there. I saw them do it. I heard his neck crack like a whip. One of these days the English will get around to notifying her, but they're not in any hurry."

A black-and-white cow stood in the road. Its udder was heavy with milk. Around its neck hung a leather collar with a brass ring at the throat. It was eating tufts of grass that grew between rocks in a wall.

Crow smoothed his hand along the cow's flank. "She's from the dairy. They must have set the animals loose before they burned it. Look. There's three more."

I saw the black-and-white clumps of Holsteins in the distance. "I don't understand burning a dairy."

The cow ground its jaw back and forth, spying with huge dark eyes for more grass.

"It was a cooperative dairy. Our local business." Crow raked his fingers up and down the cow's neck, talking to it with a sound like a huge cat purring.

He and I were the only people on the road. Tarbox had walked with us part of the way, then taken a short cut home across the fields.

I saw Tarbox's house in the distance. It was a tin-roofed shack, with no walls to fence in his plot of land. Instead, the house lay in the middle of the largest vegetable garden I had ever seen. Elephant ears of rhubarb wobbled on their red stalks in the breeze.

Tarbox's wife was bent over, pulling up carrots. She slapped them against her thigh, beating off the dirt. It was too far to focus on her face, but I saw how her back was broad and strong and I saw the outline of her smile as Tarbox ran toward her.

"The Tans burned the dairy for a reprisal. We kill one of theirs, they kill three of ours. If somebody even looks at them the wrong way, they arrest him. If he gets away, they burn his house. Then sometimes there isn't any formula to it. They just get pissed off about something and burn a whole town, loot the shops, burn down the bloody dairy. It's the damnedest thing about the English. They'd burn the dairy into cinders, but they wouldn't harm the cows. I saw Englishmen over in France in the war, blubbing their eyes out from having to kill a wounded horse, but I seen them cackling like old hags when they shoot some Irishman. Look there." Crow pointed at a field. "That's where your parents used to live."

The only way I could tell that a house had stood on the spot was from an iron gate that stood propped between two lengths of collapsed wall. A few of the foundation stones remained, jutting like broken teeth from the ground.

Crow stood with his arms folded, red-faced from the wind. "Did you think there would be some grand home?"

"I didn't know what to expect."

"It was a nice old house, with a strong slate roof and stone walls. After the storms, there'd be smashed slate all over the road. They'd kill you if they hit you. Chop you in half like an ax. Your mother's kitchen was back there facing the fields. She'd bring vegetables right in from the garden and sometimes I'd see her washing the dirt out of leeks on the back step. When they were married, the whole town came marching up this road with them at the front and we had a party in the garden here. And Tarbox and I dressed up as straw men and came to call. And the music went on all night. I carried Tarbox home on my back. And after they'd left, for America, the house burned down. It was never proven that the soldiers did the job. The wind was blowing the way it's always blowing up here and nobody could do a thing to stop the blaze. Sparks were rolling down that road like marbles into town. My cabbages had little grey specks of ash all over their leaves. And when the fire was over, one by one, the stones from this house began to disappear. I don't know who took them. They're probably scattered all over the walls and houses and shepherds' huts of this town. Here"—Crow reached across and buttoned my coat so that it covered the thick brown gun belt—"hide this a little better. Make your dad proud of you."

I stared at him, remembering how angry my father had been when he found out about Bosley and me shooting pie tins in the woods. It struck me silent to think of how differently we had both known the same man.

Crow stood back. "What? What did I say?"

It made no sense to hide it from him anymore, so I told him about the fire at Dillon's fishhouse, and how my father had been burned. I told him about the transfusion and how my blood had killed him. Then I explained what Melville told me about blood types and Arthur Sheridan not being my father.

Crow's eyes thinned into slits as he heard about the fishhouse. He nodded in sympathy for Dillon and his business gone to hell. And his mouth opened in an "Ah" when he heard about my father blown out through the wall. But when he heard about the transfusion, his eyes began to open again. He breathed in, ready to ask about my mother, but I knew what was coming and told him. Crow's eyes grew very wide and then he dug the heel of his palm into my back. "Well, what do you want to go believing a doctor for, anyway? The bastard probably made some mistake that did your father in and then blamed it on some chemistry he knew you wouldn't understand and wouldn't be able to prove." Then he made a noise in his throat, a "so there" noise to show that he knew he was right.

"But what if the doctor wasn't lying? There have been enough lies told already."

"Not lies. It sounds to me more like your father's just not telling you about the time before you were born. He left for America with his wife, settled down, had you and then put the past behind him. That's all there is to it."

"But they had me before they left Ireland. I was born here." I waved my hand across the far-reaching fields. "Somewhere here."

Crow began bumping his knuckles over his chin again. "No you weren't. I saw your mother up until a week before she left the country. And she wasn't pregnant then and she didn't have children before that. They said you were born over here, did they?"

I nodded. The news barely reached me. It was only one more

lump of rock to be rolled away into the darkness at the back of my mind.

"Well, that's one lie I suppose you could say that they told you."

"I was hoping one of you would know the truth. I guess I had hoped it would all just fall into my lap."

Crow started walking again. "Well, it's not me who's your father. I can tell you that for a start. If you're not Arthur Sheridan's son, then as far as I'm concerned you could be anybody's child." He turned suddenly, heels grinding into the road. "But that doesn't matter to me. Arthur raised you and called you his son, so who cares what your blood has to say for itself?"

The way I heard people talk about Arthur Sheridan, it was as if he still clung to life in this place. To Crow and Tarbox and the others, he had somehow survived the blaze that reduced him to ashes. To them it was something like prophecy. He said he would come back and they held him to his promise. Now I was the promise come true.

I had tricked myself into believing that this would be easy. I'd heard the warnings from Willoughby and Harley, but I was not listening. I expected it all to come clear in one long story from some gravel-voiced old man or woman. But now for the first time I saw the possibility of failure, how I could pull away shadow by shadow hiding the truth, and still not know at the end.

We walked on toward Lahinch. The holster made a lump in my jacket. My elbow brushed against it when I walked.

The cow still stood in the road, a black-and-white road block, chewing grass.

"As soon as the soldiers know that you came off that boat, they'll come for you. We'll just have to put you up with someone in the town. Someone who will say you're part of their family. We'll get you a job. That will keep you out of trouble for the time being. I'm taking you to Guthrie. He's Clayton's father, the one we're buying out of prison. So he owes us, you see. He can't refuse. He was my commanding officer in the war."

"Did he know my father?" I couldn't help calling him that, and neither could Crow.

"Guthrie knew your dad better than any of us."

We walked past a roadside temple. Under a stone arch was a figure of the Virgin Mary, moss-crusted hands held out as if waiting for rain. She stood behind steel bars and her clothes were painted black.

A shadow passed suddenly over Crow's face and he stopped in the middle of the road. He reached his arm out to make me stop as well. "You'd better stay here for a minute."

"Why?" I thought he was going to make us get down and pray to the statue.

"The reason everybody talks about your father coming back here isn't just because they've been waiting all these years to get another look at his smiling face. And it's the same reason the Tans will tear the place apart looking for anyone by the name of Sheridan." Crow watched me very carefully, as if waiting for some glimmer of knowledge in my eyes, so he wouldn't have to be the one to unravel the secrets that my father had kept all these years.

But there was no glimmer. I stared at him and waited for the truth, telling myself that this was what I'd come for, no matter what it cost me.

"Your father ran guns for us in the winter of 1897, and when he left for America around the time of your birth, he said he'd come back with more guns. So all this time, we kept him to his word. Until now. People see you and they see the guns that came off the *Madrigal*, and it's as if he kept his promise after all."

I lowered my head, as if my skull had become too heavy for the muscles of my neck. On the horizon in my mind, I caught the last glimpse of myself as I'd imagined I would be when I found out the truth. Somehow I'd thought it would make me happy. It would make things fit together and leave me stronger than I was when I started out. But now I began to feel like the butt of some vast joke. I waited for Crow to burst out laughing and for more laughter to reach me like the cackling of witches from every house and stone and tree. But when I looked up at Crow, I saw no mockery on his face. I saw only how he wanted me to know all of what he had to say, now that he had begun.

He ran his fingers across the bars of the statue's cage. "We used to meet here, your dad and I and others, when we were planning to bring in the guns. This was in the summer of 1897. A group of Americans, some of them had been young Union officers in your Civil War, managed to gather up a good number of guns. They were all members of organizations that supported Irish independence. The Hibernians. The Clan na Gael. Others. They'd been ready for the rising in 1867, but the rising never came to anything and now with them getting old, they thought it was their only chance of seeing something done. They had it planned for the hundredth anniversary of the rising of 1798. They sent word that we should go across and pick up the guns. They'd help us charter a ship. They'd keep us safe when we were there. So your father volunteered. He went across in the winter of '97. Then, in the spring of the next year, we had word that a ship had been chartered and was leaving Boston. We were to meet it off a place called Spanish Point, just down the coast from here.

"The ship left Boston, but somewhere between its leaving and arriving in Ireland, the English found out about what it was carrying. It was a man named Hagan who told us that they knew. He was working for the English at the time as a policeman. The same as Stanley is now, except Hagan didn't charge us for information. We had no way of getting word to your father. Spanish Point was crawling with the English. Guthrie and I couldn't get near the place. The English were going to wait until your father landed. Then they'd get everything. But the ship struck rocks and sank in the middle of the night. They were the same rocks a Spanish galleon struck hundreds of years before. That's why they call it Spanish Point, and there's people here with black hair that they say are descendants of Spanish sailors. We thought that your father had drowned. But he showed up a month later in Galway. He said he'd swum to shore and made his way north. He told us that only half the shipment had come over on that boat. The rest was still in America, because the Yanks had been worried about the boat getting stopped and they didn't want to risk losing everything in one blow. Your dad said he'd go back and bring the other half; another two hundred guns. He left with your mother, smuggled away in some ship with the help of Tom Hagan. They left and they never came back.

"I'm thinking he must have found himself finally safe in one place and changed his mind about running the guns. He had a better life there. It could only have been better than the one he left behind. They had a price on his head in Ireland, and you can't trust anyone when there's a price on your head."

"Isn't there a price on *your* head?"

"Not yet, although God knows they've arrested me enough times and kept me in prison on suspicion of various things. But so far, they've always let me go, because of lack of evidence." Crow spoke with surprise in his voice, as if he couldn't understand himself what had stopped them from putting him away once and for all.

"And they didn't burn your house?" I imagined pictures eaten off the walls by fire. Bottles of alcohol exploding in the heat. Chairs and tables vanished in the flames.

"They haven't burned it yet. When they burn your house,

you may as well just go to the Connemara hills and live in an old shepherd's hut. The English can't find you up there. Sometimes they try rounding people up, but it never works. You can disappear in the hills. You can vanish into thin air. Tom Hagan did when the English found out he was keeping us informed. He lost his wife and child in a fire when the English burned his house. I hear rumors that Hagan's got a group of men with him now. But all they are is rumors. And there's other rumors that Hagan died some years ago. Either way, he just vanished." Crow made a movement with his hands, joining the tips of his fingers together and then spreading them slowly apart. "Vanished."

"Is that where Tarbox is going?"

Crow laughed, his hand finding its way to his mouth as if he was ashamed of his teeth. "When they burn his house, he'll go. And you might, too. Hagan used to help people get out of the country. He'd find them ships with captains who would let them stow away. He might be the only one who could help you." Crow stopped suddenly and pointed at the horizon.

Part of Lahinch was burning. Columns of smoke stuffed the sky with dirty grey.

"In the end, the soldiers will make too many people angry. There's a line people cross where all they can think about is making the soldiers go away. Dead or living, it doesn't matter. Every day there's more of us crossing that line. That's where I am, and Tarbox and Clayton Guthrie and his da. You'll be there, too, if you stay here long enough."

At the sound of Crow's voice, the scattered hulks of wandering cows raised their heads and stared.

CHAPTER 8

Sun cut the water into blinding shreds.

The *Madrigal* lay tilted to one side, wedged in the sand. Waves slapped against its open portholes. Where cannon shells had exploded, its hull was peeled back like the skin of a huge fruit.

Small boats rowed out to the wreck, waves swinging their bows in the air. Crates of rifles salvaged from the cargo were stacked at the high-tide mark and guarded by soldiers.

The dunes were scattered with people. They wandered across the sand like sleepwalkers, as if gathered in some dream and led by visions out toward the sea.

"Those are people from Lahinch. If they stayed in the town, the soldiers might have shot them, instead of just burning their homes."

I caught sight of two soldiers. They stood on a bridge that lay further up the road. Both carried fixed bayonets on their rifles.

I felt a jolt in my stomach, telling me to turn and run. But they had already seen us, so we had to stand our ground.

And as if Crow had felt the jolt, too, he rested his hand on my arm. "If they ask, you're Guthrie's nephew. He's got one who's supposed to be coming over on a visit from the States sometime soon." Crow spoke with his chin against his chest, eyes peering up through the black shrubs of his eyebrows.

The soliders would listen to me if I told them the truth. For a moment, I was sure. I nodded hello as we came close.

The muddy brown uniforms smudged their bodies back into the grass and stones and the river bubbling under them, as it headed out to sea.

The hands of the soldiers knotted around their canvas rifle straps. They stared right through us, and I knew that there would be no talk. I put away the smile and looked down at my shoes. My hands edged toward the stitched-shut pockets of my trousers.

A truck was moving down the road. It jolted over the potholes. As the truck passed, Crow and I had to climb up on the wall because the road was so narrow.

The truck-driver's face was pink in a breeze through the open window. More soldiers filled the back, rifles between their knees.

I could call to them. The whole story wedged in my throat, ready to spill out fast if they would listen. For a moment, I didn't care about Crow or Tarbox or sad-faced Mabel Fuller. The soldiers would hear me out. I could tell them everything now and soon be going home. The chance would vanish, as I hid myself away in the basements and attics of Lahinch. If they found me after that, there'd be no point in explaining.

Then I saw Crow's hand in the corner of my eye. He had twisted the grass around his fingers, cutting off the blood. His fingernails drained white. He was watching me and he knew what I was thinking.

I saw his face suddenly stripped of age, the way my father and mother would have known him, in the days before they went away and never came back. Then I imagined all of them, Tarbox and Fuller and Mabs, all young again and friends and handing around Willoughby's letters that told about my growing up.

I couldn't turn them in. Not even to save myself. My face grew hot from the shame of having thought it.

The chance was gone now. Before long I'll be one of Crow's people, I thought, moving across the fields at night, wrapped in a trench coat and leather gaiters.

"Harold!" A woman's voice called from somewhere in the crags of sand. "Harold Crow!" It was the voice of an old woman, high-pitched and jabbing our ears.

First I could see nothing. Then the woman drifted over a ridge. She wore a dress that came down to her feet and a shawl covered her shoulders. In her hand, she was carrying a mug. "Harold, I've brought you some soup!"

"It's Mrs. Gisby." Crow stared at the approaching mass of cloth. "She owns the hotel in Lahinch. She's my boss, believe it or not."

Mrs. Gisby had a smile-wrinkled face. She was flushed from the work of moving across the sand. At the wall, she stopped and Crow helped her down to the road. Then she held out a tin mug of something brown and clear. "I saw you coming up the road." She held the mug up to Crow's mouth. It clinked against his front teeth.

Crow winced and stood back. He took the mug and looked into it.

The old woman panted and grinned. "Have you seen the ship?"

"Yes, ma'am." Crow handed me the mug. "There's a lot of soldiers about today."

Mrs. Gisby snapped her head up the road and then down the road, as if someone might be coming who would hear. "They're taking the guns!"

"Guns is it, Mrs. Gisby?" Crow lifted her up and sat her on the wall. "Now how do you know that?"

"The soldiers are saying so. An officer walked among us, asking if we'd seen any of the sailors."

"And have you seen them, ma'am?" Crow brushed off the sand that had clotted at the ends of Mrs. Gisby's dress.

"I have seen them, yes. But they're all dead. They washed up on the beach and the soldiers laid them out in the sun to dry."

"To dry?"

"That's what they said." She nodded and leaned forward. "And there's another thing. Arthur Sheridan has come back with his army."

Crow grinned at me, then turned back to Mrs. Gisby. "So you remember Arthur Sheridan, do you?"

"Well, of course I do, Harold." She batted him on the arm, rocked back and fell into the dune grass. "I'm not so old as I forget. They say he's come with his army of Yanks and he's armed to the teeth is what I hear. Those guns the Tans have on the beach, those are just the ones his army couldn't carry."

Crow helped her up. "Has anybody seen them?"

"Of course they have!"

"Who, ma'am?"

She rested her hands on her knees and thought for a minute. "I don't know. But he's been seen." Now she beamed at me. "Are you one of Harold's friends?"

I nodded, amazed at the depth of creases in her skin.

"Well, drink the soup then." She flipped her hand.

It was cold beef bouillon. Bitter saltiness pinched at the corners of my mouth. My stomach was too empty to care.

"Is everybody from the town all right, Mrs. Gisby?" Crow gathered her hands into his. Her fingers disappeared in the folds of his palm.

"They burned the creamery . . ."

"I know, ma'am. But is everyone all right?"

"Broke every window in the high street. They say McCusker, the glass man in Ennistymon, will be rich from fixing all this smashing and burning."

"Casualties!" Crow shouted. "Is anybody dead?"

"No, dear, except for a couple of Tans." Her hands worked their way out from the grip of his palms. They fluttered in front of her and came to rest against the lapel of Crow's jacket. "We all ran to the dunes as soon as the shooting started. But the houses, Harold. They burned the poor houses."

"We'll have to give them a black eye or two, won't we, ma'am?"

She tightened her grip on the coarse wool of Crow's jacket. "I say you kill every last bastard Tan in Ireland. Won't you do that for me, Harry?"

Crow looked down at her brown-spotted hands. "We'll give it a try."

"And have you brought your friend along to help, Harry?" She jerked her chin toward me. "Will he do the job for us?"

"This is Guthrie's nephew from the States."

Mrs. Gisby's face was fierce as she could make it. "Have you come to help us, then?"

"Give it a try." I hoped that would be enough. I breathed in the sea spray, the drift of breaking waves beyond the dunes.

Mrs. Gisby's face lost its tiny fierceness. "Now you tell your uncle that he should come and work with me at the hotel. I've been asking him for years but he won't listen. He could work with Harry here or do anything he wants. You tell him to stop fussing with that fat old sheep of his and that cow he keeps tethered in his garden. Tell him he needs the company of a lady like myself. His old wife's been dead almost ten years now, and it's time he moved on from that." Her face went blank for a moment, as if she had forgotten everything she'd said. Then she kissed Crow on the chin. "Are you my one and only, Harry Crow?"

"I thought that Mr. Guthrie was the man you had your eye on." He grinned and hid his smile.

She stretched out her arms. "Marry me, Harry."

Crow stepped away, still smiling. "I already love you too much."

The houses were empty. I knew from the silence.

Each window frame carried the shark's teeth of smashed glass. Light snagged on the teeth as Crow and I moved through Lahinch.

Chairs and chests of drawers had been dragged from the houses and left. The drawers were open and clothes speckled the road. I saw shoes and a hairbrush and the trodden-on rag of a tartan dressing gown. In brightly painted doors, I made out the dents of rifle butts. The shiny brass fingers of spent bullet cases lay everywhere.

Only one of the houses had been burned. Its paint had bubbled and peeled and slate roof tiles lay in splinters on the road. Still-smoking beams jutted from the rubble like the blackened ribs of a huge dead animal.

A man on a bicycle pedaled toward us. He swerved around smashed chairs and an overturned table, moving more and more slowly, until he had to put out his foot to stop the bike from falling over. "They shoot looters, you know." The man was a priest. A white collar gleamed at his throat.

"I didn't come to loot." My voice bounced off the houses.

"I don't know you." The priest's trousers were tucked into his socks to stop them catching in the gears. "Who are you?"

Suddenly I couldn't remember. Nephew? Whose nephew?

"I asked who you were." The priest had a sharp nose and pale-blue eyes.

"Guthrie's nephew!" Crow slapped his hand on my shoulder. "He's come over from the States to see his uncle. Benjamin, this is Father Petrie." Crow's thick hand reached out, palm up, pointing the way to the priest.

"You're responsible for this, Harry Crow."

PAUL WATKINS   136

"For what?" Crow's hand curled shut and dropped.

"For this!" Father Petrie swung his hand above his head, taking in the wrecked houses and gun shells and smoke. "For the killing of those Tans down by the bridge last night. I know what work you do."

"I work at Gisby's hotel, Father. You ask anyone."

"That's got nothing to do with it. You work there in the daytime and at night you go out and start wars!" Petrie stepped forward. The wheels of his bicycle clicked.

"I'd be grateful if you didn't spread rumors, Father."

"Spread rumors to who? Everyone's out hiding in the sands. Rumors is all I've been hearing since I heard the first gunshots last night. They're saying Arthur Sheridan has come back with a gang of Italian assassins from Chicago. They say it's his ship that went down in the harbor. They brought guns with them. And that's not a rumor. I saw them. I don't like the Tans any more than you, but what good are you and your thugs to the people of Ireland if you shoot and then run away, leaving us to fend for ourselves?"

"There's people who'd be happy to fight a pitched battle if the sides were even, Father. As it is, and you know very well, the Tans would wipe out the Republican Army in half an afternoon."

"So how can you blame the Tans? They don't know who's out to kill them and who's just trying to get on with their lives."

"I can find plenty of ways to blame the Tans."

Petrie gave up talking to Crow. Now he turned to me. "And you're Guthrie's nephew? How long will you be staying?"

"Just a little while." I found myself almost whispering. Smoke from the burned house slid over the rooftops.

"You don't look like Guthrie's blood to me, boy." Petrie wheeled his bicycle down the road. Its chain *tic-tacked* across the gears.

Crow stared at the brass door knocker bolted to Guthrie's front door. It was in the shape of a hand, with the fingertips held together. "It gives me the willies, that thing." He banged on the door and stood back.

The white lace curtains rippled as someone looked out.

Footsteps crunched on gravel in the alley that ran by the house. Then a man poked his head around the corner. A mustache bunched under his nose.

Crow cleared his throat. "Mr. Guthrie, sir."

"What do you want?" The man rummaged in his pocket and pulled out a pair of glasses. He put them on and squinted at us. The lenses were so thick, it seemed as if he was looking down the wrong end of a pair of binoculars.

"I wanted to talk to you, sir."

"What about?"

Crow made a tiny choking sound in his throat. "If we could talk inside, sir?"

"Come around back."

Tethered to a post in Guthrie's garden was a fat sheep and a cow. I had never seen a sheep this fat before. It looked like a barrel that had been rolled in fluff. The two animals had been lying down, but they stood as we entered the garden. They had looks on their faces as if they expected to be introduced, or at least given something to eat.

Guthrie pulled two sugar lumps from his pocket. He gave one to the cow and then one to the sheep, the lumps held out on the flat of his hand. "I'm busy," he said to us over his shoulder.

"This is business, sir."

Guthrie ignored him. He turned, holding out a hand to me and I felt the strength in it. "I haven't met you before."

"Ben."

"Well, this is my sheep and her name is Roly Poly. And this is my cow named Margaret." The collar of his shirt was too big, and it made his neck look thin and scraggy.

The veins stood out on Crow's forehead. "Sir, this is Ben Sheridan, sir. Ben *Sheridan*."

The pressure changed in the man's grip. It grew stronger and then suddenly let go. "I hear Arthur's come back."

Crow cleared his throat again. "Mr. Guthrie, sir, it appears that the rumors surrounding . . ."

"Shut up your babbling, Harry. Where's Arthur? I just heard that your dad came ashore with fifty hired mercenaries. Italians. Father Petrie told me that not ten minutes ago. The Tans have gone berserk trying to find him. There's lorry loads of them down at the beach."

I made out the shadows of old age on Guthrie's face, the hollowness around his eyes. "He's dead, sir. I came here to scatter his ashes."

Guthrie nodded and his hands clenched by his sides. His back was crooked, as if the weight of his shoulder blades was too much to carry. "I should have known that as soon as I saw you. You'd better come inside."

Guthrie lived alone.

There was a way a house smelled when a man had the place to himself. I knew that from my father, just as I knew the smell of a widow's home from Mrs. Gifford, across the street from where my father lived.

The distance from here to America didn't seem to matter. I breathed in the same earthy, smoky mustiness that my father left behind. I wondered now if he had brought it with him from Ireland, the sea spray and the peat tattooed into his pores.

One blanket-padded chair stood by the fireplace. On the wall was a lithograph of Galway Bay. In another lithograph, a man with a deerstalker hat and a mustache waded into a stream with a fly-fishing rod.

But Guthrie hadn't always lived alone. A few props of a woman's life still perched on the window sill—a china dog and a tiny lady in porcelain, frozen as she strutted through the dust.

Crow wandered to the white lace curtains. He peered into the street. Pulled back from the glass panes were heavier curtains made of purple velvet, to close in the room at night.

Guthrie clattered into the kitchen. He dug a spoon into a jar of tea leaves. "Keep an eye on the street, Harry." The burbling kettle over the fire had softened the brittleness between them.

"I hear you knew my father, Mr. Guthrie."

"Of course I knew your father. And your mother." Guthrie's face appeared from the kitchen. "I cried when I heard she had gone."

"More than ten years ago."

Guthrie brought in the tea and set it down on a low table at the center of the room. He trickled the tea into cups and added milk from an earthenware pitcher. Guthrie sat down by the fire and pointed to another chair for me to take my place.

Crow stayed at the window. "Ben didn't know about the guns. Willoughby didn't tell him." Sun through the lace curtains spiderwebbed his scalp and face. "He told me Arthur died of blood poisoning. Some doctor messed up a transfusion and told him that Arthur wasn't his real father. Something about different blood types." He laughed and his breath clouded on the glass. He kept it up until he saw that Guthrie's face had remained stony. Then his laughter collapsed into coughing and clearing his throat.

I sat cradling my tea, feeling as if I wasn't in the room at all, and had dropped in like a ghost at the mention of my name.

Crow changed the subject. "Willoughby sent us some money. Three hundred American dollars."

"And you're looking after it, are you, Harry? Now that Fuller's underground. You may have taken Fuller's job, Harry, but you haven't taken his place." Guthrie studied the smoldering peat in the fireplace.

"We're going to get Clayton out, sir. I have a contact at the Lahinch barracks. He'll take a bribe."

Guthrie blinked fast a couple of times. "I don't want to hear about it."

"You say that, sir, but you don't mean it."

"I'm not involved." He glared at the fire, as if Crow had hidden himself somewhere in the flames. "I haven't spoken to my son in months."

"I came to ask if you would look after Ben. I know you have that nephew who's coming over from the States one of these days."

Guthrie poured more tea into their cups. "He wrote that he was coming last year and he didn't. He said the same thing the year before that. But what am I supposed to do if this is the year when he finally arrives?"

"You could tell him not to. Write him a letter, sir."

"If I was to lay a guess on it, I'd say you've already started telling people that Ben here is my nephew."

"I didn't have any choice."

"The Tans will come." Guthrie looked hollow-eyed and sad. "Burn down my house. I'm not involved in this! I'll sit here and drink tea with you, Harry Crow and if the Tans come by afterward and ask me what I did, I'll tell them. And if they ask for tea, I'll pour them some as well. Do you see the way it works, Harry? I'm out of this now. If I take a Sheridan under my wing and hide him away, I'll be as mixed up in things as you are."

"We'll get him home as soon as we can."

"No you won't. You need him here. You need him because of his name."

"That's not true."

"Of course it's true!" Guthrie picked up a poker and beat at the flames. "You heard the rumors that are already going around. Already! This boy hasn't been in the country two days and already you've got people here believing that Sheridan and his avenging battalion of Wop gangsters is here in the hills and ready to thrash the Tans out of existence. It's idiots like Petrie that do it. They spend half their time bellowing at people to be calm and the other half spreading rumors that can only bring panic. And it's people like you"—he jabbed his finger at Crow—"who keep the rumors alive! This country needs heroes and nobody knows it more than a man like you, Crow. You can't just keep spitting out the old stories about Cuchulain, and Finn MacCool asleep in the hills and ready to come down and save Ireland when the time is right. Even Mrs. Gisby won't believe those stories. But Arthur Sheridan! There you've got yourself a live one, don't you, Harry? Better than a live one! The son!"

"Are you going to shelter him or not, sir?"

I stayed silent, feeling them bat my life back and forth like a tennis ball. I thought to myself, You have never taken charity from anyone. And here you are now, not only begging, but having someone else do it for you. It would be better just to get up and leave. You are asking more than just charity. It's more than you should ask from anyone.

But I didn't get up. I knew what was outside and how long I would last on my own, with only waterlogged American money and a voice to give me away. I found myself surprised at how much sense it made to take Crow's gun and blow my head off before the soldiers got to me and made me tell them names.

Guthrie slammed his hands down onto his knees and Crow fell suddenly quiet.

They had been talking, but I hadn't heard them. I was far

away inside my head, pacing the grey corridors and wondering whether to die.

Guthrie was talking to me. "Bring your things around, Ben. I'll keep you as safe as I can."

"Thank you, sir." Crow settled his cup in its saucer. "He only has the one suitcase, and that's up at Mab Fuller's for the moment."

"I thought I recognized Fuller's clothes."

The tea was cold. It tasted sour in my spit. "I didn't mean to bring trouble, Mr. Guthrie." I couldn't even raise my head to meet his gaze.

"You can't help what you bring." Guthrie's yellow-nailed fingers drummed on the edge of his chair.

I walked to the end of the street with Crow, still numb from realizing how much it cost these people to hide me. I wondered where the hell my plan had gone, and that strong resolve that had flared up inside me as I lay in my cabin on the *Madrigal*.

It wasn't fair. I didn't come to hurt anybody, or to do anything wrong. I told myself all this, but even to me it sounded like the bleating of sheep. I wouldn't have expected the soldiers to believe me, and it seemed too late for that now. It was not fair, but fairness had nothing to do with it.

"It's been such a long time since Guthrie saw his son." Crow buttoned his coat against the chill. "Clayton went away to university in Dublin last year. Trinity, he went to. While he was there, he joined the Sinn Fein. But he decided they weren't doing enough, so he joined the IRA. They trained him and sent him back here. He'd been in charge of a local brigade for the past six months, ever since Fuller went to prison. But then the Tans arrested Clayton and I had to take over. And damn near everything I've done, I've buggered up. If it had been

Clayton here to deal with the *Madrigal*'s guns, they'd all be
ashore by now and hidden away. Instead of that, there's only
a couple of dozen. That's why we need him back, and that's
why Guthrie won't have anything to do with him. He says he's
had enough for one life."

"Why do you say that?" The sky was very pale, with clouds
that streamed like wagon tracks from one horizon to the other.
I thought it meant rain. Bosley could have told me. He knew
things like that.

Crow kicked a rifle cartridge. It jangled away down the road.
"I told you he was with me in the war. He was our company
officer. He was a bit old, but he'd been in the Territorial Army
for a long time and when he volunteered, they didn't turn him
down. Well, he was relieved of his command in 1917. He was
disgraced."

"What did he do?" It made me dizzy to stare up at the
clouds.

Crow stopped in front of a chest of drawers that had been
dragged into the street. He opened a drawer and pulled out a
neatly folded handkerchief. Then he blew his nose in it and
stuffed the handkerchief in his pocket.

"In the spring of 1915, we were in the area of Mons in France.
One night we were moving up to the line, up to the trenches.
We marched and the officers rode on horseback. It was a damp
night and we had half a moon looking down on us. It appeared
now and then from the clouds. Stretching out on either side
of the road were fields, just muddy fields as far as I could see
into the dark. It was just a piss-awful night, all cold and wet,
and it was about the time when people were realizing that the
war would go on for years and not months like they said in
the beginning. The trench war had started. We were setting
up the patterns that would go on for another three years. We'd
move up to the line, live in the parapets for two weeks, then
be relieved and go back for two weeks' rest. Every time we

went up to the line, we'd lose ten or twenty or once as many as forty percent of the company. We lost sixty-five percent when the Germans came at us out of the fog with bayonets one night and our sentries didn't see them in time.

"This time I'm talking about, it was maybe two in the morning and we were all marching along in silence, when suddenly Captain Guthrie reins his horse in and stops. I heard the bit clunk in the horse's mouth and looked up. He'd been startled by something. But then he rode on. For a while it was quiet again, nobody speaking or singing, no smoking allowed, everybody just thinking about being at the line and how soon it would be before they fall into the ten or twenty or forty percent that go back from the line all rotten in a donkey cart. Or who don't go back at all. Then Guthrie calls me up to the front. I break rank and go stamping up through the mud to see what he wants. I was a corporal, then. I see his face and he's pale. He's frightened. He leans down from his horse, and his horse is frightened, too, and his damn face is so pale, I can't stand to be that close and I step back. He says to me, 'Look out into the fields and tell me what you see.' And I saw riders. I looked and in the moonlight and shadows, I saw a line of horsemen moving in pace with us. They were heading toward the front, same as we were. 'Cavalry,' says Guthrie. 'Do you see the horsemen, Crow? Tell me I'm not mad and that there's horsemen in the fields. No, sir, I told him. You're not mad. I see them, too. I didn't know we was moving up with a cavalry group. Then suddenly he leans down at me again, his face so damn pale, you'd think he had a wound that was draining all his blood. 'Look at them again, Crow.' So I looked."

Crow's voice had turned gravelly. "They was horsemen, but"—he sighed—"but they were wearing armor. Do you see what I'm saying, Ben? Armor. From the time of the Crusades damn near seven hundred years ago. With my own damn eyes

I could see them. They had white tunics over their armor and on the tunics were red crosses. They carried swords and lances. And there they were riding slowly beside us. Hundreds of them. I swear to Christ Almighty, I saw them with my own blasted eyes! I looked back at the others, all the rest of the company, and they could see them, too. We all looked out into the fields, none of us daring to step away from the road. All of us was pale as corpses. These horsemen had ridden up out of the grave and were coming to help us. Do you see? We was all expecting to die. We knew the percentages would catch us in the end, and most of us they did catch. But when I saw those knights come riding from the dark to help us in our war, I figured then that the line between the living and the dead was no more than a fog. And sometimes the fog blows away for a while and you can see straight through. Since then, I've had it in the back of my mind that the dead can come to help us. The way your father has in a way."

I thought about the fog between the living and the dead, Arthur Sheridan strong again and not raging in pain, waiting for the fog to blow away.

"The horsemen were gone by the morning. They disappeared. Guthrie reported what he'd seen and at first they threatened to pull his rank and dismiss him right there. They thought, here's some bloody Irishman had too much to drink. But too many others had seen it, too. One company not a mile from ours said they saw longbowmen from the time of Agincourt. Guthrie never got back everything he'd lost on the night we saw the horsemen. They had their eye out for him, you see, the high command. It made a fine little story for the papers but they didn't want anyone really believing it. Fine for the people at home, you know, but not for us. A year later, we were further north, still in the trenches and it was wintertime. It was night again. One of the sentries was looking through a trench periscope at the German line. You know what a trench periscope is, don't you? You look in one piece and through a series of mirrors you can see through a tube a couple of feet up. So you can see over the top of the trench without getting your head shot off. Guthrie asked to have a look. He was watching the German line through the periscope. Their lines lay only two hundred yards away at that time. Suddenly the sentry tripped backward and let out a yell and Guthrie told me that right then something flipped in front of his periscope lens. He looked up and saw a horseman. One of the Crusaders in battle armor, riding one of those great Clydesdale horses and not ten feet from where Guthrie and the sentry stood. Guthrie said he could see the rings on the rider's chainmail vest. Before he passed out of sight, he turned once and looked down at them.

"Ten minutes later, the Germans came at us with bayonets and shovels and trenchknives. The sentries weren't ready, hadn't heard the Germans assembling in their dugouts. They just came running out of the fog with no preliminary barrage or flares or anything else. They just came at us and they were screaming when they ran. That was the night we lost sixty-five percent of the company. When the end of it came and our line held and the Germans had to fall back, Guthrie reported what he'd seen to the brigade commander. I don't know what he was thinking. He should have known what they'd do. He called for the sentry who'd been with him at the time, but it turned out the man was dead. They told him to forget about it, told him he hadn't seen it really and he was just upset was all and to go back to his company. But he wouldn't let up. He kept talking about the rider and the warning in the man's face. It was too much, you see. They relieved him of command and sent him home."

"Do you think he really saw it?" Black birds with orange beaks marched on the rooftops.

Crow shrugged. "I saw those horsemen that one night. I saw them. So if Guthrie is mad, then I'm mad, too. And everyone in that company who's still alive is mad. But as far as I know, it's just me and Guthrie and Stan. Percentages caught up with all the rest."

CHAPTER 9

"Tuppence!" Mrs. Gisby barked in my face. Then she squinted, stretching her neck across the copper-plated bar top. "Oh, sorry, dear. I didn't recognize you. I can't see without my glasses and they always steam up when I'm working."

She talked for a while longer about her glasses, how they slipped off and broke at least once a month. Then she demonstrated, putting on the glasses and waggling her head until they slid down to the end of her push-button nose.

I watched the khaki foam settle on my beer.

I had been here a week, working alongside Crow at the Dunraven Hotel, which was run by Mrs. Gisby and called Gisby's Hotel by everyone except the soldiers. Most nights, the British officers ate dinner there, in the main dining room, which had salmon-pink walls and white curtains and silver candlesticks. There was a pub at the back entrance to the hotel. The locals all piled in there after sundown.

Crow and I washed dishes from a quarter to seven in the morning until eight o'clock at night. We had a spot in the corner of the kitchen, where two huge metal sinks were bolted to the wall. There were rest times, after the breakfast rush and from two until six in the afternoon, when Crow and I lay down on the floor of the kitchen and slept with our aprons rolled up as pillows. But for the remainder of the day, I hardly ever looked up from the grey water in my sink, seeing the same pots and pans disappear hissing into the water as the chef threw them over my shoulder. I watched the sweat bead up on Crow's bald head and drip into the washing water.

I didn't ask questions because questions were dangerous here. If I asked the wrong person, or if the wrong person overheard, the Tans would come for me. I kept telling myself to be patient. I didn't say much about myself, but sometimes I talked about America, which seemed to the people around me to be a place more lodged in dreams than in the real world. They didn't seem impressed that there was no war in America. They convinced themselves that America was so violent even in peacetime that it made no difference. But you could get rich in America, they said, and you could own huge tracts of land in places with names like Nebraska and Colorado. I watched Crow and Tarbox as they pronounced these words, as if they were part of a spell. They said you couldn't get rich here and I looked around and believed them. They said you couldn't own much land, either, because it had all been parceled out to the British and the people who worked with them. I told about Harley and Newport and the huge iron gate at Belmar and I tried to explain how hard it was to make the kind of wealth that Crow and Tarbox talked about, but they didn't care. What mattered to them was that the possibility was there.

"At least you can live with the hope," Tarbox told me in his even, plodding voice.

I was lucky to have a job. I even made two shillings a day. But sometimes I looked up from the swampy dish water and remembered that I had been offered that post at the First Bank of Wickford. I remembered how I'd told myself I would be running the place in five years, and I laughed and Crow jumped back in surprise.

The chef's name was McGarrity. He was bony like a starving

man, but he ate almost as much as he cooked. He looked as if he had been a large carrion bird in another life, and here he was now, feathers plucked and stretched into the shape of a man. He had two jobs. Every morning he woke at three, delivered bottles of milk to people in the town and then showed up by six-thirty at the hotel to cook breakfast. McGarrity was an informer. He spied on us and told the soldiers what he'd heard and seen. Crow said he made more money off that than he did from any of his work.

On my first day at the job he paid so little attention to me that I began to wonder if he even knew I was there.

But the police were waiting for me as I stepped out into the alley at eight o'clock that night. They all wore their shabby bottle-green uniforms. It looked as if the only things holding the clothes to their bodies were the heavy Sam Browne belts. The three of them were Irish. You could tell them apart from the English, who wore khaki and black.

Crow told me later that McGarrity had tipped them off.

I figured they knew everything, because of Stanley. They threw me up against the wall and gave me a pat-down. They turned my jacket inside out and made me take off my shoes and pulled out the insoles and looked at my hands as if to read my palms and they even looked inside my mouth. I wasn't carrying the gun. Guthrie had taken it from me and hidden it under one of the hearthstones in his fireplace.

I didn't have time to be afraid. I wasn't even sure what was happening. My mind had been taken up with my sore feet from standing all day and my hands boiled red like lobster claws from the dishwater. With the first machine-gunning of their questions, I realized they didn't know anything except that I was new in town. Relief washed through me like cold blood, and I began cheerfully to lie, even convincing myself.

They marched me back to Guthrie's, past windows fogged

with lace curtains and dusty-backed china animals crowding the windowsills. A slice of mirror showed us back our faces.

Laundry hung in the gardens, sheets pinned to copper lines rusted green in the sea air. Rows of socks danced tiptoe in the breeze.

At Guthrie's, the policemen said hello to Roly Poly and Margaret. One of the policemen even pulled a handful of sugar lumps from his pocket and tried feeding them to Margaret, but Roly Poly knocked them out of his hand and ate them all herself.

It seemed to calm them, knowing that Guthrie was involved. They trusted him, I could tell.

Guthrie appeared in his slippers and his nightcap, shredded nightshirt hanging from his body as if he had just been blown up.

When the policemen asked for proof that I was his nephew, Guthrie brought out a black metal box. From the box he pulled a stack of letters from the real nephew, and while they shined their flashlights at the stamps and unreadable scrawls, Guthrie kept up a chatter that made me wonder if he should have been working with Arnold at the First Bank of Wickford.

The policemen didn't read the letters. Mostly they just admired the American stamps. Then they handed back the bundle, apologized, and left me and Guthrie in the garden, staring at each other.

Roly Poly lay down and Margaret rolled her over with her enormous black nose. That was a game they had, which they never grew tired of playing. Roly Poly lay down, front legs folding first and the back legs crumpling after. Then she stared straight ahead, as if she had no idea what was going to happen next. Margaret dug her nose into Roly Poly's stomach and tried to roll her over. It took a couple of tries. The first few, Roly Poly tipped, but then thumped back down right-side up.

Finally Margaret won and Roly Poly's legs stuck in the air. She sat there for a while, looking up at the sky, then climbed back onto her feet.

Tarbox also had a game which he played with Margaret and Roly. He kept borrowing them in the middle of the night. He led them out into the street and tied them to somebody's door knocker. The person would be woken up, either by having their knocker ripped off its hinges or by an insane battering sound, with bleating and mooing thrown in.

Three times in my first week, I had to go and fetch them, while Guthrie cussed out Tarbox and put the kettle on for tea.

I wasn't allowed to speak to McGarrity. Everyone knew he was an informer and he had been what Crow called Boycotted. He could speak to you but you couldn't speak to him. It was like a children's playground game, but played by Crow and Tarbox and Guthrie, the game had turned savage. You could see that McGarrity had been driven half mad by the silence.

After the Tans had searched me, McGarrity left me alone. I began to feel safe in the damp heat of the kitchen. It was like being a nameless part of a huge machine. The danger seemed to have passed. The rhythm of the kitchen and sleep and the pub clamped down on me so quickly, that it didn't leave much time for thinking. Whole days went by in which I almost forgot why I'd come to this country.

But then it would return to me in a jolt that I was no closer to finding out the truth about my father and my mother.

Guthrie knew it, too. When we sat by the dying fire late at night, and the chat had faded away, he could tell what I was thinking. He never gave me the chance to say what was on my mind. Instead, he'd tuck his pipe in a stone cubbyhole set into the fireplace, slap his knees, raise his eyebrows high up on his forehead and say "Tea?"

There was no talk of getting me home. Not even talk of a plan.

I began to wonder if Guthrie and Crow and the others thought they'd done enough for me. If I wanted to leave, I figured, I would have to set out on my own. But even with people speaking the same language, or at least knowing how, and many things familiar from my home, this place was foreign to me in ways that I did not understand at first. The more I understood about the war being constantly on, even if it didn't show its face for days or weeks at a time, the more I understood that nobody really trusted anybody. Without trust, they were always suspicious, and the suspicion lay like mantraps in the fields outside the town.

At first I didn't understand why Crow and Tarbox hadn't Boycotted a waitress at the hotel whose name was Ruth. She was the daughter of a local RIC man named Byrne, which meant that I wasn't supposed to talk to her. But everyone else did, so I knew they had made an exception. Then I found out that she had a thing going with Crow. They disappeared sometimes in the afternoons, while I took my nap on the floor.

Crow said he didn't mind washing up the officers' dishes and hearing them order Ruth around in the dining room. "It keeps me angry," he told me, "and you've got to stay angry in this."

Tarbox stopped by most afternoons, dragging his cart because he was too poor to own a horse. It turned out that the Tans hadn't cut all his crabpot lines. Some of the buoys had been submerged when the Tans went looking for them at high tide. Tarbox sold most of his crabs and lobsters to the hotel, carrying them in baskets made of reeds, which he lined with seaweed to keep the crabs damp. Sometimes his wife came with him. She was younger than Tarbox, with a broad smile like Clarissa's that sent an ache through me that I had thought was long since gone. She usually tied her long dress in a knot at the side, to stop it from dragging in the sand when she helped her husband on the beach. Her legs were long and powerful and mostly she walked around barefoot. Crow said she wanted children and Tarbox was running out of excuses.

It seemed to me that Tarbox would rather have his teeth pulled out than follow orders from Crow, but he did whatever his wife asked of him and not grudgingly, either. Around her, he carried a look on his face that made him seem as if he'd only just fallen in love, although I heard they had been married for years.

I found myself jealous of how close they seemed to be, and sometimes I wished it was me who pulled that cart up from the low-tide sand, and my wife walking beside me.

Posters appeared, offering a reward for the capture of Arthur Sheridan. They were slapped at odd angles on a notice board outside the town hall and on lampposts in the High street. Wind blew half of them away and rain took care of the rest.

I came to know people and know of them, the same way I had while I was growing up on the island. Men and women were named by their trades, or by some memorable thing they had done. Guthrie was always Old Guthrie, because he had a son, and when people spoke of him, it was "Guthrie with his Idiot Sheep Roly Poly" or "Guthrie and that Bathtub of a Cow." He was "Guthrie the man who stays out of the struggle, because of what the Great War did to him." Tarbox was the Crabman, and people only trusted him so far, because he was a looter of bodies and smiled with his mouth but never with his eyes. They didn't trust his wife, either, because they couldn't understand why such a beautiful woman was living in a tin-roofed shack with this foul-mouthed man who always smelled like seaweed and whose hands were ribbed with scars. But they trusted Crow, and knew him as the youngest of the band who had once planned to smuggle guns into Ireland and start a revolution on the wind-smacked beaches of County Clare. I

heard the name Sheridan spoken of carefully and with a gentle-
ness, as if the word was fragile like old china. My mother and
my father were the ones who dared to go across the sea in
search of the guns, and because of this, they let them keep their
youth and rubbed out the faults they might have had, like the
fault of never returning. The mention of Tom Hagan always
sent the pitch of gossiping voices climbing into questions. They
discussed whether he was still alive or dead and sunk down in
some Connemara peat bog, where sheep skulls bleached in
the reeds. Some claimed to know his hiding place among the
Maamturk mountains. He was and always would be the one
who had dressed up in his Sunday suit and gone to Dublin,
trying to reason with the British before he turned to violence
and the bringing in of guns. When Hagan's family was killed
and he fled to the mountains, he became the local saint of calm
men pushed too far. There was not much talk of Justin Fuller.
It seemed as if everyone but his wife knew he was dead. I
guessed they didn't speak about him because they were afraid
of letting something slip of the story Crow had told—when
Fuller's neck cracked like a whip. They were afraid of telling
Mabel Fuller, in a way that made them look like cowards, but
they were foolishly brave about other things. I came to know
Guthrie's son, Clayton, although I had never seen him. I heard
him called dangerous and cold-blooded, but not because of
anything he'd done. Clayton had earned a name that drew itself
from what people said he would someday do in this war.

I had no idea who was right in the war. It wasn't even clear
that a war was going on. To me it seemed more like a local
feud, with everyone knowing everyone else's name, and each
with their own agenda of revenge. There was no faceless, charging enemy, and I was too much in the middle to try and see
both sides. It seemed to me that the soldiers and the people
who fought against them had long ago lost track of why they

were fighting. Now they paid back atrocity with atrocity, each side as stubborn and vicious as the other.

Lahinch was all I knew of Ireland, and for now there was no way to find out anything more.

Time thundered past someplace beyond the hedges and dunes and the sea, while I stayed strangely motionless, the muscles of my patience growing weak.

I pulled a handful of coins from my waistcoat pocket and sifted through them. The dark walls of the pub hummed with talk. Men in overalls and black coats sat on benches, cradling their mugs.

"This one, dear." Mrs. Gisby took a dull copper twopenny piece from my hand. "And how are you liking work at the hotel?"

"Very well, ma'am." I spoke as little as I could, knowing how the strangeness of my voice still brought stares from people.

"And your uncle is treating you well?"

"He's a fine man." I drank off some of the beer, enough to carry the mug back to my seat without spilling any. The heavy drink was bitter, tasting distantly of something burnt. By now I was used to the flannelly smoothness that stayed behind in my spit.

"Oh, he is not a fine man." Mrs. Gisby grinned and threw the twopenny coin in a tray.

"He's a fine, fine man, Mrs. Gisby." I grinned at her and took another swig of beer. Its damp cellar chill rested in the back of my throat.

"You tell him to come and work for me, Ben. He thinks I'll keep asking him forever, but I won't. One of these days the offer will be closed." Then from a smoke-blackened pot at the back of the bar, Mrs. Gisby ladled some stew onto a heavy white plate. She clunked it down in front of me. "There's that for your supper. And don't be telling your uncle I gave it to you."

When I turned to walk back to my seat, Guthrie was there in his usual spot. He sat on a bench by a grandfather clock, whose dial was painted with a moon that had the face of a child.

Guthrie had told me I should make sure I went to the pub. I had to be seen. If people didn't see me in public, he said, they'd think I was trying to hide.

I sat down next to him. "How are Roly and Margaret today?"

"They broke off their tether and pulled up all my radishes."

"What's that funny smell, Mr. Guthrie?" It seemed like mint at first.

"What smell?"

"Mint. Medicine. I don't know."

"Oh, that. It's my foot cure." Guthrie smiled now. His mustache turned up at the ends and he pulled a tin from his pocket. On the lid was a picture of a black-and-white cow. Turnley's Udder Balm.

"This is it?"

"Oh, yes. Good for the arthritis. I suppose, though, it's better for udders. But it's cheaper than what they sell in the chemist's. Almost half the price."

"Well, I'll be damned." The smell made my eyes water. I was trying not to laugh.

"You can use it if you want." Guthrie took a leather pouch from his jacket. It was worn smooth and blackened with sweat. A mother-of-pearl button held the pouch closed. Guthrie dug his pipe into the pouch and with his thumb he scraped the hazelnut shreds of tobacco into the bowl.

The flame of a lit match bobbed up and down over the pipe,

as Guthrie set the shreds burning. Then he jerked his wrist once and the match flame vanished. "She gave you that, didn't she?" Guthrie nodded at the stew.

"Told me not to tell you." I was on my third beer and it had made a beehive in my head.

"Well, a free plate of coddle from Gisby. What did you do? Offer to marry her?"

"I said you were a fine man." I spooned up a mouthful of stew. It was sausages and bacon and potato and carrots, stewed with parsley in hard cider.

"You said I was a fine man?" Guthrie's voice changed suddenly. It was no longer drifting and careless, the voice of an old man who forgets. Now it had sharpened and the sharpness took me by surprise.

"Crow said you liked her a lot." I hoped Guthrie wouldn't be angry.

Guthrie took the pipe from his mouth. He jabbed the stem at me. "A free plate of stew. She must love me, then, after all. I've been meaning to ask you, Ben. Do you think I'd make a good husband to her?"

"I'm sure you would."

"And do you think she'd make a good wife? She wouldn't get bored of me, do you think?"

"Never."

"Well, it's been keeping me busy with thoughts, I can tell you. Night and bloody day."

Twilight crowded the windows. Silver threads of rain broke on the glass.

A man sat down next to Guthrie. His boots were flecked with manure. "There's a bloody funny smell in here."

"Don't you say a word," Guthrie muttered to me.

"A bloody funny smell," the man said again.

Now Guthrie began sniffing as well, craning his neck around

the room, as if it was someone else's udder balm that pinched the air with eucalyptus.

I could feel laughter swelling in my throat. I looked at my beer and then down at his shoes.

The man stood up. "Well, blast me, I must have gone and sat in something."

I couldn't help it. I roared in Guthrie's face.

Guthrie had turned away.

I realized suddenly that my laughter was the only sound in the pub.

The door had opened. Cold air washed through. Embers woken by the breeze flickered red in the fireplace.

Four soldiers stood in the room. They wore strips of cloth that wound from their boots up to their knees. Their trousers were splattered with mud. One man was an officer. He had just come in from the restaurant and one of the salmon-colored napkins was tucked into the pocket of his tunic. In one hand he held a snifter of brandy and in the other a piece of paper, which he held out toward us.

I saw my last name printed on it in black letters. My face grew suddenly hot. It was one of the posters that had been stuck up a few days before.

"We're looking for Arthur Sheridan." The officer had sleepy eyes.

It was quiet except for the slack clunking tick of the grand-father clock.

I waited for eyes to wind their way toward me. It was too crowded to run. But I knew I'd have to try and I wondered how badly the glass would cut me when I dove through the window with its neat diamond panes, some of them colored like the windows in a church, all held together with thin strips of lead.

No eyes searched me out. It was as if I had become some

stuffed animal in a glass case, ignored and not warmed by the fire.

"Hats off in the pub!" Mrs. Gisby's voice scratched at our ears.

The officer snapped his head around. "What?"

"Hats off in the pub! It's the rules and you got to follow the rules."

"Arthur Sheridan, please." The officer folded his piece of paper. He matched the corners up neatly before each fold. "We know he's here. That's why I've come to offer you a thousand pounds reward, if you'll tell me exactly where he is."

The joints of my spine crunched together. I measured the paces that would carry me running to the window and through it. And I knew that once I hit the ground, I'd have to roll and stand and keep running and not think about the pain. I knew how fast a soldier could shrug a rifle off his shoulder, chamber a round, and fire.

"Hats off in the pub!" Gisby's head bobbed up and down behind the bar.

The officer didn't turn to face the old woman. "If you open your mouth again, I'll burn this place to the ground." He spoke very quietly. "Think of it, gentlemen, a thousand pounds. You could do no work for five years on that money. Besides, we only want to talk to him."

"No, you don't." It was Tarbox. He drank off the last of his beer. "You'll take your stubby little truncheons and beat the life out of him. At least don't lie about that."

Now heads twisted painfully around. Glances fastened on Tarbox.

The officer hooked his hands behind his back. "Mr. Tarbox. I should think you of all people could do with a thousand pounds."

Tarbox looked into his mug. "I wouldn't live long enough to spend it."

The officer's mouth twitched. "You know where we are if you need to talk with us. Goodnight, gentlemen." He backed out of the room. The other soldiers were already gone. Dark sucked them into the street. Hobnailed boots shuffled away.

Tarbox stood slowly, as if his bones were hurting. Then he shouted, "Hats off in the pub!"

Slowly the purr of talk returned. Smoke wound up around the rafters.

I felt the cramped pebbles of my back loosen one by one.

Guthrie nudged me. "That officer's named Sutherland. Even the Tans don't like him. He captured a group of Irishmen over past Ennistymon two weeks ago. My son was one of them. I heard a story that when the Irish opened fire on them he ordered his men right into the Irish firing line. When the Tan sergeant said he didn't think that was a good idea, Sutherland told him, 'I'm not ordering you to advance. I'm ordering you to die.' " Guthrie nodded, stern-faced, to show it was the truth.

A new pint of beer clumped down on the tiger-striped wood of the table in front of me. I saw Mrs. Gisby's brown-spotted hands let go of the pottery mug. "Harry Crow says you're to meet him on the bridge tonight at ten." The smile creases were valleys in her cheeks. But she wasn't smiling now. Her mouth was tight-lipped and serious.

"Did he say why?"

She shook her head and beetled away in her slippers. They were too big for her feet, so she moved like an ice skater over the floorboards.

Guthrie sighed. While Mrs. Gisby was there, he had busied himself with his waistcoat buttons, fastening and unfastening the black wooden stubs. Now he raised his head. "I wonder how close they just came to taking you away."

"Should I meet with Harry Crow?"

"He may have found you a way home."

I stood up to leave. No eyes rose to meet mine. I wondered

if they were thinking about the thousand pounds and if the only thing keeping their stares away was the shame of turning me in. Then I felt Guthrie's hand on my arm.

"You can trust him, Ben. But I can tell you as his old officer that Harry was born to take orders and not give them. Once Clayton's out, the only way you'll get someone to lead you up north is by getting permission from him. And Clayton doesn't care about anyone, or any damn thing except this war. And being his father, I can tell you I know about that."

It was drizzling and the rain brought silence. I stood on the bridge, looking out to sea. The wind jabbed at me like a boxer. I thought, This is a countryside to make you believe in ghosts. Maybe not in the daytime but at night, with loose panes rattling in windows and foam scudding up the empty beaches, and the wind blowing through these stone-book walls. Then it's hard not to believe.

But if there were ghosts, I thought, they wouldn't be the same as the ones I used to believe in back home. There, I bolted the door and shut my eyes against the spirits of Conanicut Indians, padding across the fog-topped bay in their white bark canoes. I held my breath in case I smelled the smoke of their ghost fires in the black woods at the north end of the island.

Here, I imagined, the ghosts were small and laughing. You'd only ever see them in the corner of your eye. They spent their time playing tricks, like blowing the foam off mugfulls of beer and into an old man's face, or pinching the bottoms of fat ladies.

For a moment, I pictured myself swimming to America. I moved alone across the ocean, kicking through deep ocean rollers, a thousand miles from land. When I reached the other side, I trudged along the roads and beaches of Jamestown. It was dark there. A mist had come down on the place. Dew beaded and dripped from the branches of the trees. People slept deeply in the warm pockets of their beds. The waves made only a faint rustling on the sand, the way they do on flat calm mornings when winter had come to the island.

Something thumped on the road. A black, fist-sized egg rolled along the ground near my feet.

For a second, I didn't understand. Then I cried out and tripped backward. It was a hand grenade. I jumped at the bridge wall, heaving myself over. My palms scraped the rough stone and I dropped into the dark.

The sound of running water was all around me. The ground slammed into my feet and my fingers dug into the sand. I waited for the shock of the explosion.

I began to crawl, pain in my elbows and thighs. I scrambled under the bridge and reached a patch of sand between the bridge's curved belly and the river.

The grenade still hadn't gone off. I knew now that it wouldn't. And whoever had thrown it would come looking for me with something else. I backed up against the stone. The river echoed off the bridge, tumbling and boiling black in front of me. The soldiers could come from either side. They'd have killed Crow. They must have killed him quietly or I'd have heard the shooting. Or maybe it was Crow who turned me in.

I grubbed in the sand until I found a rock. Then I threw it hard into the water at one side of the bridge. In the same motion, I scrabbled to my feet and ran the other way.

Head hunched, I moved fast from under the bridge and toward the rounded hills of sand. I rolled through the beach grass, grit in my eyes. Wind pawed at the dunes.

Footsteps sounded on the bridge. It was Crow. I made out the silhouette of his stooped shoulders and the shredded trench coat draped across his chest.

"Benjamin!" he hissed. "It's me!"

I didn't move. Sea mist clamped shivers on my ribs.

Crow paced back and forth. "Benjamin! It was a fucking rock!" He picked up the stone and threw it into the river.

Now I closed my eyes and breathed out. I let my head fall slowly forward to the sand.

We crouched under the bridge like trolls.

Crow pulled a flat tin of cigarettes from his coat pocket. He set two of the white sticks between his teeth and lit them. Then he handed one to me. "I brought your suitcase with me. Mrs. Fuller carried it down last night."

The sides were all warped. It looked as if it had been put together by someone who had seen a suitcase once but didn't really know what it was used for.

We settled back against the mossy arc of the bridge. The thunder of the river filled our ears.

"Guthrie's been treating you well, hasn't he?"

The first sliver of smoke sent a humming through my head. "He treats me so well that I'm ashamed I have no way to pay him back."

"It's enough that you're company for him. You probably act more like a son to him than Clayton ever did." Crow held the burning cigarette cupped in his hand to hide the glowing embers. "I got some news about a crewman off the *Madrigal*. His name is Baldwin. He was the only one who survived."

"I know him." I thought I could see the bones of Crow's hand through the glow of the cigarette flame.

"Well, Baldwin knows you, too. And the Tans got him when he was boarding a ferryboat out to the Arans where he lives. They're holding him up near Fisherstreet. They won't touch him there because the RIC man in charge is a decent man. Until now, the Tans have thought it was your father they were looking for. That's what the rumors told them. So they're looking for an old man. But as soon as Captain Sutherland gets his hands on Baldwin, they'll find out exactly who you are."

"Well, maybe he'll tell them I didn't know about the guns."

"Not if he wants to stay in one piece, he won't. Fingering you may be the only way for him to stay alive."

"They've offered a thousand pounds for my father."

"They had a thousand for Clayton Guthrie. Five thousand for Hagan. They pay up, too. You'd think they wouldn't bother, but they do. And in cash, is what I've heard."

"I'm glad they pay their bills."

"But anyone who takes that money would be hunted like a fox. Across all of Ireland and the world. And there again, you'd think maybe we wouldn't bother, but we would." Crow breathed smoke in two grey jets from his nose. "There's other news, too. I made the deal with Stanley for getting Clayton out tomorrow night. He'll do it for the three hundred dollars. Clayton's due to be taken out of the country next week and Stan has the job of driving him as far as Port Laoise. Stan will let us ambush him. That way he won't get in trouble."

"Why do you have to spend the money to do that? Why don't you just ambush him, anyway?"

"Because it's Stan, for one thing. But also because the Tans have a trick. I've seen it before. They take a leather ammunition pouch, the kind we used to carry first-aid bandages in during the war, and they stuff a grenade in it. They make a slit in the leather so that the pin and the lever bar sticks out. Then they strap the pouch to their prisoner's chest. If anyone ambushes their truck, they just pull the pin, the lever flies off and seven seconds later the prisoner is . . . well, dramatically disassembled."

"They'd be killing themselves, too."

"They don't expect to be set free. Besides. It's one thing to set up the grenade like that, but it's another thing to actually pull the pin. Sometimes they just shoot the prisoner. That's a little simpler." The amber fire of Crow's cigarette smoothed out the crags of his face.

The noise of a truck sounded in Lahinch, changing gears as it gathered speed. It rumbled over the bridge and then stopped. The parking brake rattled.

Crow pinched his cigarette dead.

Muscles trembled in my legs, ready to explode and start me running.

Two men jumped out of the truck. They unfolded a map and looked at it under the headlights. Both men took turns pointing at the map, then one man laughed and knocked off the other man's beret. They folded up the map and got back into the cab. The parking brake rattled again and the truck headed up toward the Cliffs of Moher.

Crow walked to the river. "It's the dusk patrol. They go out every night and every night they get lost. They're not looking for us." He cupped water in his hands and washed his face, running fingertips over the smoothness of his scalp.

I heard a gasp as freezing water reached Crow's skin. "Will Stanley keep his word?"

"He will, because I'm paying him half now and half later. And it's not just for the money, either. With a hundred people like Stan, I could have won this war by now. I'm tired of running it all by myself." Crow walked out from under the bridge.

I stayed hidden in the shadows. It made me nervous to stand in the open, as if my body was locked into an Enfield rifle's sights.

"Tomorrow night, you make your way across the fields to the statue of the Black Virgin. Across the fields, mind you. If you go by the road, someone might see. You must arrive by ten o'clock."

"Why do you need me?" I thought of the Virgin's stone face.

"Because from tomorrow night onward, we'll all be answering to Clayton. You'll need one of us to take you up north to find Hagan, and Clayton is the only one who can give permission for that. Hagan is your way out of here. He's the only one in this part of the country who could find you a place on a boat going home." Crow's silhouette folded its arms against the navy sky.

"Maybe I could find him by myself."

It was as if Crow didn't hear. He stepped into the dark and vanished through the rustling dune grass.

For a few minutes longer, I stayed huddled under the bridge. I remembered how I'd promised myself before I came to Ireland that I wouldn't leave until I had found out the truth. If I didn't find out, the uncertainty would stump after me like a cripple for the rest of my life. So I couldn't go back yet.

But I couldn't stay either, because as soon as Baldwin talked, the soldiers would come hunting for me in their mud-colored clothes. I was becoming superstitious about them, believing they could smell my fear the way I'd been superstitious about people at the bank smelling fear. It sparked along the branches of their nerves. They would close in, sure of the tracks, because I couldn't hide.

Singing. A flat and tuneless hymn rose from the runner beans and squat potato plants in Guthrie's garden.

I could see a man sitting in the dirt.

The singing stopped. "I got to talk to you, boy." It was Tarbox. His hand flew up to say hello. A beer bottle was stuck on his thumb and he waved it back and forth.

Guthrie stood in the doorway. His nightshirt hung down

to his ankles. "Aren't you gone yet?" He shuffled over to Tarbox. Then he curled his fingers into a fist and rapped on Tarbox's forehead. "Hello? Hello? Haven't you got a wife at home? Hello?"

"It's because of my wife that I'm here." He swatted Guthrie's hand away.

"Sitting in my runner beans?"

"She says you should save your life and get rid of this boy here. She says the Tans will stove in your fuzzy old head. She says you can't look after yourself, let alone this boy. What's that bloody funny medicine smell?"

"Udder balm for my feet." Guthrie stood back. "I got sore feet. Now get out of my beans."

Tarbox lifted himself up. "I'm sure that's why Lily Gisby won't go near you."

"Oh no, don't bring her into it."

"You should just go ahead and marry the woman. You're in love with her after all."

"It's Lily who's in love with me. Everybody says so."

"She forgets who you are sometimes."

"Well, she loves me when she remembers. And if you must know, I have been thinking about a more permanent arrangement between Lily and myself."

Tarbox didn't reply. He wiggled a finger in his ear, as if Guthrie's voice was only a ringing in his head. He swayed in front of me. "I got nothing against you. But Guthrie's already been through enough with his son, who's off fighting a war he can't win."

"Careful what you say." Guthrie lifted the stalk of a runner bean. When he let go, it flopped back into the dirt.

"Oh, it's true." Tarbox looked around the garden, as if the rows of cabbages and Roly Poly and Margaret were an audience who would applaud him when he stopped speaking. "Clayton was always talking about the millions of Irishmen ready to rise up when they hear some magic trumpet blast. But there's not millions. There's just Clayton and Crow and me and half a dozen others, who go running through the fields at night and shoot soldiers in the back."

"You tell that to Clayton when you see him."

"Clayton is a dead man." Tarbox quickly stood back, as if he expected Guthrie to strike him. "You know it's true."

"Oh, and what an emotional speech you're giving us tonight, Crabman. It's an inspiration to every bum drunkard in Lahinch. You might want to have been speaking it louder, mind you. I don't think the Tans in their barracks on the hill could hear the last few words."

Tarbox backed up, aiming his finger at Guthrie and trying to figure out what to say. Then he tripped over the runner beans. The thin wooden support poles collapsed on top of him.

Guthrie helped him to his feet.

"I'm sorry for saying it." Tarbox wore a scarf of beans around his neck.

"It might be true."

"I have to tend my crab pots." Tarbox walked off down the alley, still wearing Guthrie's beans and with a beer bottle stuck on his thumb.

I heard waves thumping the shore. "I could go north to find Hagan. Crow says he could help get me on a ship going home. I could go now if you want."

Guthrie closed his blue-viened fist around the iron poker. He whacked the fire. Peat crumbled into marmalade-colored ashes. "Don't you listen to Tarbox. You stay here as long as you have to. And besides, Hagan is best left alone. You'd have to find him first and that could be damn near impossible. The British have been trying to track him down for years. You won't have better luck."

"Crow says he lives up in the Connemara hills."

"They say he's up there and that sometimes he comes south to the Burren. When soldiers are attacked up in that area, they always blame it on Hagan, but they never know for sure. He could have been dead for ages and all that's living on now are the stories they tell about him. And if he's not dead, then he's old. Sometimes on the winter nights, I think how he must feel the chill, now that he's getting on in life."

I tried to picture Hagan, but the man seemed only a vague presence far to the north, crag-faced and cold in the rain.

Steam puffed from the kettle in the fireplace. Guthrie walked over to it, wrapped a handkerchief around its handle, and poured boiling water into a teapot. Then he took the nightcap from his head, jammed it on the pot, and shuffled back to his seat. "It's true Hagan used to get people out of the country. But it's too far to go. You'd never reach there alive."

"I'll leave here as soon as I can, Mr. Guthrie, but before I do, I want to find out who my parents were. And I think if anybody knows, you do."

A ripple moved along Guthrie's jaw. "Is that so? Well, I got nothing for you there. Why dig up old bones, anyway?"

"You do know, don't you?"

He hobbled into the kitchen. "Tea?"

Now I stood. "You *do* know!"

Guthrie stood in the doorway to the kitchen. "Look at me now. Look me in the eye and listen to what I'm saying. I don't know a damn thing. Nothing. And even if I did, I'd tell you to leave it alone. What happened might have happened for a reason. To save you some misery perhaps. To save misery from others. Leave it alone. Please."

Guthrie had shut up like a clam, the same way Pratt and Duffy did. I knew I'd get nothing more out of him. "I meant to tell you sooner. They're setting Clayton free tomorrow night. I'll be there. It's the least I could do after all you've done for me. Maybe I can help."

"Clayton doesn't want anybody's help. I can tell you that from experience."

An army truck grumbled up the road to Ennistymon.

I lay in bed, wondering how I'd be if I'd grown up here. By now, perhaps I'd think like Crow, far beyond the line of no forgiving.

If he or Clayton wouldn't help me and help me very soon, I'd have to set out by myself. That was clear now. I had enough patience left to wait until I met Clayton, but no more than that.

I couldn't sleep. Couldn't even close my eyes. I climbed from my bed and dressed. I attached the collar to my shirt with two silver studs, one at the front and one at the back. Then I pulled the suspenders over my shoulders. From the suitcase, I took my father's cylinder and crept downstairs with my boots in one hand so as not to disturb the even snuffle of Guthrie's sleeping.

The western sky seemed plated with the colors of old bronze.

As I walked along the beach, I could make out the whale-belly hulk of the *Madrigal*, still slumped beyond the waves. Foam coasted in on the high tide. It bubbled down through the sand before it reached my feet.

I unscrewed the cap from the cylinder and threw it out into the water. With the next wave that rumbled up onto the sand, I poured out the ashes. It was dark and I could barely see them fall. The sea foam gathered them and folded them away into the tide.

I felt no great sadness. It was a man reduced to this but the man was gone from these ashes. There was no need for tears in saying good-bye.

I threw the cylinder as far as I could out into the sea. As the nickel sides trapped night-blue light and vanished into a swell, I caught sight of a rowboat on the water. It lay a few hundred yards from the shore. Oars creaked in their oarlocks. The rower stood and leaned over the side. It was Tarbox, out gathering crabs from his pots. He paddled hard to catch the waves that surfed him back to shore. He sang to himself as he rowed.

I thought about the times when I'd gone crab-catching with Hettie, at low tide in Mackerel Cove. We used sticks made from white-birch twigs to stir the tide pools, in case a crab hid there. Sometimes the mud exploded and two claws rose up out of the brown, clamping down on the stick. The crab struggled, blue-green shell with spikes at each end, flippering the shallow water with its back-leg paddles. But the crab never let go. I could pick it up and set it in a potato sack and then have to cut the end off my stick before I could go back to hunting for more crabs. The twig got shorter and shorter, and after a while I'd have to find myself a new one. When Hettie and I came home, we'd empty our sacks into an old bathtub out behind her father's garage—pinching, slow-scrabbling crabs and clots of sand and torn-off lengths of stick.

I pulled off my boots and socks and waded out to help Tarbox. The cold made my muscles cringe.

Two wire baskets lodged in the bow were jammed with scuttling crabs.

We dragged his boat up to the dunes. Tarbox lashed it to the trunk of a driftwood tree. His cart stood nearby.

Tarbox rubbed the heat back into his hands. "What are you doing here, anyway? Usually the only ones I see are the Tans when they come to pester me."

"I couldn't sleep. I was scattering my father's ashes."

"Ah." Tarbox nodded. His wide eyes blinked the strange

bronze color that glimmered on the horizon. "Last year, a man named O'Keefe came down to the sea with the ashes of his wife. He scattered them and all the while he was yelling 'Bye-bye dear. Bye-bye.' And the wind was blowing the wrong way . . . Oh, it was a hell of a mess."

I looked at the broad flat space of Tarbox's forehead, and the sharp stump of his nose. He looked as if he'd been badly chiseled out of stone.

Tarbox lifted a crab basket and set it down on the sand. "I don't mean you any harm with the things I said back at Guthrie's. It's just that I'd hate to see him end his days before he gets his hands on Lily Gisby. Or her hands on him. Or however you want to believe the story. They're both mad for each other, but neither one wants to admit it. It's been going on for so many years that if he did turn around one day and said he loved her, she wouldn't know what to do with herself. That would probably be the end of it, and I dare say Guthrie knows that. I think he keeps her away so that they'll stay in love."

I saw something glinting near the bow. It was a brass crucifix, nailed into the wood of the forward seat. The cross had been polished, while the rest of the metal on Tarbox's boat was crusted with salt spray and rust.

Tarbox kicked at the crab pot and the crabs rustled inside. "I think you're bad luck, Mr. Sheridan. You can't bring good to anyone here. And any place you go, people will be risking their lives to give you a meal or a bed. Hagan won't help you. I think he's been dead for years. I hear so many damn stories about him up in the north. People say when Hagan did as much as look your way, you could hear shovels digging the earth of your grave. But whatever you do, the longer you stay around here, the better chance the Tans have of finding you."

Now I stepped closer. "They'll find out a lot sooner if you keep talking so loud. It's my life you're juggling here."

"But it's you I'm talking to, not them." Tarbox aimed a finger at the dunes, as if the soldiers were out there, eyes reflecting light, and he could see them. "Or are you forgetting already who you are yourself? The way I hear Crow talk, you never knew to begin with."

CHAPTER 10

"**B**ugger!" Guthrie's slippered foot stamped in the hallway. Morning light through a stained-glass window in the front door spread blue and ruby light across the floor. "That damn McGarrity has forgotten to deliver the milk!"

"You could drink your tea without it." I walked out to the hall, sleep peeling back from my body.

"Tea without milk?" Guthrie lifted the empty jug that he always left outside his front door last thing at night. He waved the jug in the air. Usually, McGarrity would have filled it long before sunrise from one of the dull metal churns on the back of his cart. "Oh, don't be a heathen, boy."

"How do you expect to stay healthy anyway, with just a mugful of tea and a slab of that gnarly old soda bread for breakfast? You never buy the fresh stuff. You buy it when it's a day old and half the price. And when I bring home bread still warm from the ovens, you don't touch it."

"My bread's not gnarly." Guthrie's voice collapsed into muttering. "It's perfectly good."

"Calm down. I'll go and buy you some more milk."

"I don't have to calm down. I'm an old fart and I don't have to calm down for anyone." I watched a smile work its way through the lock-jawed grumpiness on his face. "Except perhaps for Lily."

I pulled a shilling from my waistcoat pocket. "How much milk will this get me?"

Guthrie took the coin and squinted at it, as if this shilling might be worth less than any others. "More than we need. Get the milk from Lily's Hotel. They'll always sell a pint or two. You could get it on the cheap since you work there. Mention my name and you might just get it for free."

"If McGarrity is Boycotted, why do you still let him deliver milk to you?"

"There's no place else to get it. He works for an English-owned dairy in the area. Tans burned down the others. Hurry, now." His eyebrows bobbed up and down. "Or there'll be trouble."

I walked past the town hall, my thoughts still muffled with dreams. A sign above the entrance gave names and dates of ships that had gone down near the bay. It listed the survivors and the dead, names carefully painted in yellow on a blue background.

A man sat on a crate by the door, a basket of eggs at his feet. He rolled one of the eggs gently between his palms while he waited for people to buy.

I walked with my hands clutched behind my back. It made me move with a plod. At home, I would have walked with my hands in my pockets, but I didn't dare unstitch them after what Mrs. Fuller had said about men being shot for having hands in pockets.

Jackdaws cackled in the street. They marched on the slate rooftops, feathers black and shining like splinters of coal. Their beaks were gunmetal grey.

Tarbox pulled his cart up from the beach. He stopped in front of the Town Hall and wiped sweat from his forehead onto his sleeve. The cart was jammed with crab baskets, blanketed in seaweed. He nodded at me, but did not smile.

McGarrity's cart clattered across the road and down an alley. The horse he used to pull his cart was chestnut brown and had a sagging back.

McGarrity reined in the horse and climbed down. The sleeves of his too-big jacket had been rolled up to his forearms.

An army truck rumbled down the main street, windscreen reflecting the sky.

I had learned to take the rush of acid in my guts whenever the soldiers passed by. I just kept walking, head down as if looking for cigarette butts in the gutter.

Then a boy appeared from a doorway. He stood between me and the truck. Clutched in his fingers, nails bitten down to the pith, was a sharp-edged knot of flint.

The Crossley truck was twenty feet away.

Suddenly, the boy's arm swung back and snapped forward.

A spider web of bright silver splashed onto the windscreen. The sky's reflection vanished.

The boy spun on his heel and started running. He plowed headfirst into my stomach.

The air punched out of my lungs. I tipped over backward and the boy fell on top of me.

The truck stopped. Its brakes squealed and scattered the jackdaws from the chimney pots. A soldier jumped out. He grabbed the boy by the hair and lifted him almost off the ground. Then the boy's hair tore out in the soldier's hand and a patch of white showed on the boy's scalp. "You're in for it now, you little fuck." He threw away the clot of hair and took another grip on the boy's neck.

"He's just a kid." I tried to stand up. My soda bread-and-jam breakfast was climbing back into my throat.

Another soldier jumped down from the truck. He carried a rifle. The steel of his helmet looked rough, from sand that had been sprinkled on the wet paint and then painted over again.

The boy touched his hand to the bald patch on his head. "You bloody tore my hair out. You bloody bastards tore my hair out!"

"You won't have any hair at all by the time we've finished with you." The soldier twisted the boy's arm so that the boy had to stand on his toes.

The boy's mouth was locked open with pain.

"He's just a kid," I said again. I was standing now. Chips of lightning wove in front of my eyes. "You've got no right to beat up on children."

The soldier kept the boy's arm twisted. "Well, someone's got to take the blame for this."

My temper snapped and I spoke without thinking. "Fine, I'll take the goddamned blame."

"Right you are then," said a voice behind me.

Then my head exploded.

Powder-blue sky filled my eyes. I was lying in a room and looking out through a doorway. Then the sky went away and a face cut out the sun.

It was a woman. "That Tan hit you right on the temple."

"Clarissa?" I tried to sit up.

The woman's arm held me down. "Rest a while longer."

Another face appeared. Crow. He looked watery and out of focus. "What did you think you were doing?"

"I don't know." My jaw hurt. My bottom teeth and top teeth didn't seem to match up the way they used to.

"But what did you expect was going to happen after you back-talked that soldier?"

"It was a kid. Just a kid with a rock. They tore out a clump of his hair." I saw where I was now, on the kitchen floor at Gisby's Hotel. The same place where I took my naps. There was the underside of the sink. Here were the brick-red tiles below me. Forks and knives clinked together as people ate breakfast in the dining room. "I wasn't thinking about what they'd do to me. I guess I was still half asleep."

"Damn right you didn't think. Another time, you let that boy fend for himself." Crow's white apron was painted with food.

The woman had long black hair tied in a ponytail with a blue ribbon. It was Ruth, the waitress at Gisby's, the one nobody was supposed to talk with, since her father was an RIC man. "You can't blame that boy, what with all the things they're saying in school since that ship ran aground."

Crow held a lit cigarette to my lips. "What are they saying?"

"They're telling the story of that ancient chieftain and how he never died. Instead, he took his best warriors and led them to a cave somewhere up in the hills. He made them all lie down and sleep, with a promise that he would return one day to rescue the land."

"I know that story. My mother told it to me." I thought of the old dream rising through my memory, like a whale coming up from deep water to breathe.

"And the thing of it is, these boys talk of that ship as if it were the chieftain's and it was him who walked ashore with all those guns. Now the boys in the school don't see some gold-armored knight riding down from the hills after sleeping for a thousand years. They see the IRA men in their grubby trench coats and wool hats and rifles gone rusty from being hidden in the hedges."

"Did they let the boy go?"

Gisby called for Ruth from out in the hallway.

Ruth brought her face close to mine. "Are you sure you'll be all right?"

I nodded and a fleck of cigarette ash dropped onto my chest. When she was gone, I squinted up at Crow. "What happened to the boy?"

"They let him go. But they almost took you up to the barracks. By now, they'd know who you are. Instead, they just dumped you in the alleyway outside. They said they didn't want you showing up late for work. Who's Clarissa?"

"Not someone you'd want to meet." I rested my hands against my face. "I took a punch."

Crow started to laugh. His cackling grew louder and louder until a surprised look appeared on his face and he began to cough. He jammed his fist against his mouth and spluttered. "They snuffed you out like a candle."

"Thank you, Harry. I know."

Guthrie sat with his feet in a basin full of water. Steam coiled around his legs.

I stepped into the room. It was three in the afternoon, but I thought I should still bring him his milk. The pain was a sluggish thump inside my head.

"Is that you, Ben?" Guthrie pulled the glasses from his pocket and held them up to his eyes. "I could have opened my own dairy by now."

"I got stopped." It felt as if some gargoyle was pacing on my brain.

Guthrie pulled his feet from the basin and pattered them on the floor. "Any trouble?"

"None. Did you give up on the udder balm?"

"Mrs. Tarbox gave me a recipe." Steam curled like smoke off his toes. "Damn stuff smells worse than the balm."

"But does it work?"

"I can't tell. It hurts too much." Guthrie kneaded the steam from his feet. "I've made up my mind about something. I'm going to ask Lil to marry me. I'll ask her the next time I see her. Yes. I've said it now. That's what I'm going to do."

"Congratulations. People will say it's about time."

"They can say what they like. They always do, anyway."

"Is there anything you want me to tell Clayton when I see him tonight? I don't think they'll be bringing him straight here."

"The less you tell me, the better."

"No messages?"

Guthrie slowly hooked the wire temples of his glasses around his ears. "It's dangerous for the two of us to talk. He knows that. It's the cost of what he's doing."

Old bundles of flowers lay at the Black Virgin's feet, their colors bled away.

I searched through the trees that clumped behind the shrine. Wind clattered the branches. Someone else was there. I could feel it, and started to think it might be the Virgin. She glowered at me from her chiseled stone veils.

Then a man stood up from the hedge. He wore a trench coat and leather gaiters and carried a rifle. The man raised his hand slightly, spreading his fingers, cautiously waving hello.

"Crow?" I couldn't be sure. Shadow cloaked his body and his face.

"Yes, it's me. Isn't anybody on time any more?" Thistles clung to his legs. "I told Tarbox to be here by ten. That's the trouble with him. He wants independence for Ireland, but he can't be bothered to show up on time to collect it."

Crow had dug a foxhole. We both sat in it, shoulder to shoulder.

I wasn't afraid, the way I had been crossing the open fields. With night closing in, the darkness belonged to us now and not to the soldiers. "How close are you to getting independence?"

"Depends on who you talk to." Crow pulled a piece of fruitcake from his pocket, broke it in half, and gave a piece to me. "If you read the *Irish Times*, you'd think we never had a

chance. Each time someone makes a speech about Irish freedom, they're all applause and high hopes. But then when someone actually does something toward getting that freedom, like
landing these rifles on Lahinch strand, they call us murderers
and thugs."

"So who else do you listen to besides the *Irish Times*?" I
picked out the slivers of candied cherry and ate them first.

"You can listen to Clayton if you want. He'd have you think
that independence was so bloody close you could smell it. Or
you can listen to Mrs. Gisby. She doesn't even know what
independence is. She just wants to see blood, like an old hag
at a boxing match." Crow's voice disappeared as he stuffed the
fruitcake in his mouth.

The sky was purple now. Mist crept from the hollows and
spread across the fields in slow grey ranks.

"Look at this." From his coat, Crow pulled a wooden pistol
holster. He opened it and took out a strange looking gun with
a long barrel. The number 9 was carved into its rounded butt.
"It's a broom-handled Mauser. Belongs to Clayton. They gave
it to him in Dublin when he joined the IRA. I heard it came
ashore in a German shipment of arms to Bana Strand during
the war. When the Tans brought Clayton in, I ran over to his
house and took the gun away, as I knew the Tans would search
the place and find it. I buried it out in the fields for safekeeping.
He'll have it back tonight."

I listened, ear to the wind. "I hear someone coming." My
backside bristled with pins and needles against the damp earth.

"It would be about bloody time." Crow pulled a thistle from
his trousers. He reached across and stuck it on my coat.

Then came the sound of boots on the road. And whistling.
Tarbox appeared, followed by wandering sheep with muddy
tails and splats of blue dye on their backs. He stopped by the
Virgin, poked his head inside the shrine and kissed her on the

cheek. Then he faced the hedge and threw open his arms. "I know you're in there, Harry. I can smell you."

Crow stood slowly. "I said to be here at ten o'clock. It's damn near eleven."

"It is?" Tarbox pulled a brass-cased watch from his waistcoat. It was the one he had taken from the soldier on the beach, the day I arrived in Ireland. He shook it and held it to his ear. "Oh. Well, there we are then. My wife's been on at me again about having children. I swear to Christ, I'll pay you half a crown for an excuse that will keep her off my back even for a week."

"You should just have children and stop fussing." Crow stood with his arms folded, jutting up from the hedge like the stump of an old tree. "I wish I had a daughter or a son. I daresay it would get me out of this mess for good."

"And into another one!" Tarbox jumped the wall and his boots squelched on the damp earth.

Crow took the revolver from his belt and folded out the drum to see that the chambers were loaded. Then he took off his hat and set the gun on top, keeping it out of the dew. "If we get split up somehow, we're all to meet in Mrs. Fuller's basement at one o'clock this morning. Stan's going to tell them that we headed off to Ennistymon. It should give us some time before the Tans come rooting through Lahinch to find Clayton."

Tarbox's face swung out of the dark toward me. The whites of his eyes were like flakes of dried bone. "There'll be changes now, with Clayton free. For better or worse."

I smelled the smokiness of Tarbox's clothing, hung over a fire to dry. I thought about the change that was coming, delivered in the steel and canvas wrappings of the truck. On a constant twitching balance in my head was the need to go and the need to stay and learn more, but no one was going to tell me anything here, and it was far too dangerous to ask. I decided that I would just try to get home and live with what I didn't know. I had come to think of it in the same way that Crow saw my arrival in this place. Some kind of prophecy. I was not meant to know, just as Arthur Sheridan was meant some day to come back, wading from the sea onto the wide flat beach at Lahinch.

A truck puttered out of the hills. The whine of its changing gears drifted in on the breeze. Headlights carved bolts out of the dark. It stopped when it reached the shrine. The engine clunked into neutral.

I started to get up, but Tarbox shoved me back down again, his hand sinking into beads of dew that had gathered on my coat.

The truck's engine sputtered dead and Stanley climbed out of the cab. "We've got a flat."

A head appeared from a flap in the canvas roof. "You're fucking kidding, Stan."

Stanley pointed at the tire. "See for yourself, Desmond."

The head disappeared. A moment later, two men jumped down to the road. One man was a soldier. The other was dressed in civilian clothes, barefoot and with hands cuffed behind his back. It had to be Clayton.

Desmond grabbed Clayton by the collar of his shirt, lifting him onto his toes. "I don't want any pissing around from you. All right, my old pal? All right?" Desmond bellowed in his ear.

"Yes!" Clayton hunched down, waiting to be struck.

"Lie down there." Desmond kicked him behind the knees and dropped him onto the gravel. "And don't move until I tell you, or I'll come back and pull the pin on that bomb strapped to your chest. You hear me?"

"Yes, sir."

Desmond reached down, grabbed a handful of Clayton's hair. "What's your name? The one I gave you. I want to hear you say it."

"Seamus." His Adam's apple was stuck in his throat.

"All Irishmen are called Seamus. We should rename the lot of you and save time."

"Leave him alone for now." Stanley crouched by the tire. "Come help me with this."

Desmond let go of the hair and Clayton's face smacked on the road.

"It doesn't look flat, Stan." Desmond walked across. He bent down, hands on knees. "Seems all right to me."

Stanley had stepped back. In one fluid movement, he drew the gun from his belt, cocked the hammer, and shot Desmond in the back.

The air cracked and Desmond jolted backward. Quickly, he struggled to his feet. "Stan." His voice had grown suddenly hoarse.

Stanley held the revolver out at arm's length.

"What did you do to me?" Desmond's legs started to give way.

Stanley fired again and Desmond collapsed into the ditch. For a moment Stanley stayed looking down at the body. Then he walked over to Clayton.

"No!" Clayton lifted his chin off the gravel. "No! I didn't do anything!" He kicked his feet against the ground. "I didn't . . . do . . . anything!"

Stanley lifted him to his feet.

"I didn't do anything!" Clayton's voice was a high-pitched whine.

"Harry!" Stanley still held the gun in his hand.

Crow slipped through the hedge and walked down to the road.

I sat for a moment with Tarbox. I didn't remember having

breathed in the past few minutes. I felt a sudden stillness in the air, from knowing that Desmond was dead. It was a sadness, too, and I felt it against my face like the sigh of a ghost. Then the two of us followed Crow down.

"Is that you, Harry?" Clayton's hands stayed locked behind his back.

"Of course it's him. And me as well." Tarbox dragged Desmond's body out of the ditch. He turned the body over. Desmond's arms slapped down on the gravel. Tarbox opened the pockets on Desmond's tunic and made a pile of cigarettes and coins.

"No looting!" Crow set his boot on Tarbox's back and shoved him away from the corpse. "You just don't get it, do you? There will be no looting!"

"It doesn't make any sense. There's useful things he's carrying. They'll all go to waste otherwise."

"No, they won't. They'll be sent home to his wife. Same as I hope your things would be sent home if it was you lying there."

At the mention of his wife, Tarbox slumped into silence.

Crow held his hand out to Stanley. "Do you have the handcuff key?" Stanley laid his revolver on the hood of the truck and unclipped the key from his belt. He threw it to me instead of Tarbox.

Tarbox removed a hand grenade from the leather ammunition pouch that had been strapped across Clayton's chest. He weighed the gridded apple-size bomb in his hand. Then he guided Clayton to where I stood. "I was just telling Ben here how the Tans are going to rip Lahinch apart looking for you. We might as well all be living in the dunes from now on."

Clayton stared straight through me. He didn't wait for the cuffs to be unlocked. Instead, he walked over to Desmond's body and kicked him in the chest so hard I thought I heard the ribs crack. He was shaking with anger.

I undid the cuffs and it seemed to calm him down. Clayton's hands, twisted for so long behind his back, looked crooked like the claws of a bird.

Crow held out a fist of bills to Stanley. "Here's the rest of the money. A hundred and fifty dollars."

"Hide it and I'll get it off you later." Stanley waved him away. "Let's just get this over with."

"I don't know if I can."

"You have to do it. If you don't, they'll find out what really happened. I'm trusting you now, Harry."

Crow pointed at the body of Desmond. "Did you know him very well, Stan?"

"What the hell do you care? Now shut up and do your job."

Crow cocked the hammer of Desmond's revolver. Then he shot Stanley just below the knee.

Stanley's leg jerked back. He tried to stay on his feet, spitting out breath through clenched teeth. Then he dropped onto the road. He curled up in a ball and pressed his hands to the wound.

Crow knelt next to him. "Will you be all right for now, Stan? They'll come looking for you soon. Can you hear me, Stan? I'm going to put a bandage on you. Can you hear me? It's only a nick and you'll be up again in no time. We both had plenty worse than this over in France, didn't we, Stan?"

Stanley nodded. His forehead scraped on the gravel.

Clayton pointed at me, as if singling me out from a crowd. "You must be the Yank. The way I heard it, they were looking for an old man. But it's you they're after, isn't it? Tomorrow, they'll be bringing that crewman off the *Madrigal* down to Lahinch. As soon as Sutherland has him, the crewman will talk and they'll come looking for you."

I wanted to ask now if he would help me to find Hagan. I had no time to waste and wanted to set out while the dark still sheltered me.

Clayton smoothed his fingers over his wrists, where the handcuffs had dug in. "We should be gone by now."

We left Stanley on the road, still curled in a ball. As we vanished into the ranks of night fog, Stanley's groaning reached us on the wind. Once I turned and saw a splash of white from the bandage on Stanley's leg.

The white rocked slowly back and forth, as Stanley cradled the pain.

CHAPTER 11

C layton sat in a puddle of lamplight. On a bare wood table in Mrs. Fuller's basement, he sketched a plan of the Lahinch barracks. Shadows carved into his face. Lying next to him was the Mauser's wooden holster. It had been buried so long underground the soil had mottled it.

"I'm sure this was the armory room. I was in a cell opposite, and I heard rifles being pulled off racks the night that ship went down. I heard people loading the magazines as they ran out to the truck."

Crow leaned over him, squinting at the plan. "But you've got to be more than almost sure. I can't be responsible for sending a group of men into a building with the wrong floor plan."

"That's all right, Harry." Clayton set down the pencil. "You aren't responsible any more."

I sat next to Tarbox, waiting for the talk to die down so I could ask if there would be anyone to guide me north. Veils of spiderweb coated empty jars on the windowsill. Their lids were fused by ginger rust.

Crow eased himself into an old chair whose wicker seat had collapsed and never been repaired. "I got you that dairy pump, Clayton. The one you wanted just before the Tans pulled you in. It's over there in the corner if you still need it."

The pump looked like a beer keg with a hose attached to the top.

"It's a bloody milk pump for sucking the milk out of cow's tits." Tarbox hugged his ribs. "Have you lost your bloody minds?"

Clayton pressed his fingertips together. They were black with pencil dust. "If we fill it with kerosene and invert the pumping mechanism, then smash a hole in the barracks roof and pump the fuel in after it, the whole place would go up in flames."

"How do you get close enough to smash a hole in the roof?"

"Ladders."

Tarbox held his hand out, waiting to collect a better answer. "How do you get close enough to use them?"

"We lay down covering fire. We've got enough ammunition for that."

Crow stared at the drum. "But what if they shoot a hole in it? The Tans are armed to the teeth. They've got crates of hand grenades and at least three Lewis guns and all the ammunition in the world. The place is built like a bunker. What good are we against all that?"

Clayton walked over to the milk pump. "We need to make a strike at a barracks. We need to keep up the pressure. Attacks are due to take place all over Ireland, all at the same time. The whole thing's already arranged."

Tarbox spat on the floor. "It will be a massacre. How much longer do you want to live? Or is the grey dog following you and you don't care?"

I looked at him suddenly. "What did you say?"

"I said it would be a massacre." Tarbox ground his spit into the dirt.

"About the grey dog. What did you say about that?"

"It's just another way of saying he's at the end of his rope. It's from an old story. Don't look at me like that, boy. It's just a children's story."

Clayton had gone back to his map. He shaded in the barracks with the stub of pencil. "Has my father gone and married that idiot woman Mrs. Gisby, yet?"

Before I knew what I was doing, I had stood up and barked in his face. I didn't know if it made any sense, or even what I had said, except that I was angry. I'd already given up hope that anyone would guide me to Connemara. One good look at Clayton had told me enough about that.

Now Clayton looked across, as if noticing me for the first time. "What's he doing here, anyway?"

Crow rested his forearms on the table. He cleared his throat. "I thought you should meet Ben here. He's Arthur Sheridan's son, after all. He's heading up north to find Hagan and he needs a guide. I was thinking I could take him there myself."

"Do you know where Hagan is?"

"Not exactly."

"And who's going to do your job while you're gone?"

"It won't take long. We could set out tonight. The Tans will be busy searching Lahinch."

Tarbox smacked his hands together. "Well, it's another night in the dunes, boys."

"I am giving you an order." Clayton stared, as if he could not believe they would dare talk back to him. "And you, too, Crabman. If anyone under my command leaves the area without my permission, I'll shoot them myself." Clayton turned to me. "Everything your country stands for is going on in these towns and in these fields. You're looking at a people who want their independence and a ruling class that won't give it to them."

Tarbox raised his hands and let them drop again. "Oh, don't start with this again. And don't cough up that bit about President Wilson's speech, either."

Clayton didn't hear him. His words had become like a chant. "How different is it from your Bunker Hill and York-town and Lexington? How different are these members of the Republican Army and your Minutemen? I can't see a damn bit of difference myself. Even Wilson said that in Boston, in 1919. He said 'We set this nation up to make men free and we did not confine our conception and purpose to America, and now we will make men free.' And what the hell are you doing about it, Mr. Sheridan?" Clayton folded his arms and sat back. The chair legs creaked underneath him. "The same damn thing as your father; looking for the first excuse to run away."

I lunged at him across the table and I had him by the lapels of his coat. The Mauser went flying off into the dark. I swung Clayton toward me and cracked his nose against my forehead. Then someone grabbed hold of my ankles and dragged me back until I fell off the table. I thumped down to the floor. Clayton's hands were pressed to his face and blood trickled out between his fingers. I stood up and lunged at him again, but Crow had hold of my collar, which dug into my throat and held me back.

"It's not worth any more." Crow's knuckles were warm at the back of my neck where he still held my shirt.

I tried to think of something to say, but my head was all jumbled. The right words would come later, the way they always did, too late to do any good.

Clayton took out a handkerchief and dabbed at his bloody nostrils. "I was only telling the truth. I did not deserve that."

Tarbox had stayed silent until now. "You deserved worse, you horrible little man."

Clayton ignored him. He kept his eyes on me. "And how do you like sleeping in my bed?"

————

Lahinch was empty again. I went back to fetch the revolver that Crow had given me and to help Guthrie out of his house, if he had not already left.

Clayton stayed away, in case the Tans were waiting in the town.

Guthrie was still at his house, feet wrapped in bandages because he had half-boiled his feet in Mrs. Tarbox's remedy. They looked like giant snowballs.

I put him in his wheelbarrow and untethered Roly Poly and Margaret. They would follow us down to the sand.

We set off along the high street. On his lap, Guthrie carried a tattered leather suitcase.

I thought of what Clayton had said and I wondered if he was right. Perhaps it was cowardice to leave after what I'd seen. But I didn't have a picture of the whole war, packaged neat and clear in front of me like Clayton's map of the barracks. All I had seen were the little wars, flaring like tinderbrush fires across the countryside. I doubted if Crow or Tarbox knew much about the whole war, either. Even the Tans seemed drawn into the local chaos. The freedom of the country seemed so far away that neither side could picture it.

Only Clayton seemed to know, as if he had been brought to some secret room in Dublin by others who knew the whole war, and he had been shown a vision of the free Ireland. They had also shown him the cost, and he carried it hidden inside.

"How did Clayton look, Ben? Had they beaten him badly? I dreamed that they had hurt him terribly."

"No. He's fine. He's out here someplace and he's fine." I didn't tell him about the fight.

We moved on for a while in silence. The barrow's weight

rubbed blisters on my hands. "What story does it come from, Guthrie, when people talk of being followed by a grey dog?"

"Well, now let me see. That would be the story of Cuchulain's dog. After Cuchulain had died, the dog ran away to the hills. Then what happened, you see, is it would come down again to hunt for the people who had been his master's enemies. So whenever these people saw themselves followed by a huge grey dog, they knew their time had come. It meant they were going to die. And why do you ask me that?"

I told him why.

He clicked his tongue while he listened. "I doubt Arthur could have forgiven himself completely for not coming back to Ireland like he promised. Perhaps he meant to send you in his place, the way people say over here. But perhaps, as you say, with him not being your real father, he only wanted you to know the truth."

A splash of white caught my eye. Then I saw, in arm-thick letters painted on the wall of Gisby's Hotel: GOD BLESS THE BLACK AND TANS.

Roly Poly and Margaret and I all shambled to a halt outside the hotel.

Mrs. Gisby stood in the doorway. Her head was a quilt of hairpins. "They made me do it, just before they left to find a man of theirs who's missing. And they said if they couldn't find him, they'd be coming back to burn the place down."

Wind sifted through Guthrie's grey hair. "I'll help you clean it up, Lil. After this is over. For now, you must come to the dunes."

"I'll be there soon enough."

Trickles ran down from the clumsily painted letters. They wandered over cracks in the stone.

"Won't you come with us, Lil?" Guthrie gripped his suitcase. His fingernails dug into the chafed leather.

"I'll come when I'm ready."

"Lil, I been meaning to say. After all this time . . . This can't wait, Lil. I'm going to say this now, or I'm not going to say it at all. We're getting married, you and I."

"Are you asking me or telling me, you old man sitting there in a wheelbarrow?"

I set down the barrow and pressed my reddened hands together. I was a little embarrassed to be there, in the middle of Guthrie's proposing. But just then I had no place else to go.

"I'm saying this has gone on long enough!" Guthrie banged his fist on the suitcase. "My house is too big and my time is too empty. Do you want me to drop to my knees? Is that it?" He started to heave himself out of the barrow. "I didn't think you'd want a song and dance."

"Stay where you are, old man. Wait until your feet are better. That way I won't have to walk down the aisle and see you there by the altar in your barrow."

"We could decorate it with flowers." I closed my hands on the splintery wooden handles. "I could wear a tuxedo."

"I should have stuck with the udder balm. That's what I should have done!"

"We'll be having a talk about you and your balm, Mr. Guthrie."

"There!" Guthrie's voice was almost a shout, as I wheeled him down to the sand. "I really went and did it!"

"Congratulations. I know it's the right thing to do." It was hard pushing the wheels over the sand. I knew that in a minute, I'd have to stop. I thought of Lil and Guthrie together, and realized that I'd already been thinking of them as married for a long while now.

"About time!" Guthrie waved his fist in the air. "About bloody time it was, too!"

———

Fires glowed on the beach. Smoke from burning driftwood sifted through the dune grass.

I left the barrow and carried Guthrie piggyback over the sand. He weighed nothing at all. Roly Poly and Margaret followed, chewing at grass along the way. As I stumbled down the slope of a dune, I saw someone huddled by a fire. It was a woman, her hands reached out to the crackling orange for warmth. A man sat next to her.

The man was Crow. And now I recognized Ruth. She had been beaten. Her face was puffy with bruises and her eyes had both been blackened.

Crow covered her head with his hand. His fingers caged the bluish welts on her forehead. "Ruth's father found out about her being with me. He said he'd warned her too many times already. So this is what he did to her as punishment."

Ruth's head bowed lower as Crow spoke.

Guthrie whispered in my ear. "Move along, Ben."

I staggered on through the sand and Crow disappeared behind the flames.

Low-tide sand stretched down toward the water. I saw other fires burning, and people crowded around them, but Guthrie looked so cold and tired that I decided to build him a fire of his own.

I gathered strangely twisted driftwood branches from the webs of dried-out seaweed, while Guthrie stayed in a hollow, coat pulled up over his head to cut out the sand-speckled wind. The cow and the sheep settled down. They closed their eyes and slept.

I made the fire and slowly the wood began to burn. Salt

made the flames flicker blue. It wheezed and popped and the dune grass lit up like shreds of brass wire.

There had been no time to eat dinner and I was hungry. And not knowing where my next meal was coming from only made the hunger worse. I imagined the kettle boiling on Guthrie's stove, how the tea would taste smoky and how I was used to the taste of the smoke. It seemed to be everywhere; in the meat, in the beer, in the bread. "Would you like me to go and find Clayton?"

Guthrie looked down at his snowball bandages. "He'll come to me when he's ready."

"I'm leaving tonight, Guthrie. It's only sixty miles to Connemara. I'm going by myself."

"With no one to help you?"

Smoke pinched at my eyes. "No."

Guthrie bowed toward the fire. The cold was skirting his bones. "Then you may as well know. I made a promise and now I'm breaking it. So now you wait and see if that same grey dog doesn't come looking for me. Ah, Jesus." He touched his fingertips against his closed eyes. "Arthur Sheridan is not your father. Hagan is. And Mae was not your mother. Her name was Helen, and she was Hagan's wife. Hagan put you in Arthur's care when you were six months old. You were born here, Ben, just up the road. I saw you when you weren't an hour old."

Suddenly the coils of my stomach felt like glass. If I moved, they would shatter. I didn't know why I was surprised. I think I had hoped all along that Dr. Melville might be lying and news of it would reach me any day. Or I had come to accept that I would never know. I tried again to picture Hagan, but still found only a cloudy presence far to the north. Further than Connemara. It was as if he lived out on the ice floes of the Arctic.

Guthrie stabbed at the fire and sparks coughed into the air. "The soldiers were looking for Hagan. They burned his house when he and you and your mother were still inside it. Your mother died in the fire. Hagan took you out through the smoke. I remember the blanket you were wrapped in. The wool was all scorched. Hagan went into hiding. But he knew the soldiers would find him in the end. And then what would happen to you? Arthur and Mae were leaving for America and he knew you'd be safe there. So he put you in their keeping. Hagan thought he'd be dead in six weeks. He gave you up for good, Ben. Not to have you brought back years later and have your life turned on its head. For good."

For a long time, we sat without speaking. But there was no silence in my head. Voices clamored inside. All the pictures that made up my life thundered through my mind, too fast to understand. I searched for clues in my past that should have led me before now to this knowledge. But I found no difference in the eyes and skin and bones that I had believed were an echo of my own. No tone of voice. No memory of whispered conversations rising like smoke through the floorboards to my room at night. If it had been a smaller lie, I knew I might have found it. But this stretched so vast across the years that I had never thought to question.

Guthrie had fallen asleep. His chin rested on his chest.

I stood. Blown sand sifted from the ripples of my clothes. "Good-bye, Guthrie. Thank you for helping me."

"Eh?" Guthrie raised his head. His eyes were blurry.

I thanked him again and said good-bye. I said I'd come back and see him someday.

He told me not to promise, so there'd be no word to keep, but I promised anyway. I missed him already, and it brought tears to my eyes to see him lying there all helpless. But he would be with Lil soon, so there was no need for crying. Both of us had always known that I'd be moving on, and this had come between us. His was the voice that had broken the secret, so I would never forget him, and never forget the memory of myself standing here by the fire, with no clue how to get home.

On my way out to the road, I found Clayton. He sat by himself on an old tree trunk which was half buried at the high-tide line. He had a fire burning.

Tarbox's cart stood nearby. Two pairs of shoes stuck out from a pile of blankets on the cart.

Clayton put a finger to his lips when I stepped into view. "Tarbox and his wife are fast asleep," he whispered. Then he pulled a stick from the fire and held it out to me. On the end of the stick was a roasted potato. "Hungry?"

I nodded thanks and took the smoke-billowing potato. I waited for him to say something about the fight, or even do something about it, but he seemed to have forgotten.

"Come and see this." Clayton led me to the top of a dune. The sky glowed orange over Lahinch. "It's Gisby's Hotel. The Tans said they'd burn it down if she didn't write that thing about God save the Tans. So she painted it up, then burned the bloody place herself."

I watched the distant flames. Bubbles of light from smaller fires showed across the waves of sand. Silhouettes scrabbled up and then dropped down again. I knew we were all watching it. I thought of the dining room's salmon-pink walls, of my sleeping place on the kitchen floor, the benches in the pub, and the beer-splashed copper sheets across the top of the bar. If it had to burn, I was thinking, at least it was Gisby who set the place alight.

"So you're leaving now, are you?" Clayton took the potato out of my hand and bit into it.

I nodded again.

"Good luck to you." Steam billowed from his mouth. "I think luck is about all you have left."

I pointed toward the place where Guthrie lay sleeping. "Go and look after your father."

CHAPTER 12

By dawn, I was on the way to Ennistymon. Sad crying gulls drew rings in the air above me, then dropped into the plowed earth of fields beyond the road.

Crow had made me a map the day before, on a guest receipt from Gisby's Hotel. His smoky fingerprints walked across the paper.

From Ennistymon, I would bear north to Lisdoonvarna, Ballyvaghan and Kinvarra. I'd pass through Galway to Rosscahill and Maam Cross. If I reached the Cross, Crow had told me, I'd see the Maamturk Mountains in the distance. Then I'd probably be safe. Hagan was out there, someplace among the peat-bogged hills and bottomless sapphire lakes.

I had a little money. My pockets jangled with change.

Horse-drawn carts trundled by. They were filled with seaweed. Men with pitchforks spread it on the fields as fertilizer.

A river ran through Ennistymon, water foaming cream and brown as it broke across the rocks. The trees were crowded with blackbirds, cackling in the leaves.

An army truck rumbled past and diesel coughed in my face. The driver leaned out and squinted at me.

Ennistymon was busy with soldiers and shops. Rabbits hung outside the butcher's. Joints of meat, speckled with parsley, crammed the window.

Loaves of bread slipped one by one from the bakery, carried in string bags by women with shawls on their heads.

The soldiers moved in pairs, black polish on their boots blinking silver in the sun. Sam Browne belts pinched their stomachs.

I walked up a steep hill to a churchyard that overlooked the town. The roof and windows had gone from the church and grass grew through the flagstones on the floor. From here, I could see far across the water. The houses of Lahinch bunched near the horizon.

I sat down to rest on a grave. it had been raised above the ground, the earth too crowded below. Slate panels that hid the coffin had slumped. The rotten wood showed through and I could make out the rough-edged sticks of bones. A skull, worn thin as paper by the rain and wind, lay staring at the grey roofstone.

Each time I tried to fasten in myself the knowledge that Hagan was my father, my heart beat like a clock's chimes gone mad. Understanding would come only fragment by fragment. Maybe just to see Hagan would lock all the pieces calmly into place. But I couldn't imagine it. The idea only threw me further into confusion.

I headed north toward Kinvarra. Tucked under my arm, I carried a loaf of bread.

The Crossley truck had stopped a mile north of Ennistymon. It clogged up the road. The driver and another soldier were replacing a tire. A rifle with fixed bayonet stood propped against the spare wheel.

By the time I caught sight of the machine, the soldiers had already seen me. They were from the barracks at Lahinch. One of them was Sergeant Byrne, Ruth's father. The other was an army corporal. By now, I even knew the rank badges. Two stripes for a corporal. Three for a sergeant. I knew then that I couldn't turn around. So I looked down at my shoes and tried to shuffle by.

"You."

Panic rained through my guts. I kept moving. The chafed toes of my boots appeared and disappeared in front of me.

"I'm talking to you, Seamus. You. I'm talking to you."

Now I stopped and raised my head to meet their stares. If they searched me, they would find the gun.

They stood with their hands in their pockets.

The corporal stepped forward. "You're the one I hit that other day."

I hadn't known it was him, since he came at me from behind. "Snuffed me out like a candle." I remembered the way Crow had said it.

Byrne pointed at the ground in front of him. "Come and change this tire."

"What's the matter? Don't you talk? What's your name? Don't you work at the hotel?"

"Ben." My lips had dried out. They rustled together like blades of old grass.

"What's a Yank doing here except to cause trouble?"

"No trouble." My Adam's apple had jammed in my throat. If he came any closer, I knew I'd have to shoot him. I dug my elbow into my side, trying to hide the gun.

Byrne snatched my arm from behind. He swung me around until I was facing the truck. My loaf of bread fell on the ground. "Put your hands up there. Legs apart."

For a second, my fingertips rested on the taut canvas of the truck's roof. I filled my lungs, but the air seemed thin and useless.

Then I sprang away to the side, fingers raking across the holster as I tried to pull it open.

The corporal rushed me, screaming.

I had my hand on the butt of the Webley.

He smacked me in the face and I started to fall, still trying to pull out the gun.

Byrne ran at me. He jumped in the air and his boot slammed into my chest.

The wind punched out of me. My gun went clattering down the road, barrel spinning in circles.

I heard them shouting, but pain blurred their words. A boot pressed my face to the ground. They twisted my arms. Then came the brush of hands down my legs and sides as they searched for more weapons.

A stripe of burning spread across my skull. For a moment, my consciousness fizzled. Then my thoughts came back and I knew they had kicked me in the head.

They lifted me up off the ground and I had trouble keeping my balance.

Byrne's face was close. "If you so much as breathe funny, I'll put a fucking window in your chest." They had fetched my gun and now they held it up in front of my face. "Where did this come from? Who did you kill to get it?"

Before I could think of an answer, rage spread across Byrne's face. It twisted his lips and his cheeks. His eyes vanished behind the narrowed lids. Then with great care, he brought his arm back, the revolver barrel locked in his fist.

I closed my eyes. I knew what was coming. The butt of the Webley crashed into my head. Vaguely, I felt myself falling. Then my body jolted on the ground. I thought they might be hitting me. But as the darkness settled, I realized it was my heart, trying to kick its way out of my chest.

My toes scraped along the ground. When I raised my head, I saw a large stone house with metal-shuttered windows and sandbags set out in a waist-high ring around the door. It was the barracks at Lahinch.

Byrne and the corporal were dragging me. They breathed through clenched teeth with the strain.

The hedges had been cut back around the house, so that no one could approach without being seen. Only stumps remained of trees that had grown on the lawn. Tar was spread on the stumps to stop the sap from bleeding.

A soldier sat behind the sandbags and propped on a tripod next to him was a machine gun. A bayonet had been stabbed up to its hilt into the bags. The soldier flicked away his cigarette. He put his helmet on.

A shutter squeaked open. Pale faces peered from inside.

My feet bounced up the steps and past the steel-plated door.

They dragged me down a corridor. The floor was gritty with sand from spilled sandbags. Piles of them lay by the windows.

In a room to one side, iron-rail beds were lined up against the wall. Sheet music and postcards decorated the walls. By each bed was a chair, on which the soldiers had folded their clothes and set their leather bandoliers. Rifles hung horizontally from straps at the end of every bed.

I stood facing the wall in a room with no windows, hands on top of my head. The place smelled like a locker room at a gym.

Byrne took hold of the back of my neck, pinching his thumb and index finger into the base of my skull. "Don't go away."

My shirt was soaked under the arms. I rested my forehead against the cold wall, smudging the sweat. Salt leaked into my eyes.

The door crashed shut. The only light came from one bulb that hung from the ceiling. The bulb had a shade, green on the top and bone-white underneath. It looked more like a dinner plate than a shade, and only seemed to make the light stronger. The walls were bare and duck-egg blue. A space the size of a loaf of bread had been cut in the brick, far above my head.

When I turned, I saw a table in the middle of the room. Two chairs were pulled under it.

I had to get a story straight. Any story.

The door opened and shut again. "Are you all right?" It was the officer named Sutherland, the one I had seen that night at Gisby's. "I asked if you were all right."

"Yes." I squinted in the glare.

He pointed to a chair. "Sit there, please."

I sat with my back to the door.

Sutherland folded his hands and rested them on the table. The knot of his fingers reached almost to where I sat. "Please keep your hands on the table."

I held my fingers tucked in, as if they were too fragile to lie there unprotected.

"We're going to ask you some questions." Sutherland leaned forward. "All right?"

I wanted to wipe the sweat from my forehead. It was cold and itchy now. But I didn't dare move my hands. Sutherland seemed ready to latch on to them as soon as they shifted.

Someone trampled down the stairs.

Sutherland took a notebook from his top pocket. The book was leather-bound, with pale-blue pages. From the spine, he pulled a thin pencil and licked the tip, ready to write. "What's your name?"

"Benjamin Guthrie."

He didn't look up. The pencil still hovered over the tiny notebook pages. "Your real name, please." He held out his pencil and rested it on my right shoulder. "This worn patch comes from carrying a rifle. The gun strap rubs away at the cloth. You aren't Guthrie's nephew from America. So tell me your real name."

I hadn't noticed the worn patch before.

"I know who you are." Sutherland breathed out with a small whistling sigh. "I'm going to give you one more chance to tell me your name."

"If you already know, then why are you asking me?"

"We start out asking the things we do know. We get you to tell the truth. Then we move on to whatever else you can tell us. Like who you delivered those guns to and who paid for them and how many there were and what your orders were when you reached Ireland and how your father is involved. Do you see? Because at the moment, the correct answers to those questions are all that's standing between you and a hole in the ground."

The air in the room bristled with violence. It was like static.

"Nothing to say?" Sutherland looked at his watch.

I stared at a drop of my sweat as it sank into the wood of the table.

Sutherland stood up. His chair scraped on the floor. "I'll see you in a little bit." He walked out, resting a hand on my shoulder as he passed by.

When Sutherland comes back, I thought, I will ask to be released. I'll ask if there are any charges being brought against me and if there are no charges, I will ask to be let go.

When the door opened again, I stood up. Someone walked in. I screwed up my eyes in the brightness and raised a hand to block out the tiny sun of the bulb.

It wasn't Sutherland. Byrne stood there with his arms folded. "Captain says you're not being helpful."

"Are you arresting me or not?"

Byrne's raised eyebrows were thin licks of blond. "What?"

"If you are arresting me, then I would like to know the charges. If you aren't, I am asking to be released." The breath caught in my throat. "I'm asking to be released immediately." Stand your ground, I thought to myself. Don't let him know you're afraid. I was still telling myself this when I took Byrne's knuckles full in the face.

Then I was lying on the floor and from all around came hissing and thunder. Pain clamped onto the bridge of my nose and blinded me. I breathèd in and liquid caught in my throat. It trickled into my lungs and choked me. Something burst against my stomach and the shock rolled me over. The floor dropped away and something like seasickness made me want to throw up but I couldn't.

Now I was sitting on the table. Someone had hold of my shoulders. Byrne's voice rumbled like waves breaking.

My skull seemed to drift in a slow wobbly arc out into the room and my body followed somewhere behind. I thought about protecting myself but by the time my arm reached out I'd already hit the ground. I landed on my face.

Back in the chair. My lips kept sticking together. I opened my mouth to speak and speckles of blood sprayed across Byrne's cheeks.

Byrne shouted something.

Once more my head seemed to catapult itself off into space, leading me down to the floor.

Now someone else was in the room. It was Sutherland. He yelled at Byrne and the door slammed.

Someone had me by the chin. Then something metal clinked against my teeth and fire poured into my mouth. I choked and fell off the chair.

Back in the chair. "Bastard," I tried to say. But the word came out "Bathtud." I said it again and louder. "Bathtud!"

Sutherland's voice hummed in my ears. "As soon as you answer some questions, we'll fix you up. We just need to know a few names. Can you hear me?"

"Eth." My tongue flopped in my mouth.

"Good." A chair scraped on the floor and Sutherland sat down at the table. "This shouldn't have happened."

"Eth." Pain shrieking behind my eyes.

Someone else was in the room now. Another man. I stayed looking at the table. I didn't think I could raise my head even if I'd wanted to.

"Well, is that him or isn't it?" Sutherland whispered to the new man.

"I can't see his face."

A hand rested on my shoulder. It was Sutherland's. "Would you mind looking up for a moment?"

I flexed the muscles at the back of my neck. My head wobbled a little but I couldn't raise it.

Sutherland swung out of his chair. He grabbed my hair and lifted me up. "Is this him or isn't it?"

I tried to focus on the new man. Then I knew.

It was Baldwin. His face was all beaten to hell. "How can I tell after what you've done to him?"

After what they've done to him. The words repeated in my head, then tears trickled into my eyes.

"It's him." Baldwin left the room.

Sutherland let go of my head and my nose slammed against the table. A huge pendulum inside me painted one stroke of dark after another over my thoughts. Soon there was only the quiet plodding of my heart to keep me company.

The light was on. I lay on the floor. My jacket had been taken off, rolled up as a pillow and stuffed under my head. I could hear the sea through the air vent.

Boots tumped up and down the corridor.

I raised my arm to look at my watch but the watch had disappeared. My fingers touched the bloated skin around my nose. When I raised my head, I saw my shirt crusted with blood. The blood had dried and turned brown. From the ache in my ribs when I breathed, I could tell I had been kicked. I tried to breathe through my nose but nothing happened except a pressure built up somewhere in my throat.

I rolled over onto my hands and knees, and realized that I was barefoot. They had taken my boots and socks. I crawled around the room. In one corner, blood in spots and smeared fingermarks splattered the walls and floor. People had trod in the blood and tracked it across to the table. I ran my hand across the marks where I had fallen off the chair and landed on my face. The blood came away in burgundy dust on my fingertips.

Sitting against the wall, I blinked and blinked, trying to clear the pressure around my eyes.

It was dark outside. I'd been lying there all day.

Whispering. It seemed to come from inside my head and I ground my thumb-knuckles into my temples to clear the noise. But the whispering kept up. It was coming from outside.

A door slammed in the barrack building. It thundered through the walls. Hobnailed boots ran past and a draft blew against my bare feet.

"What do you mean he's not there?" It was Sutherland, followed by someone who took shorter steps and mumbled.

"He's probably just checking the grounds, sir. But I thought I ought to tell you." It was an Irish voice, the throaty purr so different from the English.

The front door of the barrack house swung open. Its armor-plating dragged across the floor.

"Stanley!" Sutherland yelled.

"Probably just checking the grounds, sir. As I said." The Irishman mumbled again, as if he had trouble assembling the sounds into words.

"Stanley! Stanley, is that you?"

It was quiet for a moment. I leaned closer to the cold metal of the door. Then came a sound like a damp log bursting in the fire. The sound came again. Gunfire.

Someone cried out in pain.

Suddenly the barracks shook with footsteps. Shouts piled up on shouts. A long scrape traveled the length of the corridor. Then the light went suddenly away from under my door as a falling body blocked the space. Footsteps running away.

"Raid!" Frightened voices came muffled through the brick. "It's a raid!"

Bullets clanked against the metal window shutters.

I crawled into the corner and wrapped my arms around my knees. I had begun to shake. I waited for the door to burst open and for Sutherland or one of the soft-talking RIC men to drag me out and shoot me.

The man on the other side of the door was trying to sit up.

Gunshots banged at my ears.

"Oh my God." The man slumped down again.

More footsteps. Someone crouched down next to the door. "Captain Sutherland, sir? I've got morphine for you, sir." It was another English voice. "It's me, sir, Sergeant Gillis."

"Oh, Christ." Sutherland was trying to sit up.

"You've been shot, sir. I've got some morphine here. I think they might try to burn the place, sir."

"Take me home to my family."

I stared wide-eyed into the black, waiting for the fire. My blood-crusted nostrils searched for the first threads of smoke.

"Sir, I'm putting a bandage on you. This is all I can do for you at the moment. I'm going to take charge of the group, sir. Do I have your permission, sir?"

"Shoot the hostage."

"Yes, sir."

"Kill him."

"Right, sir."

The door creaked as Sutherland pressed himself against it, trying to get up. "Home to my family."

"Open your mouth, sir. I'm just going to set this under your tongue. It's morphine, sir. It's what you need for now."

Sutherland sighed and settled back against the door.

I didn't move. All my thoughts had concentrated into one tiny speckle of light. I felt as if I was staring back inside myself.

The building shook. Something swished past outside and thumped onto the ground. Footsteps trampled upstairs.

"What the fuck was that?" Sergeant Gillis stood. His voice traveled up the door.

"They're on the roof." It was Byrne. "They just blew a hole through the tiles. We'll get them off. Don't worry. The Ennistymon people are probably halfway here by now. We've only got to hold out another half hour or so."

"You listen to me," Gillis said. "I wouldn't be so sure about the Ennistymon barracks setting out in the middle of the bloody night. We'll have to hold out until morning and probably longer. Sutherland wants the hostage shot."

"You know damn well if the hostage dies and we have to surrender, they'll finish off every last one of us. You know that, don't you?" It sounded as if Byrne was about to attack Sergeant Gillis.

"Sutherland said to . . ." Another explosion tore at the roof and something clumped down the stairs.

The floor jolted under me. Chips of paint flickered down from the ceiling. I crawled to the doorway and lowered my head to the floor, hoping to see out under the door. As my face touched the ground, I felt a wetness on my cheek. It felt heavy and sticky and I realized it was Sutherland's blood.

Now I crawled to the air vent and balanced on the chair to look out. The hedge sputtered with gunfire. Sparks from the burning roof flickered down onto the grass. A hissing sound filled my ears and the bright curve of a flare sailed out. It burst and drifted. The grass lit up milky white. I made out the broken squares of loose roof tiles lying on the ground beside the house. A body lay in a gap near the hedge. The man's shirt had come untucked and his chest was laid bare. In the light of the flare, his skin had the shine and smoothness of marble. The gunfire had stopped. All I could hear was the rustle of the flare. Shadows stretched as it drifted. Then the hissing died as the flare was sucked into darkness. Immediately, the gunfire started up again. *Clank, clank* against the window plates. Two men jumped from the hedge and ran across the grass. They carried an oblong box between them.

They threw their box at the barrack wall and ran back toward the hedge.

The air in the room crunched into fire and smoke and suddenly let go. I bounced off the table and fell to the floor.

A gun went off outside the door. Another gunshot. Someone slammed into the door and fell down. The corridor outside was filled with people.

The door opened. Sutherland's body slumped into the room. Cold air poured in and the hallway was riddled with smoke.

A man filled up the doorway. He stepped over Sutherland's body and into the room. "Come on after me and keep your head down."

At first, I didn't move, so the man strode across and yanked me to my feet. I followed him to a place where the outer wall had been blown through. Smashed brick covered the floor. Once the man turned to make sure I was following. In the smoke, I still couldn't see his face. The man moved with a limp. One leg was stiff, as if a brace had been clamped on it.

People in trench coats shuffled past. All of them carried rifles. Gunfire crashed in the hall. I heard the *clack-clack* of rifles reloading. Empty cartridges rattled on the floor.

I stepped through the blast hole and out onto the grass. Dew soaked my bare feet. Now I recognized the hobbling man. It was Stanley. He still wore his RIC uniform but had pulled the two harp insignias from his lapels and he didn't have his cap. "Clayton wants a word with you."

"What happened to Baldwin. Is he all right?"

"Byrne shot him. He'd have shot you, too, if he had time."

I thought of Baldwin, pug-faced with his anger, and I wondered how long he'd held out while they were beating him.

Branches of flame spread from a gap in the barrack-house roof. Ladders leaned against the building.

Someone was shouting to cease fire. Gunshots sputtered dead inside the building. Orders barked from room to room. The front door swung open and a Tan walked out with his hands on top of his head. Another followed and another. They moved slowly, peering into the dark.

"Here's the gun they took from you." Stanley held out the revolver in its holster. "And your feet . . ." Stanley pointed at the pale stubs of my toes. He led me over to a sunken road that ran beside the hedge. On the road where three bodies. Trench coats covered their faces. Stanley crouched down near the bodies and held his hand out to me. "Give me your foot."

I hopped on one leg as Stanley matched my foot first against the boot of one dead man and then against the boot of another. He removed one man's boots and gave them to me, along with the socks. "You'd better take whatever else you need as well."

The socks were wet and cold and the boot laces clogged with mud. I strapped on the revolver and then buttoned the trench coat, hoping no one would recognize the clothes. I needed them too badly to do without some thin armor against the bramble hedges and flint-pebbled roads.

The Tans stood in a line on the grass.

IRA men stood guard. Their shredded trench coats fluttered around their knees. Flames gave them shadows which vanished when the fire died down.

Dead men lay stretched on the path, faces covered with helmets or caps.

The noise of a trotting horse reached my ears. I caught sight of McGarrity's delivery cart. It was driven by Crow and stopped outside the barracks. Rifles and ammunition from the barracks were loaded on to it.

Down the road, still hidden in the dark, I heard running. Then I saw a shape and a paleness. A flash came from the figure and the air tore open above my head.

"Cover!" Stanley dove into the hedge.

I fumbled with the holster and peered at the figure again. It was McGarrity.

"Kill him!" Stanley yelled from the brambles.

McGarrity kept running. He carried a gun. The air cracked again and dirt splattered up near my boots.

I pulled the revolver from its holster. I could hear McGarrity's breathing now. The man's head was thrown back as he ran.

"Shoot, for God's sake!" Stanley bellowed from somewhere nearby.

McGarrity's body flashed as he shot off another round.

I aimed the Webley down the road and locked my elbow straight. I breathed in once and held the breath in my lungs, then fired and lost sight of McGarrity behind the blur of gun smoke. The heavy kick thumped back through my bones. I kept firing until the drum clicked empty.

McGarrity stood only a few paces away. His eyes were open wide. All of the buttons had popped off his jacket. The cloth lay in shreds across his chest. Now through the holes, McGarrity began to bleed. Dark lines ran down his stomach, falling in drops to the ground. He twitched suddenly, as if something had exploded inside him. He dropped to his knees and pitched forward onto his face.

Stanley crawled out of the bushes. It took him a while to get to his feet. His stiff leg got in the way.

I stepped toward McGarrity, but felt Stanley's hand hold me back. "Don't you worry about him. Worry about yourself

instead. McGarrity came to the barracks as soon as the trouble
started in town. He figured it was the only safe place for
him." Stanley pulled the ammunition bandolier from across his
shoulders and draped it over me. "You'd better go find Clayton.
He's in charge now. He'll tell you what to do."

I stayed looking at McGarrity's body. I found myself waiting
patiently for him to get up and walk away. The bandolier's
leather was warm where it had rested against Stanley's neck.

"Go." Stanley's voice climbed above the rustle of flames.

My boots crunched over sand from spilled sandbags, rifle
cartridges, and clods of brick chipped off the walls. It was dark
inside the barracks, except for the wobbling light of an oil
lamp, which barged an orange glow across the walls.

Tarbox stooped over the body of Captain Sutherland, going
through his pockets. The white pocket linings stuck out like
handkerchiefs from Sutherland's trousers.

Clayton stood next to him, holding up the lamp.

Tarbox scooped his hands under Sutherland's armpits and
propped him up against the wall. Sutherland's tunic and shirt
were open and a bandage had been wrapped around his chest.
Blood had soaked through the dressing. "What do you have
for me? Eh?" Tarbox pulled out a cigarette case, turned it once
in his hand, then skimmed it away across the floor. "Anything
I can use?" Tarbox slapped him on the cheek.

Sutherland's head flopped to one side. His eyes were half
open.

"Is that you, Sheridan?" Clayton held up the lamp. "Did you
tell them anything?"

"Nothing." With my nose blocked and useless, my voice
vibrated in my head.

"Who beat you?" Tarbox took hold of Sutherland's cheeks
and squashed them together. A trickle of red saliva dribbled
out onto his hand. "Is this the man?"

"It was an RIC sergeant. Byrne."

The oil lamp quivered in Clayton's hand. "It's a shame we can only kill him once."

I breathed in the smoke that pillowed the ceiling. "I was leaving to find Hagan. They picked me up outside Ennistymon."

Tarbox stood. "We're all heading north now. There's been a change of plan. So you've got company for the trip after all."

"I heard them saying that the troops at Ennistymon barracks would be coming."

"They are." Clayton walked toward me. "I want them to."

"Thank you for getting me out."

"We didn't do it for you. We did it for the guns. On schedule. And now we need your help. The Ennistymon Tans will be here in an hour. If we don't drive them back, none of us will get more than a few miles up the road and that includes you. They'll set barriers on every road between here and Connemara and no one will be able to pass. But if we hit them hard now, they won't return until they've gathered reinforcements and that will take a couple of days. By that time, we'll be up in the hills, which is the only safe place for us now. At least until things settle down. We need everyone we can get."

I said I would do what I could.

Clayton nodded. "My father . . . he says to take care of yourself."

Byrne's eyes strained in their sockets. He watched as Clayton approached.

The Tans had all been searched. Their tunics were open, brass buttons like yellow pebbles on the khaki cloth. They still kept their hands in the air and the muscles were tense in their faces.

Clayton pulled Byrne out of line.

"I was doing what Captain Sutherland told me . . ."

"Shut your face." Clayton pointed at me. "Look what you did to this man."

Smoke peppered my skin. It made me flinch to catch Byrne's eye, as if another beating would thrash me to the ground.

"Look at this man." Clayton's voice was a rumble. "You damn near painted that cell with his blood."

"I was doing my job," Byrne shouted. "Captain Sutherland . . ."

"You people!" Clayton howled at the soldiers. He spent all his breath in the two words and had to fill his lungs again. "You know the rules by now. You know you'd never stand for this from us. Well, we won't stand it from you." He led Byrne towards the barracks, signaling for two IRA men to follow him. They took the handcuffs that dangled from Byrne's belt and cuffed him to an iron railing that ran up beside the barrack-house steps.

The two IRA men unshouldered their rifles. One of the men was Crow. They stood only a few paces away from Byrne's twisting body.

Crow chambered a bullet. The rifle bolt clacked into place.

"Oh, for Christ's sake! I was following orders! Sutherland told me to rough him up." Byrne tugged at the handcuffs. They scraped against the railing.

The two men tucked the butts of the rifles into their shoulders and their heads hunched over the stocks as they took aim.

"For Christ's sake." Byrne's arms strained at the railing. His mouth twitched out of control.

The rifles kicked back into the men's shoulders. The noise of gunshots clapped off the barrack walls.

Byrne flew across the railing. One of his arms dislocated. His body shook, then slumped. Slowly the handcuff chain slid down the railing, dragging Byrne with it, his hands still pinched in the cuffs. He moved inch by inch until his body settled on the ground.

A moan came from the line of British soldiers. A Tan dropped to his knees. His fingers dug into the ground.

No one moved to help him.

The soldier began to crawl forward. The tendons stood out in his neck. His cap fell off and he crawled over it.

Still no one moved.

The soldier's arms gave way and he rested his forehead on the ground. He began to cry.

I heard someone barely a foot away draw in breath.

"Get back in line!" The shout was deafening. A Tan stepped out of rank. He was a sergeant, with three chevrons and a crown stitched to his right arm.

The IRA guards didn't move. Nobody did.

The sergeant's face was crooked with rage. "Stand up and get back in line!"

The soldier rocked his head back and forth, still sobbing.

Then the sergeant walked across and picked up the man by his collar. The soldier shook his head. His jaw locked open and the moaning sound crept out. The sergeant spoke to him in a voice that only the two of them could hear. Then the soldier moaned louder and shook his head again.

The sergeant smacked him in the face with the back of his hand and dragged him to the ranks. The two Tans on either side of the soldier had to prop him up. He stood with his knees half bent, ready to fall if the others let him go. His head hung forward. The sergeant went back to his place, raised his hands in the air and stared in front of him.

Clayton said nothing. He made no gesture to show that he had even seen what happened. He shouted for the IRA men to fall in on the road.

There was a sound of heavy footsteps on the grass as people followed his order. I ran with them.

Then the hammer of a machine gun sent me down on my face. The others dropped, too. I lay pressed to the ground with my hands covering my head.

The Tans were crying out.

Their shrieking paralyzed me. I realized that they were the ones being shot at.

The gun's stitching thunder continued for long after the shouting had stopped. Then I heard Clayton yell to cease fire.

I raised my head from the dirt and saw others doing the same.

The Tans were all down, their bodies cripple-twisted and lying on top of each other. There wasn't even the movement of a wounded man.

Byrne's corpse had settled on the ground, as if his skin was already blending with the grass.

A Lewis gun had been set up in the hedge facing the Tans. Clayton must have ordered it. The two men who had manned the gun, one carrying a sack of spare magazines, sank back through the hedge and lined up on the road.

Crow stamped toward Clayton. He looked as if he had gone mad. "What is the fucking point of executing Byrne in front of all these people, and then shooting them as well?" He screamed in Clayton's face.

Clayton talked back too quietly for us to hear.

Crow was shaking with rage. "There's a corridor in hell for people like you!" Then he spun around and walked back to the road.

"What did he say?" I asked him as he passed me.

At first Crow didn't know who I was. Then he said in his old quiet voice, "Clayton told me he wanted it to be the last thing those Tans saw on this earth."

I found myself almost untouched by the bodies on the ground. There were too many of them. It dug into me more to have seen Byrne there by himself, or McGarrity facedown in the mud. But the carpet of khaki-clothed men left me with only a numbness, and I was already numb from the beating.

We set out across the fields, loaded down with guns and bandoliers.

Clayton caught up with me. He had been running and was out of breath. He carried two Lee-Enfield rifles and gave one to me.

I slung it on my shoulder without breaking stride. I didn't want to talk. All the violence I'd seen since I walked ashore seemed to come from Clayton. It sparked off his fingers like lightning.

I had hoped somehow to stand outside the war, and even thought it was possible. But with the killing of these Tans, it made no difference what I'd believed. It seemed as if I had crossed the line so long ago, I could no longer recall when it was.

Clayton knew what I was thinking. "They got what they deserved," he said.

I didn't answer. I raised my head and watched the moon spread silver across the black sky.

CHAPTER 13

The dark was filled with whispering. Fog had settled in. I sat against a low stone wall, sheltered from the wind. One by one, I pulled bullets from the bandolier and loaded them into the rifle. I set my thumb on the brass bullet cases and pressed down until they clicked into the magazine.

Men in trench coats drifted past. From close by came the scrape of wall stones being rearranged.

The field beyond the wall sank down to a hollow. A stream ran through it, and trees clustered on the banks. The Ennistymon Tans were down there somewhere. They had come across the open ground, avoiding roads. Now they were forming a battle line. Shards of voices traveled on the wind as the soldiers regrouped in the dark.

When the magazine was full, I chambered a round and settled the gun across my lap. I tried to calm myself by thinking of home. It had been a while since I last imagined the daily movements of Willoughby, Hettie, and Harley, and the tides around the island. It used to be that every time I found myself with any room to think, standing half-asleep over the grey dishwater at Gisby's, I had traveled home in my daydreams.

The daydreams had ended, but I couldn't remember when. The point had come and gone without my noticing. The island and the people I knew there had lost their clarity. Now they seemed blurred at the edges and half formed, like the products of my sleep.

A part of me had already given up hope that I would reach home again. That part began to call this place home, and had sunk roots into the black soil. Even now, it didn't want to leave.

I wondered if Guthrie would be all right. Perhaps the word of him sheltering me never reached Ennistymon and now, with the Lahinch Tans gone, there would be no one left who knew.

Someone passed a canteen down the line. I shook it to see if there was anything left. The canteen was cloth-covered, with a wine-cork for a stopper. When I took a mouthful, I felt my eyes open wide with surprise. Whiskey. Perhaps even Dunhams. It sent the same bright fire down inside me.

Mist billowed across the fields and I could no longer make out the shapes of men lying near me. I only heard the rustling of their clothes, as if the fog itself had voices. I corked the water bottle and slung it on my back, then crawled along the wall to where another man was sitting. I had met him once at the pub but couldn't recall his name. Coogan, maybe. Culligan. Cadogan. I held out the canteen.

The man pulled out the cork with his teeth.

Culligan. Countryman. I still couldn't remember.

He wiped the mouth of the water bottle on his sleeve, then drank three heavy swallows. "I'm going home." He breathed alcohol in my face. "The Tans have turned around and left. A while ago, you could hear them down in the hollow. Now there's nothing. They've all buggered off."

It was true that the voices had stopped.

"Besides, I have to show up for work tomorrow." He tucked the rifle under his arm and set off towards Lahinch.

I stood by myself, barely breathing as I listened to the fog. Then I returned to my spot by the wall.

Stanley and Crow were there. Stanley carried a Lewis gun. Its barrel was as thick as Stanley's leg. In a satchel on his back were spare magazines, round like plates and two fingers thick.

Crow unclipped the bayonet from his rifle. He ground its blade a few times on a stone. "It'll be like old times, Stan."

"So it will indeed, Harry." Stanley swung the Lewis gun back and forth on its stand.

My mouth still tingled from the whiskey. "I just talked to a man who said the Tans have turned back. He was on his way home."

Stanley looked up. "You're fucking kidding."

Crow scraped his thumb across the bayonet's blade and then clipped it back onto his rifle. "They're still out there. They can walk around like ghosts. And the last thing the Tans are going to do is turn around and go home. They're probably looking forward to this. Bloody useless, isn't it? Have to fight the damn war by ourselves, Stan." He stepped back into the fog and his footsteps faded away.

Stanley fixed a drum of bullets onto the Lewis. "We shouldn't be here at all. There's only about twenty of us and there must be at least fifty of them. When daylight comes, hundreds of them will be crawling all over this place. We should just get up into the hills."

I stared at the fog. It wove into shapes that I recognized, then scattered and left me straining to make out what I'd seen.

Stanley took three grenades from his pockets. A bar stretched along one side of the dull gridded surface, held there by a pin. He brought one of the bombs close to my face. "It's a Mills bomb. All you do is keep your fist wrapped around the bomb and the lever bar. Then you pull out the pin. Don't let go of the lever. Once you do, you've got seven seconds. Do you see?" Stanley set the grenade back on the wall. The grid pattern stayed printed on his palm.

"When are you leaving for America, Stanley?"

"Soon as I can. I've had false papers made up. Passport. Work permits. I paid to have it done."

"But they'd recognize your face."

"Not after I'm through with it." Stanley grinned. Then suddenly his smile collapsed. "I can hear them."

All I could make out was the far-away burble of the stream. The saliva wouldn't go down my throat, so I spat it on the grass.

Something rustled by the wall. I grabbed the rifle and aimed it at a patch of fog. Stanley swung the Lewis around. His legs were braced to take the shock. The rustling kept up and then we saw a man moving toward us on all fours. A rifle was strapped to his back. It was Clayton. When he saw the Lewis aimed at him, he rose to his knees and waved his hands in front of his face. "They're here." His voice was scratchy with whispering. "Tarbox just caught one of their forward scouts up on the ridge. We found these on him." Clayton pulled a clip of bullets from his pocket. The copper tip of each bullet had been filed down so that it looked like the end of a chisel. "Dumdums. If one of them's done that, then they all have."

Clayton set the bullet in my hand, then curled my fingers over, as if the bullet was a gift. "They don't fly straight through the air. Instead, they cartwheel end over end. So when they hit you, they don't just leave a little hole. They tear out a space the size of your hand. Are you sure you didn't tell them anything at the barracks?"

"If I say I didn't tell them anything, then I didn't."

"It's good for you that you didn't talk, Ben." Then Clayton's head snapped around towards Stanley. "It's you I don't trust."

Stanley used his sleeve to rub damp off the barrel of the Lewis. "Well, you don't have a lot of choice, do you?"

"Give the Lewis to Sheridan."

"He doesn't know how to work it."

"Well, teach him."

"No time." Stanley's voice was growing hoarse.

"I don't trust you with the only decent weapon we've got."

"Look you." Stanley held out his hand. His fingertips rested against Clayton's chest. "I got as much to lose in this as you do. More, if they catch me."

Clayton watched Stanley's hand. The space between them had vanished, cut off by the outstretched arm. "If you break formation before you get the order from me, I'll have you shot." He didn't wait for a reply. He continued down the wall, with the slow, loping tread of a hunchback.

I settled back into the quiet. Hagan's face shimmered in front of me, as if seen from underwater. I was afraid to finally set eyes on him. It seemed as if I had never thought past the idea that he might exist and never dared to give him shape and character. I wondered if he knew that I was here and plodding my way north to find him. People in Lahinch spoke of Hagan as if he knew everything, watching down from the treeless rock of the Connemara hills. He had gone away and left them years before, but they would not leave him. They made Hagan keep them company in the stories that they told.

There had never been anything in my life that I thought worth fighting for. But having come this far, I would do anything to finish what I started. If people stood in the way, I'd do whatever it took to push them aside. It was all that mattered now, and for the moment I didn't care if I keeled over dead the second after I caught sight of Hagan, because it was as far ahead as I could think and as much as I dared ask for.

Stanley jerked his chin at the place where Clayton had disappeared. "It's him you want to watch. Not me. I been in worse places than this." He'd been muttering to himself for a while now, but I had not been listening.

"Why?" The damp rested in my lungs.

"Because he thinks he's got the whole bloody war planned out in his head. Who's going to die. When they're going to die. Why they're going to die. I think he must sit down at his desk every night with a slide rule and figure it all out."

Noise came from the fog. I crouched down behind the wall.

With my thumb, I pushed forward the gridded metal stub of the Enfield's safety catch. I flexed my hand, trying to drive out the chill.

The noise came again, metal on metal. Whispering. A rustle as someone crawled forward.

Stanley hugged the butt of the Lewis against his chest.

There was a shout. Then a slow growl came from the fog. The growl rose to screaming. Footsteps thumped toward us.

I shouldered the rifle and tried not to blink.

Howling echoed around us. Boots trampled the ground.

Fire burst along the wall. Shapes appeared from the fog. Running men. They held rifles out in front of them, bayonets fixed on the ends. Their mouths were open and the dew was wet on their helmets. Bayonets swished through the mist.

A blast of wind struck my head. Then the hammer of the Lewis gun surrounded me.

The Tans all jumped back at once, rifles spinning through the air. The flash of the Lewis's firing reflected off the fog. Soldiers slammed into the ground.

Boots scrabbled over the wall. Then came howling and the thud of bodies colliding. A man appeared from the fog. He ran toward me, helmet shoved back on his head. The chinstrap dug into his throat.

I pulled the trigger and the air blurred for a moment. When it cleared, the soldier was gone. I pulled back the bolt and sent the empty, smoking cartridge flying over my shoulder. Then I looked again for the soldier, but the man had fallen. His rifle lay across his chest. Hobnails shone on the soles of his boots.

Orders boomed at the Tans to regroup and right wheel and keep moving.

Stanley began firing again. He swung the gun, stabbing light into the fog.

A long scream rushed out of the dark. I raised my rifle and stood waiting.

Stanley scooped his arm under the barrel of the Lewis and lifted it off the wall.

A khaki blur rose up in front of him. He cried out and the shout suddenly quit. A shred of silver punched through Stanley's back. It was the point of a bayonet. Stanley dropped the Lewis. He staggered.

The Tan screamed in Stanley's face. Their bodies were touching. Then suddenly he turned and saw me. He stepped away, trying to pull out the bayonet. But Stanley's hands were clenched around the gun barrel.

I swung my rifle butt into the soldier's head and the Tan's arms flew up. He dropped his gun and fell.

Stanley sank forward. The Tan's rifle dug into the earth and held Stanley there on his knees. He made no sound. His hands still gripped the stock, hands red where the web of his thumbs held the rifle. Blood leaked in streams across his wrists.

The Tan was trying to get up. He moved like a blind man, hands groping against the wall stones, but couldn't find a grip.

I raised the rifle high above his head and brought it down like an ax on the Tan's uplifted face.

Stanley hadn't moved. He stayed on his knees, held there by the bayonet. I could see from his eyes he was dead.

I couldn't bring myself to touch his body. Each time I tried to make my hand go forward, the muscles locked. My breath slipped out around his head.

The sound of an engine echoed across the fields. It strained uphill in low gear.

The stock had broken on my rifle, so I dumped it. I picked the hand grenades off the wall and stuffed them in my pockets. My eyes passed once more over Stanley's body. Dew spread across the dead man's back in a cape of silver beads.

The noise of the truck slowed and then stopped. Its engine puttered in neutral. It had to be a captured truck. All the roads from Ennistymon were blocked. Clayton would be using it to bring back wounded. I ran toward the sound, the grenades weighing me down. I hoped Crow would know about Stanley before I saw him again. I'd rather have done anything than tell him his best friend was dead.

Darkness faded from the sky. Grey blue sifted through the clouds.

A wall of brambles gathered in the fog, blocking my way. Behind it lay the road. I stopped and listened. The truck was coming toward me. Then it appeared, sliding past behind the brambles. I brushed back the spiked vines of the hedge.

A dull mass of metal rolled by and I stepped back in surprise. My heel caught a root and I fell. The machine moved very slowly. It was something armored, painted the same dark green as the Crossley trucks. In the dingy morning light, I made out the welding of its metal panels. Its hatches were shut and mud clogged the heavy-treaded tires.

Brambles scraped at my face. I waited for soldiers to follow, but the road stayed empty and blurred in heat from the armored car's exhaust.

I took a grenade from my pocket and pulled the pin. The lever bar flipped over my shoulder and a thin sliver of smoke leaked from the grenade. I threw it at the machine. The Mills bomb wobbled out of my hand and clattered on the road.

I turned and sprinted, sucking in breath through clenched teeth.

The explosion slammed through my body. Sheep-trampled mud rose up to meet me and my hands smacked into the dirt.

The armored car's engine changed pitch. It plowed into the hedge. The engine stalled and stopped. Immediately, its ignition began to cough as the driver tried to start again.

I took out another grenade and pulled the pin. Bitter smoke from its burning fuse wafted into my face.

The fat egg wobbled over the hedge. It clanked off the armored car's roof and someone shouted inside.

The air clenched and burst open. Metal clanged against metal and shrapnel sliced through the brambles.

It was quiet now. I lay flattened against the earth. Dark smoke puffed from the car's engine grill. Several minutes went by and I didn't dare to move.

The armored car's top hatch squeaked open. A head peeked out. It wore a black beret. Then the shoulders appeared, and a hand holding a revolver settled on the top of the car. "I think they're gone."

"Are you sure?" This voice came from the belly of the machine.

"I think so, sir." The man climbed higher. He wore a brown leather coat and had goggles around his neck. On his belt was a Webley revolver. "We're leaking petrol." He jumped down to the road.

I pulled out my revolver and breathed in the heaviness of dead leaves and earth. Bramble vines crisscrossed in front of my eyes.

Another man appeared from the hatch. He wore an officer's peaked cap. "I don't know where the bastards went. I can't see anyone from here. I don't even know where we are."

The driver on the ground crouched down and dabbed his fingers in the spilled gasoline. "Our back tires are gone as well. We should head back to Ennistymon on foot."

My chin rested in the dirt. A snail wandered its sticky path along a branch right by my face.

The driver took off his beret and used it to wipe sweat off his forehead. "Shall we head back then, sir?"

"No." The officer climbed down to the road. "I'm going to stay here with the machine. You'll have to go back and get help."

"What? By myself?" The driver stuffed the beret on his head. "It's a good two miles back to the barracks, and I don't know who's between us and home."

"Look, Parsons. I'm not asking you to do this as a favor. I'm ordering you to run like hell back to Ennistymon and get someone out here with a Crossley so we can tow in the armored car. We're going to catch hell as it is. We've only had this bloody machine for a week. And do you think I'm looking forward to spending the next hour by myself in the middle of nowhere with all these Paddymen creeping around?"

"No, sir. I don't suppose you are."

The officer climbed back up to the turret, dropped back inside and screwed the hatch shut.

Parsons turned around. For a moment, he just stared along the road. Then he began a slow, flat-footed run toward Ennistymon.

I'd be safer with a hostage, I was sure of that, so I followed the man. The road led down toward the hollow and crossed the river at a small stone bridge. Parsons picked up speed as he went down the hill, but at the bridge he stopped. He fetched out his gun. "Who's there?"

I crouched in the tall grass. My clothes were splattered with mud.

Parsons wiped his face again with the beret. "Fuck." He peered up through the brambles. Then he put the gun away. "Fuck!" He started across the bridge.

I slid down a dirt bank to the road, held out the Webley and cocked back its hammer.

"Oh, Christ!" Parsons heard it and stopped. He didn't turn around.

I walked toward the man, gun held out.

"I'm not moving." Parsons's shoulders hunched down into his neck. "I'm just standing here. Oh, Christ."

I rested the Webley's barrel against the back of his head. "Take off your gunbelt and then hold it out in your right hand."

Parsons unstrapped the belt from around his coat. "I'm undoing the buckle. I'm doing it slowly. See? I'm doing it slowly. Christ." He took off his belt and the revolver.

"Throw it in the river."

Parsons tossed the belt and the holster's dark slab of leather into the water. "I got a family." Sweat ran down from his temple to his cheek. "I never hurt anybody, I swear. I only been here two weeks."

Water rustled underneath the bridge.

I kept the gun at the back of his head while I patted the damp leather of his coat, searching for other weapons. When I found nothing, I stood back. "Now we're going toward Lahinch."

We walked along the river bank. Trees with mottled bark grew by the water.

Parsons stumbled over the rocks in his hobnailed boots. He still kept his hands in the air. "I got a little baby girl at home. I've been married almost two years. My wife's name is Thea." He talked without pause, as if only the words were keeping him alive. "I joined up in the Oxford and Bucks Light Infantry in '16. I got shipped over to France in two months and when I got back in '19, I couldn't get a job. Not anything. I even applied to be a tea server at Fortnum & Mason. And the buggers turned me down and all."

"All right, pal," I had to raise my voice over the rushing of the stream. "I've heard enough about it for a while."

"I can't help it. I'm sorry." Parsons stumbled and fell to his knees, but stood again and kept walking. "I'm sorry." He started to cry.

A fish jumped in the river. It was swimming upstream, and in the second it spent in the air, I saw the gold-spotted belly of a brown trout. Both of us looked at the place where it had disappeared. The ripples folded quickly away into the current.

I thought of a stream not far from my home. It ran past

Gilbert Stuart's mill in Saunderstown, across the bay from Jamestown. Buckeyes spawned there in the spring. The water ran so thick with fish that sometimes I could catch them with my hands.

"I got . . ." Parsons let his tired arms settle on top his head.

"You got what?"

"I got a first-aid kit in my pocket if you want it. I see you've got blood on you."

"It's not mine."

"Oh, Christ." Parsons started babbling again. "My daughter's name is Evelyn. She got little blond curls and . . ." His head sank forward. "Little blond curls . . ."

I stopped walking. The hostage idea was no good. "Look, Parsons, why don't you just go home?" I sat down on a rock and spat on my boots.

"I'm sorry. I can't help it."

"Go home, will you? It's that way." I waved the Webley's barrel toward Ennistymon.

"You'll wait until I'm running and then you'll shoot me in the back."

"Well, you can stay here with me if you want. I don't give a damn. I don't know how the hell your wife puts up with all your talking."

Parsons backed up toward the stream, hands still raised in the air. He stepped into the shallow stream. Fast-running water frothed around his knees. "Thank you, sir. Thank you very much." He bowed slightly forward as he spoke. Then he waded to the other bank. The river was only waist deep. Once he reached dry ground, he started running. He disappeared through the trees and his boots squelched into the distance.

I sat on the rock for a while, thinking of the things I'd told myself the night before; what I'd do to anyone who got in my way. It wasn't true. I couldn't have killed that man, no matter what was at stake. "Clayton could have done it," I said to myself. "He wouldn't have thought twice."

I headed out across the fields, toward the house of Mrs. Fuller. If anyone had stopped on their way north, I knew I'd find them there. I'd find Mrs. Fuller there too, still waiting for her husband to return. I saw again the brave and useless patience on her face.

CHAPTER 14

Smoke curled in witch's fingers from the chimney of Mrs. Fuller's house.

A group of men had gathered in the garden. They were getting ready to leave. Clayton was there with Tarbox and Crow. They were arguing, Clayton shaking his fist at Crow, and Crow had gone stony-faced with rage. Tarbox stood back, leaning on his shotgun as if it was a walking stick.

Wounded men lay on the garden path. The front door was open and I could see wounded lying there, too. Some were covered in blankets and others had their trench coats tucked under their heads as pillows. Mrs. Fuller walked among them, handing out apples. The apples were puckered and dry from storage in a barrel.

As soon as Clayton saw me, he stopped talking. He waved Crow away with a brush of his hand and walked over. "Where's your rifle?"

"It's bust. I threw it away." My boots had soaked through. The laces were clogged with grass and peat.

"You were issued with a rifle, which is either going to be used by us or against us. Have you thought about that? Did you at least destroy the mechanism before you abandoned it?"

"It was already broken." Wind twisted my hair.

"How exactly?" The front of Clayton's trench coat was plastered with dried mud.

"How? It didn't work. That's how I know it was bust." I

couldn't even bring myself to be angry at Clayton. None of
what he said surprised me. It wouldn't have occurred to him
to be glad to see me or ask how I was. "And I blew up one of
their armored cars, so you could call it a fair trade."

Crow had left the group. "That was you, was it?"

"He lost his gun." Clayton's face didn't budge.

"Leave it alone." Crow threw me an apple. "Don't take this
all out on him."

"All what?" I bit into the apple. Its skin was leathery against
the roof of my mouth.

"There were attacks planned to take place all over Ireland.
But a lot of them didn't go through, including one planned
against the Ennistymon barracks. That's why we had to stay
and fight them off."

Clayton spoke as if it was his fault. Someone had to take
responsibility and because he was in charge, he took it on
himself.

"The Dublin office called off the raids because of inadequate
ammunition supplies. But they left it too late for all the raids
to be canceled. The news didn't reach us until after we'd taken
Lahinch barracks. By then, we were already committed."

"Do we have a lot of wounded?" I wished I could sit down.
At least take off my boots and rub the blood back into my feet.
But the other men were already lining up on the road. They
were impatient to be gone.

"Not a lot of wounded. They were using dumdum bullets.
We have a lot of dead. Casualties were heavy on both sides.
We figure to have killed almost twenty men between the La-
hinch and Ennistymon Tans."

"But how many of our own?"

"We don't know yet." Clayton threw his apple core across
the road and a sheep ran over to inspect it. "Between those
who are dead or dying and the wounded who'll be captured,
we reckon perhaps ten."

Mrs. Fuller shoved Crow out of the way. "It's a shame! Terrible shame! There's whole families that will die out now because of what happened last night." She jabbed her finger at Clayton. "You've got no right doing this. You knew they'd all be killed." Her face was the color of a radish. "My husband always said if . . ."

"Your husband . . ." Clayton spat out.

For God's sake don't say it, I thought. I closed my eyes and waited for hell to break loose.

Suddenly the anger left Clayton's face. "We're lucky to have made it out with as many as we did."

"We should give in, then. Let them have what they want. At least, then, we'd all still be alive." She walked inside and clumped up the stairs.

Crow followed, trying to calm her down.

I'd been watching Clayton. I wondered what had scratched the coldness from his eyes and replaced it with something almost gentle. Perhaps some memory of himself much younger came barging into his mind. Mrs. Fuller standing there had sent him back for a moment to his childhood, where he could not find enough cruelty to tell the woman that her husband was dead.

I couldn't imagine a childhood for Clayton. I couldn't imagine him younger or older or any way except the way he was now. To me, Clayton had begun to make sense. He didn't try, like the others, to live as if the war could be forgotten from time to time in the dark-paneled walls of Gisby's pub or in front of a fire at night. Clayton lived in black and white. He saw no boundary to violence. The war never quit and his instincts for war never rested. He had no other instincts. Everything else had been put away in a warehouse in his mind. He claimed no friends or love of family because he could be hurt by people who hurt them.

Now I thought of Guthrie, living in the vast bell jar of his

loneliness. And I wondered if it was the same loneliness that
Hagan felt, with family gone and son not knowing his name.

"Do you think Mrs. Fuller will talk?"

"Talk about what, Clayton?" I pulled off my boots. I had to
take them off, even if only for a minute.

"About us. To the Tans."

"And what if she did? Would you shoot old Mrs. Fuller?" I
looked at the blood-soaked toes of my socks, where blisters
had burst and rubbed through.

"It would be necessary." Clayton scratched at the mud on
his chest.

Twelve of us set out from Mrs. Fuller's house. We walked
all afternoon and into the evening.

I washed my face in a cow trough by the road. The water
was tea-colored with peat. When I caught sight of my reflection
in the water, I saw that I had two black eyes. The puffed skin
was purple with a yellowiness around the edges. I figured my
nose was broken and without a doctor, it wouldn't heal prop-
erly. Some day it would have to be broken again in order to
set it back straight.

Lavender twilight spread across the fields.

I carried a satchel filled with a raincape and a mess tin with
an army spoon inside. I also had a portable stove with some
fuel tablets. It had all been taken from the barracks at Lahinch
and given to me just before we left Mrs. Fuller's house. Clayton
said it had been issued. He said if I lost it, I would be punished.

All the wounded who could not walk by themselves we had
left behind. That was what Crow had been arguing about with
Clayton. Crow wanted the wounded to be brought along, on
stretchers if need be, but Clayton wouldn't allow it. They had
watched us as we left, knowing that they would be rounded

up in a few hours and stuffed into prison forever or killed right where they lay.

Breaths of cigarette smoke sifted down the line. Some of the men wore bandages. Sheep followed, bobbing on the road like puffs of grounded cloud.

We walked in silence deep into the night. Wind-carved hedges curled over us like the crests of breaking waves.

Crow dropped back and walked beside me. I knew what he wanted to ask, so before he opened his mouth, I told him about Stanley. I only said he was dead. I'd made up my mind not to tell him more than that. Crow didn't ask, anyway. He continued to walk beside me in silence, staring hollow-eyed across the fields.

The line slowed as we moved past a farmhouse. A black-and-white dog ran out barking into the road and nipped Crow on the heel.

"Now then!" Crow shook his finger at the dog. The dog shrank away. Then it came back and bit him on the heel again. "You stop that!"

"Just give it a kick."

"He's only doing his job. That's the way they're taught to herd cattle, biting the cows on the heel. Seeing us all in a line outside his farm, he's probably trying to herd us into the yard." Crow held out his hand. The dog sniffed his fingertips.

Cows crowded up to a barbed-wire fence. Steam rolled from their noses and mouths.

Then a door slammed in the farmhouse. A lantern wobbled toward us. "Well, it's about time!" It was an old man. He held out the lantern to Clayton. "They passed through late this afternoon."

Clayton stood backed against the hedge, the strange long shape of the Mauser in his hand. "Who did?" He squinted in the glare. "Who are you?"

"I'm Alan Cottrell. Captain Sutherland knows me." The farmer had a spiked grey beard and wire-rimmed glasses. He wore a black wool coat and heavy boots with no socks. "The men you're looking for passed through here not six hours ago. I counted fifteen of them."

Nobody spoke. I realized that Cottrell had seen Clayton's military belt and mistaken him for a Tan.

Clayton screwed up his eyes. "Fifteen men?"

Cottrell nodded. Lantern light splashed across the road.

"Which way were they heading, did you say?"

Cottrell's arm shot out toward the north. "Same direction as you. Is Captain Sutherland here?"

"Not tonight."

"You tell him Alan Cottrell says hello." The gate creaked and the sheepdog scuttled out. Cottrell told it to sit. Immediately the hind legs gave way and its tail swished at the road.

Clayton touched his fingers to his lower lip. "Are you sure these men were Republican Army?"

"Well, if that's what you want to call them. They were armed to the teeth and they weren't Tans, so who else could they be? Where's Captain Sutherland? He ought to be here if you're going after so many men."

"Sutherland is . . ."

"He's slacking off, if you ask me. He ought to be out here leading his men. If you don't keep moving, you'll never catch them. They were marching two by two all up the road with one man at the front."

"What did this man look like?"

"It was hard to see. My cows kept getting in the way. He was tall. I don't know what else."

"Are you alone?"

Cottrell fiddled with the buttons on his coat. "It's just me and the wife and the dog. Has been for some years now. My wife is up in Galway with her sister for the week. I got people who come by in the day to help me with the cows."

Clayton turned away from Cottrell and waved the column on.

As I walked past, Clayton pulled me out of line. He talked in a murmur, so that Cottrell couldn't hear. "Sooner or later, the real Tans are going to come marching up this road and when they do, that farmer will tell them exactly how many of us there were and exactly how many guns we have and exactly what direction we're heading in. This man needs killing. Do you understand?"

I nodded.

Cottrell nodded back and smiled.

Clayton rested his arm on Cottrell's shoulder. "This man will take down the details of what you saw, Mr. Cottrell. The rest of us are moving on."

"Captain Sutherland . . ." Cottrell cleared his throat. "Well, he usually makes some kind of compensation for any assistance. Nothing big, mind you. I did get up out of bed and all." He raised the lantern and it lit up his gap-toothed face. "We had an understanding."

Clayton tapped me on the arm. "You heard what the gentleman said. Compensation for assistance."

Cottrell waited until the column was further up the road, as if he didn't want them to hear. "Well, as I said, there were fifteen of them. And they all had rifles, as best I could see."

I thought of the Tans writing down what Cottrell said. Anger crackled through me. I put my hand inside my coat and grabbed the Webley's barrel.

"Are you going to write any of this down? Sutherland usually pays me five pound. I was wondering if you could do a little better this time, seeing as it's, you know, useful information. You'll catch them all with what I'm telling you."

In one movement, I pulled the gun from my coat and smacked it across the old man's head.

Cottrell spun around. He fell against the gate. His lantern broke on the road and its fuel burst into flames.

I dragged Cottrell into his house and put him in his chair by the fire. He was still breathing. I looked around for a telephone, in case he had one. I was going to rip it out of the wall. But he didn't even have electricity. The dog sat and watched us. Then I walked up to the column, which had stopped around a bend on the road.

Clayton was waiting. "Is it done?" He took hold of my elbow. "Is it?"

"Yes."

"But you didn't kill him, did you?"

"He'll be out for long enough." I looked back. The lantern's fire was an amber bubble in the black.

"I wanted him out for good."

"Then you do it." I knew there was reason for what he wanted, but I could not convince myself.

Clayton didn't say another word. He pulled the Mauser from its wooden holster and went down and shot the old man. I could see muzzle flashes through the windows. When the dog started barking, Clayton shot it as well.

I walked on. A dull and thumping numbness spread out through my veins. The dead farmer and his dog and his steam-breathing cows dropped back into the dark and we left them there. I moved in step with the column. My body slipped into the rhythm of the march, while in my thoughts I drifted far across the sea.

CHAPTER 15

A ruined church stood black against the sky. It had no roof or windows and the churchyard bristled with stone Celtic crosses. Figures in tattered clothing seemed to drift on the wind-scalped fields.

By the time I ducked through the doorway, people had already lit their stoves and were cooking rations. White fuel tablets burned with a salty blue flame. From all around came the rattle of mess tins and mumbling talk and the bobbing suns of lit cigarettes.

I crouched down next to Crow and set up my stove. I borrowed a match off him and held it to the tablet. A twitching violet flame crawled across its surface.

Crow leaned over, a cigarette hanging from his mouth. He uncorked his water bottle and half filled my mess tin. Then he pulled a can from his satchel. "Now you see this stuff? It's called Maconochie." The cigarette waggled in his mouth. A clump of ash fell into my mess tin. "You boil this can in the water before you open it. You have to eat this stuff hot or it'll give you the cramps. When it's done, throw your biscuits into the water. Where are your biscuits?" Crow reached in and grabbed them from my bag. "Boil them into mush. You can't eat them any other way. One of these packets will have raisins in the biscuits. They're called Squashed Flies, because that's what they look like. Mash it all up and have that for dessert, and throw in everything else you can find." Crow turned back to his own stove. He pulled his rain cape over his head, using his rifle like a tent pole.

"Crow?"

"What?"

"Those people back there. The ones the farmer saw. That was Hagan, wasn't it?"

"Could have been anyone. That old fart's probably so blind, it could have been the Tans that he saw and mistook them for us and then when we came along, he thought we were Tans. But I daresay it was Hagan. I heard he sometimes comes down to the Burren, which is close to where we are now. I hear rumors that there's peace talks going on, and maybe that brought him down. There's always rumors, and they're never quite lies but they're never quite the truth, either."

Dew had settled everywhere.

The fuel tablet's smoke was like grit in my eyes. I used a spoon to roll the Maconochie back and forth. Tiny bubbles rose to the surface.

Crow hummed to himself. Smoke billowed from the anthill mound of his cape.

Some men had lit a fire with wood gathered from the hedges. Its light bled across the church's fieldstone walls. They hung capes across empty window spaces, so the fire wouldn't show outside. Wind moaned through the stone crosses.

I spooned my Maconochie tin out of the water and jammed a knife twice in the top, making an X. Then I prised back each of the four triangles. The tin was hot, so I held it between my palm and chest.

Meat stew with potatoes and turnips. It reminded me of school lunches, wedged on a bench between Bosley and Hettie, scooping the food from tin plates with a spoon too big for my mouth.

Crow's head poked from his raincape. It seemed to have

come loose from the rest of his body. "I ate Maconochie stew for a hundred days straight in 1917."

"I suppose you get used to it after a while." I let biscuits fall like chips of tan-colored slate into my mess tin. Then I mashed them with a spoon.

"You do get used to it. To this and everything else. It's trying to get used to having things be normal again that you'll find hard. I learned that when the war ended in France." Crow knocked a fist against his chest to help himself swallow a lump of potato. "On the day the war ended, we were in trenches only two hundred yards from the German dugouts. We were expecting a raid in the morning. But no raid came. We stood there on the parapets in the pissing rain and waited and nothing happened. At first we thought maybe some new Germans were coming in to take the place of the old ones. Perhaps that's why they'd canceled the raid. But it wasn't time for a rotation. There was something queer about it. Why eleven o'clock? They never rotated in the daytime, always at night."

Crow looked at his hands as he talked, turning them over and back, studying the lines. "There was a machine gunner in a pit opposite from us. Since sunrise, we'd been plinking away at him. Every now and then, he'd have a go back at us and chop up the sandbags we were hiding behind. He had a Maxim gun. It was a thing on little wheels with an armored plate up front. Every time we hit the plate, we'd hear a *ping* noise and then we'd cheer. Then came eleven o'clock. The officer blew a whistle. I heard whistles from the German side, too. All up and down the line, we heard whistles. The officer said there'd been a cease-fire. The war had ended. He had to keep saying it to us because we didn't understand. Then this German Maxim gunner started shooting up in the air. He fired until his barrel melted. When it quit, there was no noise from anywhere. Then this German gets up out of his pit. He stands up right in full view of us and takes a bow like an orchestra conductor! After that, he just turns around and starts walking back to Germany. And more of them and more of them and soon enough the whole German company is walking home. They dropped their helmets and their guns. We started cheering. And then in the middle of all the shouting, Stan turns to me and says, 'So what do we do now?' And you should have seen the smile fall off my face. I hadn't thought about it. But now I realized how difficult it was going to be heading home. And it was. It is. Sometimes I think I like it better out here in the rain."

The mushed biscuits boiled and plopped. I blew out the white fuel cube. The flame slithered back and a gust of acid smoke struck my face.

Clayton stood in the church doorway, hands in the pocket of his coat. No one had spoken to him since they reached the church. They shifted nervously when he walked past. Their talking ground into silence. Clayton even seemed to make himself uncomfortable.

I draped the raincape over my head and smelled the rubberized cloth. For a while I watched the other men. They knelt by the fire, hands stretched out to the flames and drawing in warmth. Shadows seemed to make the bones jut from their faces. Suddenly I wished I knew them better. I wished there was time to be friends.

The rancid smoke of fuel tablets drilled into my sleep.

It was morning. Crow had thrown back his cape. He stood stripped to the waist, slapping a soap-lathered shaving brush across his bald head.

Tarbox held up a pocket mirror. In his other hand, he held out a mess tin of water, which foamed with shaving soap. He was bare-chested under his trench coat. His shirt lay draped over a gravestone, warming in the sun.

"Hold the mirror steady." Crow held the razor to his forehead, then scraped the blade slowly back across his head.

"Morning, Ben." Tarbox nodded. "Ready for a fifteen-mile march across the Burren?"

"Stop wobbling the damn mirror!" Crow shook his razor and shaving soap splattered the grass.

Four men were out in the field, throwing peat at each other. The spongy clods exploded on their chests and backs. Their out-of-breath laughter echoed through the church.

"Stop wobbling the bloody mirror, Crabman!"

Tarbox looked out toward the field. The hand that held the mirror dropped to his side. "What's that noise?"

Crow grabbed Tarbox's hand and held it up, so he could see himself again. "It's me yelling at you, you silly bugger."

"No." I stepped to the door of the church and looked out at the vault of blue sky. "Something else."

The men who had been throwing peat stood still in the field. They all looked toward the horizon.

Worry brushed through me.

Crow's shaving soap smelled of sandalwood. The razor was a stripe of silver in his hand. "For God's sake, what is it?"

Now we could hear it. The buzz of an engine, coming from one place and then another, shifting on the breeze.

The fields were empty and bright.

Then a beetle-winged speck popped into view. It grew quickly. The sound grew with it. A plane, flying in low to the ground.

The men in the field were already running. Their untucked shirts flapped behind them.

Crow spun around. "Run!" He grabbed his rifle and swatted away a raincape that covered a window. He dove out and rolled away onto the grass.

"Run!" they were shouting in the field, eyes wide and terrified.

The plane took shape. The noise of its engine was loud.

I could make out the crossed threads of its wingstruts and the leather-wrapped ball of the pilot's head. I turned and followed Crow out through the window, thumping down hard on the grass and running now, already breathless. But there was no place to go. The fields gave no cover and the engine filled my ears. Then came the clatter of its guns and I pitched myself down on the ground. Grass dragged between my outstretched fingers.

A shadow jumped on my back and passed over. When I raised my head, I saw the plane bank sideways.

It was a two-seater. There was a fixed gun that fired between the propellers and the man in the back had a gun mounted on the fuselage. He stood in his cockpit, bundled in leather and his face hidden behind the two insect eyes of his goggles. He swung the gun around and fired at the church.

The plane was painted brown with red and blue circles on its sides and wings. Pale blue like a robin's egg coated the underbelly, a paler blue than the sky, as if the paint was made to hide it on a different day than this. The machine swept back at the church and smoke poured from its guns.

Men crouched down and fired at the plane. The soil burst open around them. One man flew against the church wall. Pieces of rock chipped from the stones. The men panicked and ran in all directions across the empty field. Stitches of earth exploded at their feet as the gunner fired at them.

I sprinted for the hedge. I'd seen Crow heading that way, and in the place where he had dived through the brambles were peeled back and broken.

The engine grew louder behind me. Then the air snapped open and a clod of grass sailed past my face. The albatross shadow cut out the light and then the plane's wheels flipped past, wobbling crookedly. The gunner was aiming straight at me, hunched over the fat ring of the gunsight. Again the air split apart and I dropped at the base of the hedge. Bramble leaves thrashed over me as the bullets ripped through and punched into the earth.

Then gunfire came from the road as Crow shot at the plane.

I heard the sharp clack-clack of reloading and the clink of empty cartridges that bounced off the stony road.

The plane was over the church again. Its pilot turned and looked down. His gloved hand pointed at the building. The gunner sent bullets chopping through the gravestones.

A man stood, arms raised, and fell back to the ground. His rifle spun in the air and came down on top of him.

The plane banked once more, sun on the tight fabric of its wings.

Tarbox broke from the churchyard and started running. He had dropped his gun.

"Here!" I waved.

Tarbox changed course. Now he was running toward me.

Crow shouldered his rifle and fired over the top of my head.

The plane dove at Tarbox.

"Keep running, Crabman! Don't look back!" I pulled out my Webley. The drum clicked empty after four shots. "You're almost here, Crabman!"

The plane tipped slightly to the side as its gunner took aim.

"Oh, Christ!" Tarbox yelled as he ran. "Oh, Christ almighty!"

"Run, Crabmaaaan!"

Then the gun began firing. It sparkled through the propeller.

Tarbox cried out, his short arms flailing as he ran. A bursting trench of earth flew up where bullets struck. They raced in toward him, sputtering soil and ripped grass.

Crow dove into the hedge.

I stood, the revolver in my hand, and emptied my lungs with a shout. "Crabmaaaaaan!"

Tarbox's right shoe blew to pieces off his foot. His body

rose in the air. Then Tarbox's chest exploded and his still-flailing arms carried him down to the ground.

A line of bullets chopped past and smacked into the road.

I didn't move. I stared at the pile of trench coat that covered Tarbox's head. His hand stuck out twisted from under the cloth. A piece of his shoe lay nearby.

The plane dove once more on the church and then headed off over the fields. Its engine faded away.

Crow crawled out of the hedge. He ran over to Tarbox and pulled back the trench coat.

Tarbox's eyes were like mirrors. All his blood ran out. It smeared and beaded on the grass, luminous against the green.

Clayton rose up from the middle of the field, as if he had been hiding underground and had clawed his way out of the soil. He started walking toward us.

We buried Tarbox and two others in the peat-dark earth. We dug the grave with our hands and laid the bodies side by side. We covered them quickly, raking back the soil with crooked fingers, because we had to keep moving and there was no time to waste.

"May the Lord bless you and keep you," Crow was saying. "May the Lord make his face to shine upon you."

I knelt with the others, dew soaking through my trousers, and I tried to remember a prayer. But nothing came to mind, not even a song. All I could think of were Tarbox's bright-painted crab-pot floats, bobbing in the water off Lahinch. And now Mrs. Fuller's words sank into me, about whole generations dying out. I saw how it would be. Tarbox's wife would move away and their tin-roofed shack would fold back into the earth. There would be no children to inherit the land and keep the name alive. The faint scratches that Tarbox had left on the earth would be rubbed out by a year or two of wind and rain.

I had not liked him much. If he had lived and I'd gone back home again, I would not have remembered him kindly. But now I cried for Tarbox and for his wife, because I had been jealous of how much they were in love.

The rock of the Burren spread like barely cooled lava across the ground.

We waded through ferns in the stone-stubbled fields. Gorse bushes dragged their needle leaves across our legs.

Clayton said that now it was too dangerous to move along the roads. So we walked in a straggling line across the open ground.

Sometimes he climbed up on a wall and pulled out a compass in a silver case. He pressed a button at the top and the lid popped open. Then he held the compass out on the flat of his palm to take a bearing.

Towns clustered in the valleys. Through Clayton's binoculars, I saw a woman hanging laundry in her garden. She held clothespins between her teeth. Wind molded the wet sheets against her body.

In another garden, a man had set his compost heap on fire. Thick scarves of smoke climbed from the mulch. Sparks had caught in the gorse and set it burning. The man beat down the flames with a shovel. The charred gorse branches smouldered, pain-twisted like the legs of a cripple.

Distant ocean snubbed the Burren rock.

Once, in the corner of my eye, I saw a crooked wing. I hunched down fast beside a wall, thinking it was another plane. But it was only a raven, gliding off toward the water, feet tucked into its feathers.

It was evening when we heard the sound of a truck.

We crouched in the brown-edged ferns and watched it putter through a town. Its canvas roof was tied shut. A staff car followed after.

People ran from their houses when the machines had passed. They stood at their garden gates and watched.

Clayton rose from cover. His shadow stretched along the ground. "We'll stay here tonight. These people will give us shelter."

The thought of staying under a roof and perhaps even in a bed made me feel almost dizzy. I walked down the slope with the others. Sunset blazed through the grass.

Sheep raised their heads and peered at us. Their monotone laughter passed from field to field.

A woman looked up from her garden, where rosebushes burst with pink and yellow flowers. She pointed at us and called to her neighbors.

Gunfire. The dry clap of rifles.

I flopped down in the ferns, pulled out my revolver and realized it was empty. So I rolled onto my back and pulled spare bullets from my pocket. Some of them slipped out of my hands. I fished for them among the fern stalks, and jammed the bullets into the Webley's cylinder.

"It's in the next valley." Clayton snapped his fingers at me and we both ran down to the village. Ferns had jammed in the wooden holster of his Mauser.

A man walked out to meet us. He said his name was Gracey. He wore blue overalls and a grey coat. "They're at Tolliver's farm about a dozen of them. They all moved in there last night. That truckload of Tans has gone after them."

"All who?" Clayton looked over Gracey's shoulder at the people in the street.

"I don't know who they are, sir." Gracey wiped his palms on his chest, as if he meant to shake Clayton's hand. "All I know is that they came by looking for shelter and Tolliver gave them his barn to sleep in."

"Was the man in charge named Hagan?"

"I never heard him mentioned, sir."

"Who told the Tans they were there?"

"I don't know, sir. I know it wasn't me."

"How far are they?"

"A ten-minute walk, sir. Five minutes if you run."

We ran toward Tolliver's farm, boots clattering on the elephant-grey stone.

My joints ached as if I'd been running all day.

The gunfire continued, shots echoing over the hedges. Then the slate roof of the farmhouse slid into view.

We rounded a corner and saw a Crossley truck jamming the road. Its canvas back was open and the truck looked empty.

An English voice shouted orders and the firing grew sharper. Glass broke in the farmhouse. The tangled branches of the hedge hid everything from view. The light had left the road and now it swam in shadows.

Clayton looked over the top of the hedge and then ducked down again. He signaled for us to move up.

Four Tans crouched behind a wall. They fired at the farmhouse. One shot, then ducked down and reloaded. Another popped up and fired. Their helmets had been taken off and lay like upturned birdbaths on the ground.

Crow shouldered his rifle. His cheek pressed against the dark oiled wood of the stock. He wrapped his arm through the black canvas sling and took aim.

Then a Tan appeared by the truck. His tunic was undone and his brass buttons seemed to glow in the failing light. He was carrying two cans of ammunition. As soon as he saw us, he dropped the cans and turned to run.

Clayton swung his arm up and the Mauser jumped in his hand.

A sudden wave of fire poured across the road. A screech filled my ears and after that there was only ringing. Heat thrashed at my face. It threw me to the ground. I'm on fire, I thought. I beat at my chest and legs. Oh, Jesus, I'm burning.

Someone had hold of my collar and was dragging me back down the road.

I wasn't burning now, but smoke climbed from the wool of my coat like dust off a trampled rug. The truck was outlined in flames. Its canvas roof hung in shreds, dripping like liquid from the steel frame of the roof. The tires boiled black smoke. I put my hands to my face and felt the skin raw, as if it had been rubbed with sandpaper. Flecks of burnt hair crumbled dull orange onto my chest.

It was Crow dragging me. He pulled me into a field and we lay in the ferns. Smoke skimmed over the hedge. It twisted and coiled and blew away out to sea.

"Clayton hit the fuel tank." Crow pulled a handful of copper-headed .303 bullets from his bandolier and started to reload his rifle.

Night pressed dark-edged blue around the corners of the sky. The last streaks of sun touched the water out to sea.

Now the Tans came running down the road, bayonets fixed on their guns.

I sat up, ready to fire and Crow heaved me back into cover. The smell of my burnt hair made me wince.

Footsteps crunched by.

Then came a volley that set my ears ringing again. I crawled to the edge of the road, elbows and knees pasted with mud.

The soldiers had fallen. They lay with arms outstretched, like swimmers on the land.

Clayton jumped from the hedge in a waft of ripped trench coat. He took the soldiers' bandoliers and the revolvers in their belts. Then he waded through the gorse and ordered us into a firing line. With a wave of his hand, he pointed me down toward the water.

I dodged across the road and started to crawl, following the thump of waves against the rocks. The gunfire had stopped. No commands came shrieking through the breeze. After a few minutes of pawing through the musty jungle of ferns, I raised my head and looked at the farmhouse. Its windows were all broken and the shutters hung smashed on their hinges. The truck still burned, throwing shadows on the silhouettes of men.

One of them had to be my father. I wanted to call out his name, but a heavy silence had sunk down on the fields, drowning our voices away.

CHAPTER 16

Lazy waves rode up the beach. They rumbled through a bank of empty mussel shells.

The beach was short. Rocks crowded down to the shore.

The Tans lay somewhere between here and the farmhouse. If they broke out of the ring that had gathered around them, they could run for help. When daylight came, the ring would close in. Then the Tans would have no place to hide.

My job was to guard the beach and make sure no one passed through in the night.

Moon-bright water lay calm on the horizon. The scrape of boots on stone echoed clearly across the Burren. Whispers slipped through the ferns.

The white-painted walls of the farmhouse were like a sheet of bone. The place seemed empty. I wondered how many people were hiding inside and whether they knew yet who had come to help them.

The night dragged my patience away. I wanted to cross the distance to the farmhouse in long sprinting strides and not wait for the sun to come up.

As the cold picked its way through the fibers of my clothes, I began to think of what would happen tomorrow. The Tans would come back with their plane. Perhaps they were already loading the Crossley trucks with men whose anger and instincts still lived in the trenches of France. Then even Connemara wouldn't hide us. I imagined Crow and Clayton and the rest of us all filing into the mouth of a cave someplace in the treeless hills. There we would lie down to rest and the cave would be sealed until long after the Tans had stopped searching and gone home and died of old age. And when the time of our sleeping was over, we would unseal the cave and walk out into a world of strangers.

The even rustle of the waves through the old mussel shells broke suddenly as someone jumped down to the beach.

I peered from the rocks where I was hiding. I lifted the Webley slowly from its holster, hearing its forward sight drag across the leather.

A man stood ankle deep in the shells, looking out to sea.

My eyes blurred from staring. The dark seethed with tiny geometric shapes.

Then the man dropped down to one knee. He held out an arm to steady himself. It was Clayton. He moved as if to stand up, but fell back. Shells crunched under him and the next wave brushed at his legs.

I left my cover and crawled across. My palms dug into the brittle mussel shells.

Clayton turned. A wave doused him with foam. He reached out, as if to push me away. His fingers raked down my face. They were covered in blood. Clayton's breathing popped and spluttered, as if he was gargling spit. His throat had been cut. He kept raising his hands to push me away. The wet fingers dug into my cheeks, hard at first but growing weaker.

A wave soaked us and rumbled away, stirring the mussel shells in flickers of opal and black.

I held my hand against the gash across his throat. It didn't do any good.

Slowly his eyes closed. His hands fell away and lay half curled by his side. Another surge of water stole the heat from our bodies. Clayton kicked out at the next onrushing wave. Then he was dead.

Strange how heavy he became in my arms. The next wave washed over us and as it pulled back, the clear water poured from his mouth like molten glass.

I felt strangely cold at seeing him this way. It seemed to me that Clayton had long ago given himself up for dead. He had prepared himself, pushing friends away so that he wouldn't be missed when the time came. Everybody knew that his place was in the war, but no one seemed to think he would survive it.

For a long time, I listened, waiting for the swish of someone moving through the ferns. But I knew that whoever had killed Clayton was already through the ring and on their way to find help. No shape looked familiar in the silhouette tangle of rock and grass and trees inland. I knew I would have to get to the farm and let them know that the ring had been broken. We'd all have to move on before the Tans returned.

I crawled to the place where I knew Crow was hiding, in an outcrop of rock that overlooked the road. As I slithered through the ferns, I saw Crow's darting silhouette as he closed in on my movements.

I stopped him from killing me, but not by very much. He had his straight edge razor out.

For a moment, I wondered if it was Crow who had killed Clayton. I could have thought of half-a-dozen reasons why he might. But I said nothing. Instead, I just told him what happened.

Crow said Clayton had been carrying maps that we would need on our way north.

Clayton was gone when we got there. The tide had pulled him away. We could see his body drifting on deep water, hands seeming to trace the arc of tiny waves as they swelled past him. He was too far out to try and bring him back.

We moved toward the farm. I crawled after Crow's muddy boots, stopping and listening and crawling, then stopping again a while later. When the breeze blew, we moved more quickly, our movements hidden in the shuffling of fern branches.

There was no way to find every man in the ring and tell them what had happened. We just had to hope that they didn't shoot us by mistake.

It took half an hour to reach a wall that ran behind the barn. Through the stones, I could see the barn's corrugated roof. Its rippled iron was the color of pewter. A stretch of mud lay between the wall and the open barn door. Puddles reflected the moon. The farmhouse still looked empty.

Crow raised his head over the wall. "You in the farm!" His voice was deafening in the quiet that covered the fields. "We're from the second Clare Brigade. I'm coming in."

The farmhouse stayed silent and dark.

I sat with my back to the wall, looking up the slope. I watched for the blink of knife blades or the moon catching light off gunmetal. For a moment, it occurred to me that everyone had gone. Not just the Tans. And perhaps the only ones here were me and Crow, creeping in fear of our imagination.

Crow cupped his hand to his mouth. "Can you hear me?" he called to the blank farmhouse windows. When no answer came, he slumped down behind the wall. His voice was a whisper again. "We'll have to hope they heard us. We could always just run, Ben. Just you and me heading for Connemara. We'd be safer than in the group." He turned to me, wanting me to agree. His eyes were silvery. "We'd stand a better chance."

I hadn't told him about Hagan. It was a private thing that

I didn't want to share until I had met with the man. "We can't just run out on them."

"No, I don't suppose we could." Crow nodded.

I said I'd go first and Crow didn't try to stop me. I stood, blood storming in my head, jumped the wall and sprinted. The mud seemed to spread out forever. I dove at the barn's open doorway. My legs lifted high in the air and then the ground crunched against my chest. I skidded along the floor, through dirt and scattered straw. Then for a while, I lay still. The huge-treaded wheel of a tractor arced up in front of me.

Outside, drops of water clung in silver bubbles along the door frame.

Crow's grubby face appeared and then the rest of him. He flew into the barn and belly flopped onto the straw.

Then a bullet snapped into the wood over our heads. The drops of water lined along the doorway shuddered and fell. Another round hit the barn. Wood chips scattered across the floor.

Crow covered his neck with his hands. He buried his face in the dirt.

As I scrambled under the tractor, I caught sight of helmeted men advancing across the fields, running and crouching and running again.

Then the walls of the barn flew apart. Bullets punched fist-sized holes through the wood and clanked across the corrugated iron roof. The air became foggy with dust. Volley after volley crashed in from the field. A bullet struck the tractor's radiator grill. Musty water poured onto my head. Then rubber-smelling air from a punctured tire burped into my face.

Gun flashes gouged at the dark from the farmhouse windows. The men in the field dove for cover.

The tractor's radiator water trickled down my chest in clammy streams.

Crow brushed woodchips from his shoulders. "We have to

get to the farmhouse before this whole place falls down on top of us."

The door to the house stood open, across the cratered farmyard mud. Someone crouched in the doorway. The paleness of a hand waved toward us.

Crow lunged across the yard and I followed. A feeling of nakedness surrounded me. My boots splashed through the puddles. The air seemed filled with cracking whips.

The snarl of Crow's breathing suddenly rose to a cry. He fell and rolled over. A puddle shattered like a mirror as he splashed through it.

I grabbed hold of his collar and a jet of earth sprang up beside me. I dragged him toward the door. His trailing legs left a broad path through the mud.

A chunk of the doorframe vanished. Grit spattered my cheeks. Then I was inside, let go of Crow and fell forward. Bullets thumped into the walls. It was dark in the house. A pair of boots clumped to a stop near my head and I looked up.

A man held a shotgun to my face.

"Are you Hagan?" I didn't try to get up.

"No." His teeth were chalky pegs in the dark.

"Then bring me to him. Please." I used up all my breath.

After a moment, the man lowered his shotgun. "Hagan's not here. I'm Tiffin. Hagan left me in charge, so if you've got a message, you'd better give it to me."

Crow hugged his shin, eyes shut tight. We carried him down to the cellar.

Tiffin's clothes hung in rags. He looked more like a scarecrow than a man. "When we came through town last night, the people there said that the radios were talking of an armistice. So as soon as this farmer Tolliver had us bedded down for the night, Hagan went back into the town to hear the radio's evening news. Then the Tans came through and I haven't seen him since."

"What did Hagan look like?" I thought maybe I'd seen him in the town.

"Last I saw, he was wearing a green corduroy coat."

I didn't remember any green corduroy. "The Tans have gone for help. That's what we came to tell you. We've got to break out now, while it's still dark."

"There's too many of them out there. We can't break out. And you almost died breaking in. They'll be coming at us again any minute."

A staircase made of flagstones brought us down into a dirt-floored cellar that was already crowded with wounded. A woman who must have been Mrs. Tolliver pointed to a clear space on the floor and we laid Crow there on a bed of potato sacking.

"I don't have any more bandages," she said to Tiffin. Her voice was quivering, as if she expected Tiffin to beat her for running out of supplies.

"Just do the best you can. All right?"

"But with what?" She held up her hands and they were shaking. Her hair was wrapped in a flower-print scarf. It gave her the face of a child.

Tiffin pulled off his flannel shirt and handed it to her. He said she could tear it up as a bandage.

I took off my trench coat and waistcoat and heaped them all on the floor while I unbuttoned my shirt. The collar was stiff with dried blood and old sweat.

Now all Tiffin had was an undershirt, so I gave him my coat and he had to roll up the sleeves.

Crow had turned very pale and he was sweating heavily. A gouge on the top of his head had spread a bloody sunburst across his weathered skull. Through the tear in his trousers where the bullet had gone through, I could see his kneecap exposed. I knew that if we moved on, he would have to stay behind. I think he knew it, too. His eyes stayed shut and his crooked mouth did not show pain as much as it showed disappointment that it should all end here for him.

Tiffin pulled me away.

I followed him upstairs and into the front room. A table had been tipped against the wall and chairs lay in a pile. Our boots crunched over broken glass. Tiffin stood beside the window. He broke open the shotgun and slid two copper-ended cartridges into the breech. Then he closed the gun again and handed it to me. "You're a Yank." He said it as if perhaps I didn't know myself.

I shivered without my coat. "I need to find Hagan."

"You might have come too late. The Tans will be here any minute." He held his hand out at the patch of grass beyond the window frame. "This is your ground. Anybody that moves out there, it's your job to put them away." He pulled a stiff leather cartridge bag from his shoulder and set it on the floor beside me. then he walked into another room.

I dragged a chair across the floor and sat down by the window. Pain like an old man's arthritis began to loosen from my legs, like bandages unraveled. I felt myself falling asleep. Then my foot shifted and I knocked over the cartridge bag. The noise of shotgun shells rattling inside jolted me awake.

The land outside seemed empty and calm again. But when a breeze came wandering through the gorse, I heard the rustle of bodies as Tans closed in on the farm.

A rock seemed to shift by the wall. Then a face appeared.

I jumped up out of the chair, squeezed the shotgun's trigger and realized the safety was still on. I released it and fired, stunning myself with the blast inside the room. Cordite smoke billowed around me.

The face disappeared. Footsteps. Now the fields seemed to shudder with movement.

Suddenly helmeted heads rose up from behind the far wall and gun flashes burst in my eyes. The window frame shattered. Stone dust peppered my skin.

Men were running towards the house, doubled over and carrying guns.

I felt the stun of a bullet pass by my face and rip a chunk of plaster from the wall.

Something flipped past from one of the other windows and I heard one of the soldiers cry out.

The blast of a hand grenade was like a door slamming in my face. It knocked me back into the room and my lungs were outlined with pain. I crawled back to the window and could see nothing but smoke.

When it began to clear, I saw two men lying just in front of the window. Another was dragging himself back toward the wall. His leg was twisted the wrong way.

I broke open the gun and started to reload. Then a shape swung in front of the window and someone lunged through the frame.

It was one of the soldiers. He grabbed my hair and pulled me to him. He had hold of my throat and made me drop the gun. I cried out and jabbed my elbow into his chest but he held on. He was breathing in my face. I smelled old tobacco. He dug his fingers into my windpipe and blue flashes burst behind my eyes. I couldn't cry out any more. He hooked one knee into the window frame and started to crawl into the room. I smacked him in the jaw with my elbow and for a moment his body grew heavy as if I'd knocked him out. But then he sank his fingers deeper into my throat and I could feel my consciousness bleeding away. I threw myself at the window frame, jamming his body against the glass. I heard the pain in his voice and his fingers slipped away. I jammed him once more and heard the frame crack with his weight. His fingers came at me again and scratched at my eyes. He had hold of my wrist so I bit him, sinking my teeth in and feeling the blood well into my mouth. He yelled and deafened me and as soon as he let go, I tugged the Webley out of its holster. I swung it up toward him. He grabbed my arm, but his grip didn't hold. I set the barrel under his chin and for a second I could see the brightness of his eyes in the dark. He spat in my face and thrashed forward and I pulled the trigger. His head jerked up and his jaw shattered. Fragments of his teeth dug into my face like shards of broken pottery. Sparks flew out of the Webley's cylinder and blinded me. Then, while his muscles still shuddered in the last sputters of his dying, I stuffed his body back out the window and heard it fall heavily on the grass.

It felt as if his fingers were still sunk into my throat. I spat out his blood and cocked the hammer on the Webley, in case someone else tried to climb in.

But no one did. One man still dragged himself back toward the wall. His tunic was shredded. He groped his way up the stones and then fell down on the other side.

I hunched down to reload the shotgun, fumbling with the brass buckle of the cartridge bag. Sweat cut trails through the dirt on my face.

The firing continued on the other side of the house. Its thatched roof was held down with heavy ropes that had been weighted with stones. They dangled like strange jewelry and the Tans seemed to be using them for target practice. I heard the ricochet of bullets off the stones and then a thump as the rock smashed back against the house. Orders barked from room to room and another man was dragged coughing to the basement.

I held my hands to my throat and gagged. The muscles twitched in my arms and legs and I could not calm them down. It hurt to swallow. Anger kept flaring up inside me. I wanted to lean out of the window and shoot that Tan a few more times and kill him all over again. I couldn't help it. My nerves were

buzzing with rage. Then suddenly it left me, and all I felt was
tired.

My killing ground stayed quiet. If I stared for too long at
one spot, it seemed to shift and come alive. The only things
that remained still were the dead men lying on the grass. The
dew collected on them, just as it had on Stanley.

I was thirsty. The smoke had dried me out and my stomach
was sour and empty. Part of me waited for Tans to rush screaming out of the dark, and the rest of me daydreamed about
porridge with brown sugar and slices of apple.

Hagan was probably gone. Or the Tans had caught him.
They would have sent for reinforcements and at first light they
would attack again. Our ammunition would not last. If they
brought an artillery piece, the farm would be blown in around
us. We could not break out, because now they owned the ring.
And even if we did, they would catch up with us after a few
miles. For a while I tricked myself into imagining the others,
lying dead in the bomb-smashed beams of the house, while I
ran safe and invisible through the fields to a place where my
father was hiding.

But it was this simple: There would be no running away.
After what had happened in the Lahinch barracks, there would
be no giving in, either. All of us knew that.

I had come this far, but I would not meet my father. I told
myself it was enough to know the truth and enough to have
had a man and a woman raise me as if I were their son. Surely,
with this war about to swallow me, that had to be enough.

During the Great War, as I read the headlines of Ypres and
Verdun and the Somme, I was never able to picture the grand
strategy. For me, it always boiled down to single faces in the
mud, frozen by a photograph or by the way someone told it
in a story. That was how I understood the war. Instead of
considering the world's new order when the war was over, I

found myself wondering how it must feel to be there in the trenches and know almost for certain that death was coming with the great rolling thunder of artillery and the iron-hooded soldiers rushing in.

What I realized now was that although the chances of surviving were nearly zero, still they were not completely zero. The pathetic thread of possibility grew in my head until it outweighed any chance of dying. I would be lucky. I would dodge and duck and run and be shielded by angels. I would head for the cave where no one could find me and sleep with the promise of returning to the light someday far into the future. It did not seem possible to me that all my thoughts could be snuffed out. I could imagine almost any degree of wounding and maiming and pain but not the simple vanishing of my mind. It had built a wall between itself and death and the wall would not give in.

The first thin bolts of sun spread whiskey-colored light across the fields.

I heard a truck sound in the distance. It was the Crossleys winding along narrow roads with their canvas roofs battened down. I knew people would be running from their gardens to stand in the trails of exhaust as they watched the trucks move by.

The farmhouse seemed to shudder. Half-asleep men threw themselves at the window. Rifle bolts clacked.

The trucks mumbled toward us. Sheep stopped grazing and raised their heads.

Tiffin's voice boomed through the house, telling us to wait until the soldiers were in close before we fired.

I wondered about the shotgun's range. The Tans would be over the wall and halfway across the garden before I could be sure of a target. The world had been reduced to the view from this farmhouse window. I wanted it to begin. I shoved away the clutter of worry and planning for when it was over. It made no more sense to drift on paths of daydream, where I kept myself safe and alive. All that remained of my senses was a tiny, flickering pilot light that fastened me to life.

A truck slipped over the hill on the horizon. It showed itself for an instant, as it dropped into a lower gear. The rest must have stopped on the other side of the ridge. The soldiers would be piling out now, forming in their sections on the road. Soon they would set out across the fields.

In another room, a handful of bullets dropped on the floor. Someone scrabbled to pick them up.

"Let them get close," Tiffin shouted.

I wiped the moisture from my palms on my trouser legs and rested my hands in the stone dust, chalking them to dry up the sweat.

The truck appeared on a rise. But it seemed too small for a truck. It was a staff car and a man stood in the back seat with a shred of white cloth tied to a stick. Two men sat in the front. The car slowed as it drew near to the house.

Tiffin ran into the room. He pushed me aside. Stubble jutted from his chin like slivers of ivory. "They want us to give up without a fight."

The car brakes squeaked and it stopped in front of the farmyard.

An officer stepped out. He took off his cap and tucked it under his arm. His short black hair was combed straight back on his head.

Behind him, a soldier stood in the car with the white cloth raised.

The driver kept his hand on the steering wheel. His cap had a red and white checked band and two tassels hung down at the back of his neck.

The officer walked into the farmyard. Mud covered the shine on his boots. He breathed in deep and shouted, "I am Captain

Houston. Send out whoever is in charge." His eyes passed from window to window. "I don't have all day."

Tiffin jammed his thumbnail in his mouth. He muttered into his fingers. When he pulled his hand down, he bit off half the thumbnail and spat it on the floor. Then he took hold of my arm. "You follow me out. I want you standing right behind me all the time and bring that shotgun with you."

We walked down the hall to the door.

I saw men in all the rooms. They crouched by overturned furniture, guns locked in their hands. Then something grabbed at his foot.

It was Crow. He had crawled halfway out of the basement. His face was still sweaty and pale. "Don't you trust them. You keep looking at their eyes. It's their eyes that give them away."

For a second, Tiffin stopped in front of the door. Then he tucked in his undershirt and smoothed the hair back on his head. He gripped the door handle, pressing the latch with his thumb, and swung the door wide.

Houston flinched when he saw the door swing open.

Tiffin walked to meet him, his back stiff and his arms held straight at his sides.

I followed, ducking from the shadow of the farmhouse roof into the bright sun. Puddles flashed and blinded me.

Tiffin stopped and I almost piled into him.

Houston saluted.

"What do you want?" Tiffin breathed as if he had walked miles to meet the man.

Houston snapped his hand down to his side. "There will be no attack. Neither do we require your surrender. We heard on the radio at five o'clock this morning that a general armistice was signed last night. We have been ordered to cease all hostilities immediately. And so have you."

"How do you expect me to believe that?" Tiffin's feet stirred in the mud.

The shotgun was impossibly heavy in my hands.

Houston fitted his cap back on his head. He had said what he came to say, and he had no more time for talk. "I could have rounded you up in half an hour with the men I've got waiting in that town over the hill. But I'm not doing it. That should tell you something. We're pulling back now. You will not fire on us as we depart or I shall consider that a renewal of hostilities." He saluted again. "See you again some day." Then he spun on his heel and walked back to the car. The engine started up.

The car turned and backed up and turned again. It sped away down the road. The white cloth snapped in the wind.

Men stood up from their hiding places in the fields. Two Tans appeared from a bank of ferns. They looked at the car and then at the farmhouse.

A man in a trench coat crawled out of the hedge.

The Tans started running toward town. They kept looking back.

Tiffin turned to me. "It can't be true. It's been going on too long just to end like this. Go into town and find out if the armistice is real. If you're not back in half an hour, I'll know they were lying. Leave the gun. You've got a better chance without it."

I left the shotgun behind and walked in the middle of the road.

As I reached the crest of the hill, I could see down into town. People filled the streets. Two Crossley trucks and the staff car were parked in the village square. Tans sat in the backs of their trucks.

A woman poured tea into the white and blue tin mugs that the Tans held in their outstretched hands.

Houston was talking with Gracey, who still wore his overalls and black coat. The officer took a black cigarette case from his pocket and offered it to Gracey.

Gracey picked a cigarette and nodded thank you. He struck a match and held the flame cupped in his hands to Houston, who bent forward and puffed.

Houston breathed in the smoke and then pulled the cigarette from his mouth. He smiled and nodded and rocked on the heels of his muddy boots.

One soldier stood on the thatched roof of a house. He held the white flag above his head and waved it back and forth over the town.

The armistice had come, even if just for a while. I felt the cautious reaching of my thoughts toward home, the distant rhythm returning.

A man walked up the hill, hands in the pockets of a green corduroy jacket. He stopped when he saw me.

I saw my own face looking back, with a haze of age across it. The man took his hands from his pockets and shielded the sun from his eyes.

I walked down the hill. In a moment I started to run. I had a sense of rushing past the frail shell of my body, treading lightly through distance and time.

ABOUT THE AUTHOR

PAUL WATKINS, in addition to being one of the best-reviewed new writers on the American literary scene, is also one of the most colorful. The California-born son of Welsh parents, Watkins grew up on the shores of Narragansett Bay in Rhode Island, and was educated at Eton and Yale. His widely praised first novel, *Night Over Day Over Night*, the story of an SS soldier's coming-of-age during the Battle of the Bulge, was published when its author was just twenty-three, and was nominated for a Booker Prize. To research the book, Watkins hiked through the Ardennes forest, where the battle took place, and interviewed veterans of both sides. *Calm at Sunset, Calm at Dawn* was awarded Britain's Encore Prize for best second novel. It reflects several seasons Watkins spent working on trawlers off the New England coast. For his third novel, *In the Blue Light of African Dreams*, Watkins learned to fly a biplane and spent months in the Moroccan Sahara. And before he wrote *The Promise of Light*, he made four trips to Ireland, lived in the towns of Lahinch and Ennistymon, wore clothing from the period, interviewed Irish citizens and scholars, and drew upon a vast body of historical literature in order to study the Irish independence movement from all angles.

Watkins makes his home in Princeton, New Jersey.

ABOUT THE TYPE

This book was set in Galliard, a typeface designed by Matthew Carter for the Mergenthaler Linotype Company in 1978. Galliard is based on the sixteenth-century typefaces of Robert Granjon, which give it classic lines yet interject a contemporary look.